Buffy could P8-AYG-659 **in blackness. And what she felt was totally alien: like no skin she had ever touched. It was slick and scaly and tough, all at once.**

She clawed her way across the thing, finally finding an opening. Her fingers closed on the side of the opening—like a great maw of some kind. She pulled with everything she could, and heard a sound like flesh tearing. Then the beast made its first noise, a high-pitched keening that sounded like it came from everywhere at once.

Since she couldn't see the creature, could only vaguely sense its whereabouts and dimensions, she made sure to keep at least one hand on it at all times.

She turned to face it again, still holding one arm, and threw herself on top of it. She felt something that seemed enough like a neck to take a chance on. Letting go of the arm, Buffy grabbed the neck and twisted.

The monster went limp in her arms.

Buffy, stood, panting, hands on her knees, trying to catch her breath.

Which was when the next one hit her.

Buffy the Vampire Slayer™

Angel™

Available from ARCHWAY Paperbacks and POCKET PULSE

Buffy the Vampire Slayer ™

Child of the Hunt
Return to Chaos
The Gatekeeper Trilogy
    Book 1: Out of the Madhouse
    Book 2: Ghost Roads
    Book 3: Sons of Entropy
Obsidian Fate
Immortal
Sins of the Father
Resurrecting Ravana
Prime Evil
The Evil That Men Do
Paleo
Spike and Dru: Pretty Maids All in a Row
Revenant
The Book of Fours
The Unseen Trilogy (Buffy/Angel)
    Book 1: The Burning
The Watcher's Guide, Vol. 1: The Official Companion to the Hit Show
The Watcher's Guide, Vol. 2: The Official Companion to the Hit Show
The Postcards
The Essential Angel Posterbook
The Sunnydale High Yearbook
Pop Quiz: Buffy the Vampire Slayer
The Monster Book
The Script Book, Season One, Vol. 1
The Script Book, Season One, Vol. 2

Available from POCKET BOOKS

Buffy the Vampire Slayer™

ANGEL™

UNSEEN

THE BURNING

NANCY HOLDER AND **JEFF MARIOTTE**

POCKET BOOKS

New York   London   Toronto   Sydney   Singapore

Historical Note: This trilogy takes place between the fourth and fifth seasons of *Buffy,* and between the first and second seasons of *Angel.*

This book is a work of fiction. Names, characters, places and incidents are products of the author's imagination or are used fictitiously. Any resemblance to actual events or locales or persons, living or dead, is entirely coincidental.

An *Original* Publication of POCKET BOOKS

POCKET BOOKS, a division of Simon & Schuster, Inc.
1230 Avenue of the Americas, New York, NY 10020

ISBN: 0-7434-1893-X

First Pocket Books printing May 2001

10 9 8 7 6 5 4 3 2 1

POCKET and colophon are registered trademarks of
Simon & Schuster, Inc.

Printed in the U.S.A.

This book is for Maryelizabeth, our Hart.

—Nancy and Jeff

Acknowledgments

The authors very gratefully thank the casts, staffs, and crews of both *Buffy* and *Angel*, especially Joss Whedon, David Greenwalt, and of course, Caroline "Coy-woman" Kallas. Thanks also to George Snyder of Mutant Enemy and Debbie Olshan at Fox. Many thanks to friend and agent Howard Morhaim, and Stacy Schemehorn, his assistant. At Pocket: we love you, Lisa "Termineditor" Clancy, Micol Ostow, and Liz Shiflett.

On the home front: thanks indeed to Maryelizabeth Hart, David and Holly Mariotte; Belle Holder; Elise Jones and *ohana*; the one and only Ida Khabazian, Lee Sigall, Andy Herron-Sweet, Karen Hackett and family; and the Mysterious Galaxians: Terry and Todd Gilman, Patrick Heffernan, Beth Orvis, Linda Tonneson, and Elizabeth Baldwin.

Prologue

Sunnydale

In Sunnydale, it was hot as hell, and that was no joke.

A week into summer and the deceptively placid-looking little town was like a blast furnace, even closing in on midnight. In Weatherly Park, the trees sweated and the sidewalk along the fence was ready for scrambling a few eggs. Touch the chain link and one would get a painful burn that resembled a tattoo, or the diagonal grill patterns on the steaks at Steer Town.

In the twelve graveyards within the city limits, friends and foes alike rotted faster.

Buffy wiped her forehead with her hand, glad she had picked the T-shirt and lightweight pants instead of the long-sleeved shirt she'd been thinking about. This was no weather for sleeves.

This was no weather to be on patrol. But that wasn't up for negotiation. She was the Slayer, she patrolled. End of story.

Although there hasn't been a whole heck of a lot of slayage to commit, the last few nights. Since the end of school—well, since the end of the Initiative, and Adam, and Maggie Walsh, if one wanted to get specific—Sunnydale had been positively somnolent. The way people who really didn't get it thought Sunnydale always was.

But, quiet or not, she was the Slayer so she went through the motions, going out on patrol at night to see what manner of creepiness might be skulking in the dark. Elsewhere, Riley Finn was doing much the same. Usually Slayer and Boyfriend of patrolled together; other times, to cover more territory, they split up. Tonight, they had split up. Leaving Buffy with no one to talk to and nothing to kill.

And just what kind of person am I, she wondered, *that I would wish for creatures of the night to inhabit the planet just to give me something to do?*

As if in answer, someone screamed, in a fairly coy way.

Buffy tried not to smile. *Earlier days of slayage, major faux pas,* she thought. *About now, I'd have dashed off to majorly intrude on some lusty couple, and they'd both look at me like I was a psycho.*

There was another scream; same screamer, totally different message. This was not a fooling-around-scream, this was truly a something-is-trying-to-eat-me scream if Buffy had ever heard one.

And in her time, Buffy had heard more than a few.

She ran, ran like the oh-so absent wind.

The scream sounded like it came from a couple of blocks to the east, pretty close to downtown Sunnydale. It sounded again—definitely female, and terrified. Then it was cut short.

Buffy poured it on.

As soon as she came around the corner she knew where the victim was. There was an alley, midway down the block, and open on both ends. People sometimes used it to shortcut from Main Street to their car, if they'd parked a block or so away. Someone had probably been walking back from the Espresso Pump, or dinner, and been accosted by, well, something.

A vampire? A demon from the darkest pits of Hell? No telling, around here, she thought.

Sneakers providing traction, Buffy swung around the corner into the alley. She vaguely registered the stench of broiling garbage as she leaped over a limp cardboard box oozing with oranges and lemons.

Midway down, she saw them: a woman, struggling, a dark shape hulking over her, tearing at her with flailing arms.

Vampire.

Buffy slipped a stake from her belt, adjusting her grip as she ran.

Before she could reach the bloodsucker, she was blinded by lights, blasting at her from the other end of the alley. First white ones, then flashing red. A police car, she realized, being someone who had intimate knowledge of being pursued by same; *well, not intimate, exactly,* but in her line of work, she had learned how to avoid them.

The car was barreling toward the struggling couple, its headlights washing over them and its roof-lights flickering against the alley's brick walls like flame in a fireplace.

As the light beamed at Buffy, she hugged the wall.

The vampire released his victim, and the woman yanked her purse from his grip by its strap.

Two Sunnydale police officers leaped from their squad car, guns out and aimed at the guy. He quickly raised his hands in compliance.

"Don't shoot!" he pleaded.

He's no vampire, Buffy realized. *He's a garden-variety*

purse snatcher, performing a dark-alley mugging on a summer's night.

And he was surrendering to the cops.

A Slayer wasn't required here, after all.

She didn't think they'd seen her yet, so focused had they been on the mugger and his prey. *This is crazy,* she thought. *I'm going nuts here.* Resolving to go find Riley, just to have someone to talk to—and maybe with some kissing mixed in—she slipped from the alley, unnoticed.

Unneeded, she knew. *Extraneous. Unnecessary. And all those other words that mean useless.*

Unseen.

Chapter 1

"Look," Willow Rosenberg said, making a scrunchy face and shaking her cute red hairdo as she shivered theatrically. "And also, ick."

"Ick?" Buffy asked her, looking around, semipoised for battle. "What ick?"

"This ick."

Willow pointed to a sign on the cosmetics counter. The model on the sign was stick-thin, with sunken cheeks and bruise-colored makeup ringing her eyes, and she was draped over a tombstone in a dress that may or may not have been made of old dust rags. "Dead girl chic ick."

"I don't get it," Buffy said, shaking her head. "I mean, looking good is one thing. We all like to be fashion forward, right?"

"Some more than others," Willow observed.

"But what's the point of looking like you've already died?" Buffy went on, idly picking up one of the lipsticks, pulling off the cap and swiveling it open. It was the exact shade of Sunnydale graveyard dirt.

Grimacing, she showed it to Willow.

Willow shook her head, nowhere close to testing it on her mouth. "Vampires leave you alone?"

"Sure, but then the vultures picking at you are just as bad." Buffy picked up another tester and revealed the truly unappetizing bluish-black color to Willow.

"And I say it again," Buffy's best buddy added. "Ick."

They were in the Sunnydale mall, browsing but not really buying at Robinson's-May, the department store that anchored the west end of the shopping center. Neither had much need for new clothing or makeup right now, but they hadn't had much opportunity to spend time together of late. Willow had been hanging with her girlfriend Tara pretty much nonstop since finals week, and Buffy . . . well, Buffy hadn't been far from Riley.

So, the afternoon shopping trip. They'd started at one end of the mall, and were working their way toward the other. Shoes, dresses, even eyeglass frames—there was nothing that was out of bounds for trying on. By now, each carried a paper shopping bag with a few small purchases inside. Buffy had been telling Willow about the relative scarcity of monsters and demons on the street since the cataclysmic collapse of the Initiative, the paramilitary demon-hunting unit of which Riley Finn had been a part. Her fear was that the nasties would take the disappearance of the Initiative's hunters as a good reason to flood the city, but instead they seemed to be keeping their distance. Now that classes were over for the summer and she had time to worry about the Hellmouth, it was all quiet.

Buffy was sniffing a bottle of Charlie—it smelled like her mother—when Willow called out, "Oh, Buffy, look!"

"Another ick?" Buffy inquired.

"No, not at all." Willow held up a tiger-striped vest of some fuzzy, remotely furlike fabric. A fuchsia zipper ran up the front. "Look. Is it me?"

Buffy regarded it carefully. Her slender, redheaded friend clutched the vest against her body. "I don't know if it *is* you," Buffy finally said. "It *could* be you, I guess. If you were, you know, somebody else. Who isn't you."

"But I want it to be me," Willow said plaintively. "I want to be one of those women who wear the really amazingly cool clothes and look great in them."

"There's no law that says you can't change," Buffy pointed out, flipping over the tag. "Except maybe for the law against stealing, since that's probably what you'd have to do to get your hands on something like this."

"Humph," Willow said. "I . . . could have the bucks."

"Yeah, for fall tuition and books," Buffy countered. "Besides, you look fine, just the way you are. Wonderful."

"I guess," Willow agreed, looking at the price tag. "But this . . . this is calling my name."

"A leopard can't change his spots," Buffy said. "But maybe a tiger can change her stripes if she wants. Okay." She nodded eagerly, loving the thrill that inevitably came on when a fellow consumer nailed a buying decision. "I definitely think you should go for it."

"It'll mean doing without for a while."

"Without what?"

"Pretty much everything," Willow said glumly. Then she brightened. "Water's cheap, though. And on the bright side, if I starve myself for a few weeks, I could start to look fashionably dead."

"Buy the vest," Buffy urged. "You love it. You may not want to wear it until the weather cools down, but it will. Someday. And when we're finished here I'll treat you to a scone. Or one of those great big carrot muffins."

Willow's face broke into a smile that Buffy found infectious. Willow threw her arms around her friend and crushed her, with the vest imprisoned between them.

"Thank you, Buffy. You're just the corrupting influence I need in these trying times of growinguphood."

Buffy's eyes widened as the hug continued.

"Um, Willow?"

"What?" she asked joyfully.

"I think you're imprinting tiger stripes in my skin."

"Oh, sorry." Willow released her and backed away.

"Not to mention zipper," Buffy added, rubbing herself. "But I think, unlike a tattoo, zipper marks fade with time."

"Let's go pay for this," Willow said, all resolve face. "I mean, I'll pay for it."

"Right," Buffy said. "I pay for the food."

There was a coffee shop a few stores down from Robinson's-May. Buffy tugged open the glass door and held it for Willow, who was still fairly beaming from her purchase. The scents of fresh-brewed coffee, cinnamon, and baked goods on the air drew Buffy like iron filings to a magnet. Soft jazz emanated from unseen speakers like music from heaven.

Once inside, Buffy headed for the shiny wooden counter to place her order. It took her a moment to realize that Willow had paused behind her. Buffy turned and looked at Willow, but Willow was staring hard into the farthest corner of the deep, narrow coffee shop.

"I think I know that girl," Willow said quietly.

Buffy followed her gaze. There was a young woman sitting alone at a table in the back. She was pretty, with onyx-black hair and smooth olive skin, but tears had streaked her eyeliner down her cheeks, and she dabbed at her nose with a napkin. A coffee cup steamed on the table in front of her.

"Looks bummed," Buffy observed.

"She's one of the happiest girls I know," Willow said, concerned. "I mean, she used to be. I thought."

"I can see that," Buffy said, speculatively tilting her chin. "Not."

Willow said, "I need to talk to her."

"I'll give you guys a minute, then join you. Bearing yummies."

"Okay," Willow said. Then she was headed toward the crying girl. Buffy turned to the counter to place her order.

A few minutes later, Buffy put two cups of iced mocha on the table, then returned to the counter for her three scones. She brought them back, warm from the oven, and put them in the middle.

"Maple oat nut, currant, and cranberry," she announced. "Dig in." She looked at Willow's friend and held out her hand. "I'm Buffy."

The girl managed a smile that revealed even white teeth. Even though she was dressed very casually, in a UC Sunnydale T-shirt and a pair of jeans, she exuded class. She had her hair up, held in place with a simple tortoise-shell comb that looked old and expensive. A simple gold crucifix hung from a chain around her neck, matching two reddish-gold bangle bracelets, and a gold signet ring on her right middle finger. One small gold post per ear finished off her look.

"Hi, Buffy," she said. "I'm Salma de la Natividad. Willow has told me so much about you."

"Salma was in my world lit class," Willow explained. "She did a great paper on the impact of magical realist literature on election cycles in Latin America, and . . ." She must have seen the glazed look that Buffy could feel inching across her face, despite her best effort to appear interested. "She has kind of a problem."

Which doesn't take a genius to figure out, Buffy thought. *And I don't think it has anything to do with her final grade in world lit.*

"Oh?"

"It's my brother, Nicky," Salma told them. Her lower lip quivered, and Buffy was afraid she was going to break out crying again. Buffy could battle outlandish beasties all day long, but the emotional outbursts of strangers were close to terrifying for her. "I haven't seen him for days."

"Do you usually see him?" Buffy asked.

"He's been staying in my apartment with me for a while," Salma explained. "But now he's missing."

"What do you think, he's run away? Kidnapped?"

"I . . . I don't know," Salma replied. She looked across the table at Buffy, regarding her with serious brown eyes. Buffy felt like she was being sized up. "I didn't go to high school here in Sunnydale," Salma continued. "But I have heard stories about you, Buffy. Not from Willow, but from others. Kids who speak of your high school graduation day, when you . . ."

"Well," Buffy said, picking up a scone and tearing off a little bit. She always felt strange to hear that civilians knew about any of her Slayer exploits. Most people in Sunnydale had made a lifestyle choice of looking the other way. There had been, after the graduation incident, some recognition from her fellow students of her role in keeping them alive, but it had faded quickly, and she had become invisible girl again. "People exaggerate, you know."

"I don't think so." Salma regarded Buffy very seriously as Buffy nibbled on the scone. "I think you are truly something special."

Buffy shrugged uncomfortably. Praise wasn't her preferred position in a conversation.

That's more up Faith's alley, she thought, chilled for a moment, then let it go.

"Buffy's mom feels that way, too," Willow said to Salma.

Salma took a breath. "The reason I bring it up is that I am afraid for Nicky. Afraid that he has become involved with something . . . something supernatural." Unconsciously or not, Salma touched the crucifix around her neck.

"Why do you think that?" Buffy asked.

Salma started to speak, and then the floodgates opened. Tears filled her eyes and spilled down her cheeks. She bowed her head and began to sob quietly. Willow took Salma's hand, and they let her cry for a few minutes. When she was able to bring herself under control again, Willow handed her a tissue. She blew her nose and looked shyly up at them.

"I'm sorry," she said meekly. "I'm such a baby."

"Don't be silly," Willow insisted. "You're worried."

Salma dabbed her eyes and twisted the tissue between her hands. "Yes, I am."

"You said something about the supernatural," Buffy prodded gently.

"Yes," Salma nodded. "My grandmother . . . she has some experience in these things. I am afraid that Nicky is following in her footsteps, without really understanding what he's toying with. I believe there are forces—dark forces—at work in the world."

"You're not kidding there," Buffy said. Willow glanced at her but kept her silence.

"And if Nicky has become involved with them, as I fear, then he may be in more danger than he can imagine."

"Or there."

"You do know about these things, don't you?"

"A little," Buffy admitted. Nervously, she sipped her mocha, pulled some more crumbs off the currant scone.

"Nicky has always been a dabbler," Salma told them both. "He takes up a hobby, spends some money on it, then moves on to something else. Like skiing. He decided one winter that he wanted to take up skiing. He subscribed to three magazines, bought the most expensive Rossignols he could find, ski clothing, special sunglasses. Now it all collects dust in his closet. By the next winter, he was on to snowboarding."

"And you think this month's diversion is demonology or something?" Buffy asked.

The distraught girl smoothed back her perfectly smooth hair. "He was living with me, at my condo. But he was calling Doña Pilar, my grandmother, a lot. Asking her questions. And I found some books, in his room."

"What kind of books?" Willow asked.

"Books with strange names," Salma replied. "I remember some of the titles. *De Vermis Mysteriis. Brotherhood of the Dawn. The Book of Eibon. Culte des Goules.*"

"Giles has that one," Willow interjected, a little excited.

"Willow . . ." Buffy's tone was a warning one.

"Well, he does." Willow snatched up her cup and drank, then set it down indignantly.

"Okay. So he left these books behind, and they freaked you out."

Salma hesitated. "Yes . . ."

"That's the technical term," Buffy explained. "Freaked out. Sorcerers and black magicians use it all the time."

"You think I'm being foolish," Salma said. It wasn't a question.

Buffy instantly regretted being flip. "No, not at all. I believe you're genuinely worried about him."

She took a moment. Willow was sending *help her* via the magic of serious face, and who was she to deny that she'd been looking for something to do?

Not to do, she corrected. *To slay. I'm a vampire slayer, not Sherlock Holmes.*

And a grown-up guy who's been living with his sister, away from his parents ... I hear mere road trip in this equation.

"If he's been reading those books, I also believe that you might be right," Willow said. "He might be messing around with things he doesn't understand. Bad things."

"And then, three days ago," Salma continued, "He didn't come home. I called our family in Los Angeles, and all of his friends that I know. No one has seen him, or heard from him. This isn't like him at all. He is very much a family person, always in touch."

"Couldn't be something like he got a new girlfriend?" Buffy queried.

Salma shook her head. "He would have called, or something. He would have brought her over." She gripped her coffee cup.

"You really are scared, aren't you?" Willow asked her.

"Do you think you could—no, never mind." Salma looked at her lap as if she had lost something there. "I'm sorry. I don't have any right to ask."

"There's nothing to be sorry about," Willow chimed in. "Of course we'll help you, if there's anything we can do."

Buffy wanted to kick her. It wasn't enough that she had to live on a Hellmouth and kick demon behind her whole life, but now she was being volunteered to assist a friend of Willow's track down a brother who had probably just gone surfing in Baja for the weekend.

But that wasn't what she said. What she said was, "Sure we will. Whatever we can do. I mean, any friend of

Willow's . . ." She left the thought unfinished because she wasn't really sure how to end it.

Salma flashed another smile. Buffy realized that when she did smile, the girl was past beautiful and into stunning-model territory. Her rich olive skin set off the whiteness of her teeth, her deep brown eyes almost glowed with passion, all topped off by that lustrous black hair. She seemed very alive, all in the moment, but very sad. Suddenly Buffy found herself wanting to help Salma as much as Willow did.

After all, there was no summer job ahead for her, no special plans, just patrolling and spending time with Riley, and while those things were good—the Riley part especially was great—it wouldn't hurt to have a goal. A challenge. Something to make the days go faster.

"Of course," she said at length. "When can we get started?"

"I think you're right, Buffy," Riley told her that night. They were patrolling together, making a circuit of Weatherly Park. Riley, tall, darkish blondish, and gorgeous, wore his fatigue pants with a dark olive ribbed T-shirt. Buffy, remembering the stifling heat of the night before, stuck with a T and cargo pants. "He's probably just off partying with some buds. Got caught up in the adventure and forgot to call home." He flashed a smile at her. "Hey, teenage guys can be irresponsible sometimes, right?"

"Most of them," Buffy said. "Most I've known, anyway."

"So in a day or so, her brother will probably remember and give her a ring. In the meantime, it's nice of you to spend some time looking around. She give you any idea of where to begin?"

Buffy thought about it a moment. "Not really," she said. "Her brother had some books, you know, the kind Giles likes to keep around for light reading? How-to guides for the spirit world, and so on. But nothing as handy as, say, a road map fell out of them when she shook them. So I'd have to say that's a big no."

He was scanning the perimeter, a bit distracted. He was a well-trained combat guy, but he didn't have Slayer reflexes; every once in a while the multitasking tasked him.

"What are you planning to do, then?"

She shrugged. "Mostly keep Salma company, I think, is the plan. Until Nicky comes home on his own, or we think of something. Willow and Tara are hanging with her tonight. Weepy movies and ice cream on the agenda." She smiled wistfully. "Chubby Hubby ice cream."

When he smiled, he had dimples. "Wish you were there?"

Buffy looked down at her stomach, then at Riley. She took his hand. "I think I'm right where I want to be," she said.

There was a glance of smolder, as Willow had taken to calling them. Buffy and Riley were not lacking in the chemistry department. Nor in the respect department. He knew she was stronger than he was, and that was kind of cool, in his book.

And that was incredibly cool in hers.

He gave her hand a squeeze and took a final look around the park, turning in a slow three-sixty. His practiced eyes didn't miss a thing. Buffy loved watching him work—the way he triangulated his field of view: near, middle, far, so that he would see anything that was there to be seen. He was methodical, dividing up the landscape into sections, dismissing one before moving on to the next.

At one point he stopped, gave a nod. "Young lovers on the grass over there," he pointed out.

"Cute," Buffy said. They were probably making with the big smoochies.

They shared a look: *there but for patrol go we.*

And also except for the fact that they had access to indoor smoochie facilities, namely Riley's place.

Riley chuckled softly—he was reading her mind, or else her body language—and Buffy knew it was time to get back to business.

"Come on," he said. "Let's cut across the park toward the playground, see if anything's happening over there."

"I thought those two would never leave," Burt said, meaning the petite blonde and her tall militia-type boyfriend, or whatever he was, wearing cammies. He and Aimee were sprawled on a blanket on the grass. They'd had a nice picnic as the sun set, and then had been sitting and talking quietly ever since.

It was their third date. The first two had been a little more traditional—dinner and a movie, then a weekend lunch and a game of miniature golf. Now the picnic. Burt had great hopes for the picnic. He knew Weatherly Park closed at ten. But he also knew that there were spots inside the park where the groundskeeper who locked the gates couldn't see someone who was waiting quietly. And once the gates were locked, privacy was assured.

It had worked for him before.

Not with anyone quite as hot as the lovely Aimee, though. Burt sold cars at the Ford/Lincoln dealership, and Aimee was the new chick on the lot, working as a cashier in the service department. Since her first day on the job, Burt had kept an eye on her. It was impossible not to. She was tall, built, and had he mentioned built?

Her hair was red and thick, piled on top of her head at work but loose and free-flowing now. He had started flirting with her during her second week on the job, casually, taking it easy, not pushing as so many of the other guys had done.

That was the way Burt sold cars, too. He kept things loose, easy. Let the customer sell himself. Let the car sell itself. When the customers ran from the high-pressure techniques of the other salespeople, they ran straight into the arms of Burt, who acted like he didn't care if he never sold another car—just as long as people left the lot with smiles on their faces.

And his no-pressure system made him the highest volume performer on the lot, month after month.

Now, he was about to find out if it worked with Aimee, too. So far, so good.

And she'll leave with a smile on her face, too. No problems with that kind of performance, either.

Guaranteed.

Aimee was watching the incongruous pair hop the fence. Burt watched too, anxious for them to be gone. They were surprisingly athletic, particularly the woman, who had looked too small and slender to be making the moves she was making. Trick of the light, or something: he could have sworn she shimmied up the eight-foot fence like it was a stepladder. Then she hopped over like no big deal, with a nice, easy landing.

"You're sure there's no one else around?" Aimee asked.

Her voice quaked a little. *Good,* Burt thought. *If she's nervous, that means she's game.*

"Absotively," Burt said. That was one of his favorite words. Sometimes it was followed by "posolutely." But not tonight. Because as soon as the first word was out of his mouth, Aimee's tongue was in his mouth.

Wow. Talk about horsepower.

Breathlessly, she turned to him, pressing his shoulders

against the blanket. "Oh, Burt, that's so good," she said, panting. She smiled at him. "I've been waiting long enough."

He felt her hands roaming over him, his shoulders, his chest, his legs. He was a little taken aback—he liked to be the aggressor—but not enough to object. *Hey, I can be a piece of meat just as much as the next guy.*

It was only because he was lying on his back, eyes open, that he could see anything at all. It had gotten that dark. Aimee's cheek, in the forefront of his vision, was illuminated by a stray beam from a streetlight just outside the park fence. But suddenly, as he watched, the spot of light that defined her cheekbone disappeared into shadow.

Someone standing over us? Cops?

Burt pushed her off and sat up quickly.

"What's the matter?" Aimee asked. "I thought this was what you—"

"Shh!" He looked around. There was the streetlight. But he couldn't see what had passed between there and here to block its light. Couldn't see anything but the shadows.

And then, the shadows came to life.

A black shape, nothing more than dark against dark, moved across his field of vision. Aimee clutched his forearm, her fingers biting into his skin. *She saw it, too, then.*

"What is it?" she hissed.

"No idea."

There was no way to determine its borders, its boundaries. One shadow slipping across another shadow, black on black, moving with absotive, posolute silence through the benighted parkland.

Burt couldn't say why, but he believed it was getting closer to them.

If only I could see it clearly, he thought.

Aimee let out a hushed whimper. Burt wouldn't have minded if she'd screamed.

He felt the tiny hairs standing up on his arms, his neck. It was definitely getting closer. He thought he could hear something now, but then he realized it was just a breeze fluttering the leaves of the trees that he couldn't see, the trees that were also in shadow.

Just before it struck, he smelled it, though; an exhalation of dank, fetid breath that washed over them. His stomach knotted.

A moment later sharp claws ripped it from his body and spilled it onto the ground.

Finally, Aimee screamed.

Then it was her turn.

Chapter 2

THE WHOLE GANG CONVERGED AT GILES'S APARTMENT AT noon—the "gang" consisting of Buffy, Riley, Willow, Xander, and Anya. Giles had called Buffy early in the morning, awakening her, and insisted that she gather them together first thing. She had agreed, then fallen back to sleep in Riley's arms.

Twenty minutes later, she awoke with a start and a guilty conscience. She made some calls and took a quick shower. And here they were, almost like they were having a come-as-you-are party, because Anya, for one, had some serious bedhead going, and Xander hadn't shaved.

In a wrinkled jeans skirt and a nice fuzzy sweater, Willow covered a yawn and looked politely interested.

All were seated around Giles's cluttered living room, and Buffy was wishing she and Riley had taken the time to get a couple of lattes to stay awake. Giles, in an actual T-shirt (*Grateful Dead, yet!*) and a pair of jeans, was so not the tweedy British guy of yore, yore being high school.

He stood to one side of the group, where his stereo system was. Albums—the vinyl kind—leaned against the system. Derek and the Dominoes, Van Morrison, The Who. Buffy had heard of the British Invasion; Giles seemed intent on reliving it.

He was talking about his new hobby.

"I've been listening to, umm, police band radio lately," he explained. "It's fascinating, really. A bit of a slice of real life, you know. As opposed to those ridiculous programs you all watch on television."

"Like *Cops?*" Xander suggested.

"Precisely." He realized he'd been taunted, and blinked the way he did when he was slightly miffed. "Or—well, never mind. The point is that what I'm hearing are the Sunnydale Police Department's own internal communications. Just in case they run into something that's a bit out of their league, as it were."

Buffy watched him fiddling with his cassette recorder. She had known him for years and loved him like a father—or at least, like a Watcher, which was what he had originally been to her. The Watchers Council had kicked him out, because he sided with her, against them. So she still thought of him that way, as a kind and wise older man who cared for her and had her best interests at heart. She would do anything for him.

But boy, she thought. *Since the high school came down, Giles has sure become desperate to be needed.*

Finally he had the tape cued to where he wanted it. "Here," he said. "Listen to this."

Staticky audio came from his speakers. There seemed to be a lot of that "one Adam twelve" stuff she'd heard on TV a million times. But after a few moments, as she got used to listening, she heard a young officer's voice quivering with horror.

". . . horrible," the voice said. "I've never seen anything like it. A pack of wild dogs, maybe . . . more like a shark attack, though. Except in the middle of Weatherly Park. There are . . . there are pieces everywhere. Pieces . . ." His voice broke off then.

Giles clicked the tape off. "I wanted you to hear the emotion in the young policeman's voice," he said. "The abject terror."

There were nods all around.

"Very abject," Willow said helpfully.

"This is definitely not wild dogs."

"It never is," Anya said, stretching. She yawned. "Maybe it *was* sharks."

Giles blinked. "Anya, there are no sharks cruising through a city park, miles from the ocean."

Anya scowled.

"And then, there was another call, several hours earlier. I didn't play it for you first, because the dispatcher who relayed the call to a squad car didn't take it seriously. But in light of the discovery made this morning—" He consulted a note he had jotted down. "—at seven-thirteen, the call from last night certainly seems like something that ought to have been taken very seriously indeed."

He rewound the tape and pressed another button. Again, the static came through the speakers, followed by a voice.

"Dispatch, this is Peters. I checked out that squeal you caught over on the south side."

"The monster?" another voice asked. The dispatcher, presumably.

Peters barked out a laugh. "That's the one. Seems Mr. and Mrs. LaVeaux were taking a walk, around midnight. The old man doesn't sleep so well, unless he gets a late walk. So they were out, and they felt like they were being watched."

"Never heard that one before."

"Right. So they're walking, they're getting nervous, and then Mrs. LaVeaux, she says that there's a shadow following them down the street. That she can see it when it passes underneath the streetlights. It's big, hunched over-looking, like a big cat following them down the sidewalk, only it's twice the size of the biggest lion in Africa."

"Ain't they all," Dispatch drawled.

"Ten feet tall, twenty feet long. She can only see it when it slips through the patches of light. Like it's there, but not there, she says. Mr. LaVeaux, he sees it, too. It's behind them, but it's getting closer, catching up. Only they get home before it reaches them, turn on all the lights, and call us."

"You see anything in the neighborhood?" Dispatch queried.

"Plenty of shadows. It's one in the morning. But none of them chased me. I'm heading back in."

"See you soon," Dispatch said. "Over and out."

Giles stopped the tape again. "So you see—"

"I have a question," Anya interrupted, raising her hand like an elementary school student. Beside her, Xander visibly cringed.

"Yes, Anya?"

"If you taped that call at one in the morning, and the other one at seven-thirteen, does that mean you're totally insane, or just obsessive-compulsive?"

Xander elbowed her in the ribs. "You are the soul of discretion, Anya."

"Like you weren't wondering it, too."

Giles reddened a bit, but continued. "So you see. A report of a big catlike presence, a shadow monster of some kind. And elsewhere the same night, two lovers are torn apart by something with giant claws."

Buffy saw Willow nervously twirling her hair around one finger. "It couldn't be . . ."

"It's not Oz," Buffy assured her, even though she wasn't so sure herself.

Willow's eyes grew huge. "But it might be. What if he's back, and he's gone evil somehow? That happens, right?"

"Willow, there's no reason to think it was him. It doesn't even really sound like a werewolf attack. And even as a wolf, who would think that Oz was ten feet tall?" She turned to Giles with a plaintive expression. "But when we can rule it out for certain, I'm sure Will . . . we'll be happier."

"I agree with Buffy," Giles said. "For one thing, last night was a half-moon. Not werewolf time at all.

"Nonetheless, we must investigate every possibility. I'd like a couple of you to go to the park. Check for paw prints. See if there's any reason that we need to think werewolves are involved. I'm sure it's not Oz, but we should rule it out one hundred percent."

"Yeah," Willow agreed.

"And maybe we should find Spike, see if he's heard anything," Buffy added.

"Good idea, Buffy," Giles said.

"Any thoughts as to how the victims were chosen?" Riley asked. "Buffy and I were in Weatherly Park last night, probably around the time of the attack—we saw a couple there, before we left. It looked like they wanted some privacy."

"Were they naked?" Anya asked.

"Not yet," Riley replied. "Matter of moments after we left, I'm sure."

"I don't think we have enough information yet to . . . to speculate on that," Giles said, still a bit red-cheeked. "All we know is that one couple saw a creature, and another couple had a more unfortunate encounter with something that may or may not have been the same creature."

"I have a suggestion," Xander volunteered.

"Yes, Xander?" Giles asked him.

Everyone looked at him expectantly.

He did not disappoint.

"If we all stay inside for the next few nights, maybe none of us will run into this, this shadow monster. Then, maybe you can keep listening to your junior G-man radio set, and you can figure out how it picks its victims.

"And once we know that, then we can just not do whatever it is that its victims all have in common." He smiled brightly and raised his eyebrows.

"That's incredibly helpful, Xander," Giles said.

"I think what Xander means is that he's offering himself up as bait," Riley joked. "We'll tie him to a tree and watch from a distance to see what happens."

"Yes. With our special X-Men field glasses, so it can be a very faraway distance," Buffy added, all lilting innocence.

Anya put her arms protectively around Xander. "If anyone's going to be tying Xander up, it's going to be me," she announced. "And he likes it best if you—"

Xander shot up and clapped a hand down over Anya's mouth. "Discretion again," he said, blushing furiously. "I can see we need to make another trip to the big dictionary."

"Obviously, I need to patrol again tonight," Buffy said, changing the subject for Xander's benefit.

"We both do," Riley agreed.

Buffy turned to him. "But not together. We can cover more ground if we split up."

Riley reluctantly nodded.

"And also, we still have Salma's brother to think about," Willow reminded her. "We promised her we'd work on that."

"Unless Salma's brother is in pieces in the park, I think this has to take a higher priority," Buffy argued.

"Buffy, from what you told me of the books Willow's friend says her brother was delving into, I think you had better make him a high priority as well," Giles suggested.

Buffy frowned. He took off his glasses as he regarded her, then set to cleaning them with his T-shirt.

"Those are not beginning readers. He's playing with some deadly serious toys. I hate to suggest it, but the timing of his disappearance, with the sudden presence of these shadow beasts, suggests that there may even be some connection between the two cases."

Willow nodded at the Slayer. Capitulating, Buffy sighed. "Okay. We'll put some effort into trying to locate Nicky today. Giles, how about if you and Xander and Anya do some research, try to see if you can turn up anything about 'shadow monsters.' "

Giles looked at Anya and Xander. Buffy could see his shoulders slump a bit as he did. But he was a trooper.

"Very well."

"I'll go out on patrol and you can deal with Willow's friend," Riley said. "If I need backup, Buffy, I'll be in touch."

"Be sure you are," Buffy insisted. "This thing sounds pretty nasty."

"I'm tough," Riley reminded her, with a little wink.

"I know. I wasn't saying that you weren't."

She was abashed. She kept expecting him to not love the fact that no matter how tough he was, he would never be as strong as she was. Her defensiveness in that area was hard to let go of. Why, she wasn't too sure. It had never bothered her that she was stronger than Xander, and it had been a point of pride in the early days that she could deck Giles within minutes of any training session. But Riley was her boyfriend, her very-much-human boyfriend, and for some reason, there was the crazy notion of the other shoe dropping, and him admitting he wanted some chick in a gauzy negligee who stood in the corner and screamed while he vanquished the evil.

Maybe I just keep expecting him to find some reason to leave. Which, given my history with the opposite sex, is not an insane fear.

Still, ego.

His, or mine?

He was staring at her intently, as if trying to speak to her in the secret code of goo-goo eyes.

"What?"

"I'll call for backup if I need it," he said gently. "Don't worry."

"Not. Not worried." She made her eyes big. "Really."

His smile was slow and lazy, like the Iowa River or whatever it was. Corn-fed, normal Riley.

She thought about the magnet on his refrigerator: *Things are not as they seem. They are what they are.*

Maybe only in love, she thought.

That's sure not true of life in the Slay lane.

Los Angeles

There was something bothering Cordelia Chase as she walked down Rodeo Drive in Beverly Hills, looking into the windows of shops that she couldn't even afford to walk into, but she couldn't quite put her finger on what it was.

No, that wasn't quite accurate. She couldn't isolate it, because it wasn't just one thing, it was many. And they all added up to one big, overwhelming fact—Cordelia was having a lousy day. She had saved up enough money to buy a pair of killer pumps she'd had her eye on at Barney's, and that still held promise of turning the day around. But so far it just pretty much stunk.

There was the obvious fact, of course, that all these stores had been placed on the earth just to taunt her, to remind her of how much money she had once had, and how much she didn't have now that the IRS had taken from her father what it felt it was owed for all those years in which he had not bothered to pay his income taxes.

There was the fact that, although working in the office of a vampire private investigator had its own rewards, none of them were monetary. And it wasn't even something she could really talk about at parties.

Then there was the sighting, just moments ago while crossing the street at the corner, of Monique Breton, who Cordelia had once known as Monica Barnes. Monica had gone to junior high in Sunnydale, but since moving to L.A. she had scored a recurring role on a TV series. She wasn't even a cast regular yet, but one would never know that by the way she looked right through Cordelia on the street—even though Cordelia had been working up her fake I'm-so-happy-for-you-smile and everything.

And Monique/Monica isn't the only one who seems to think I'm transparent, she thought. *It's like no one can see me.*

Back in Sunnydale, Cordelia had been the big fish in a small pond. She wasn't universally loved, but she was universally known. Xander and Willow hadn't formed a "We Hate Cordelia" club because she was some nobody. In Sunnydale, she had been the glamour queen, the beautiful one, the captain of the cheerleaders.

In Los Angeles, though, she was just one more pretty face in a sea of pretty faces, many of which were more well-known and successful than she was.

She wasn't used to being one of the minnows. And she didn't like it.

She crossed Rodeo, intending to cut over to Beverly.

There were stores there, only a block over, where a normal human could afford to shop once in a while. Places where the shopkeepers didn't judge one by how recently a person had appeared in the trades. Cordelia could take Beverly down to Wilshire. She wouldn't feel as invisible there as she did here in glitz central.

She was just stepping up to the curb on the east side of the street when it hit.

A vision. A bad one. The force of it knocked her down.

It started with a grinding pain behind the eyes, like someone was operating on her frontal lobe with a power tool of some kind. Then it got bad. Agony that felt like hot steel rods being driven through her skull.

In the midst of it—and she never got this part, she always thought it would be much more efficient if the visions came with some kind of pleasant, peaceful sensation so she could focus more on them and less on the pain—she saw the face of a young boy. Dark skin, black hair, big brown eyes wide with terror. *Not more than ten or so,* she thought. His name was Carlos Flores. He lived on South Pembroke, not far from the intersection of Figueroa and Pico.

Then the vision was gone, the memory of Carlos Flores's face burned into her memory, and the pain was receding.

But she was still sitting on the sidewalk on Rodeo Drive. Land of the beautiful people. And now—of course—they were looking at her.

Cordelia felt her cheeks redden with the sudden attention. "Slipped," she explained to no one in particular.

A bronzed god with a swimmer's build and expensively perfect teeth extended her a hand and helped her up. "You okay?" he asked.

"Fine, thanks. Slipped," she repeated. She thought she recognized him from a guest shot on *Baywatch: Hawaii,* but since she didn't admit publicly to watching the show, she couldn't ask him. Anyway, the humiliation was too much to bear. A little unsteady on her feet, she left Rodeo Drive, looking for a pay phone.

She found one on Beverly, in front of Nate & Al's. Maybe after she called she'd go in for some blintzes, or one of their justifiably famous pastrami sandwiches. But first things first. She fed the phone and dialed the number of her apartment. Wesley Wyndam-Pryce picked up on the second ring.

"Angel Investigations," he answered.

"Wesley, can't you say 'Cordelia Chase's apartment,' and also 'Angel Investigations?' What if a casting director calls or something?"

"Let's cross that bridge when we come to it, shall we?" Wesley replied. "No need to live our lives in a delusional state."

"Very funny," she said sourly. "I need Angel."

"He's rather busy at the moment. Is there, perhaps, any way in which I can be of assistance?"

Wesley was British, a former Watcher turned "rogue demon hunter" when his charges, Faith and Buffy, turned out to be a bit more rogue than he was. He helped Angel on some of his cases, but his type of assistance tended toward the cerebral rather than the physical. She didn't think there was anything he could do now. Besides, when the Powers That Be sent a vision, they intended it for Angel, not his subordinates.

"No. Angel. Vision."

"Ahh, right. Hold on."

She heard footsteps fading from the phone, then returning a moment later. Wesley picked up again. "Right with you, Cordelia."

"Thanks, Wesley." She waited. Her head still throbbed, but the pain was going away.

After another moment, he said, "Here he is." *Master of the obvious,* Cordelia thought. Angel's voice came over the line a second later.

"Cord. You had a vision?"

"Right in the middle of Rodeo Drive," she said. "You can't imagine how embarrassing that is. I mean, it was one thing when I was in your office, which was, to put it bluntly, not heavily trafficked, you know? But here, in Beverly Hills, I'm among my tribe. One second I run into an old, old friend who's starring in a hit series, and the next I'm on the ground with my head in my hands.

"Next time you talk to the Powers That Be, try to get them to work on their timing, okay?"

"Cordelia. The vision?"

"Sure, I understand. The pain of some stranger you've never met is so much more important than mine. Sorry, that's redundant, I guess. Isn't a stranger, by definition, someone you haven't met?"

"Cordelia . . ."

"Carlos Flores," she said. "South Pembroke, near Pico. He's just a kid, Angel. And he's scared."

"I'm on it, Cord. I'll keep you posted."

"You do that," she said. "In the meantime I think I owe myself a treat."

Angel hung up the phone. Cordelia stood on Beverly, debating. *Nate & Al's? Or the bakery across the street?*

Sunnydale

"Here's the list."

Salma de la Natividad slid a piece of looseleaf note-book paper across the oak table toward Buffy. Twin red candles, cinnamon-scented, burned in silver candle holders on the tabletop. They were in Salma's condo, in a fourteen-story building a few blocks from the beach. She was no dorm kid, Buffy realized. Her place was just a two-bedroom condo, but it was light, spacious, and airy. She had furnished it in light woods and wickers, with colorful print fabrics providing splashes of color here and there.

Buffy turned the paper over and scanned it. Salma had written, in a neat, legible hand, a list of names, addresses, and phone numbers. All the friends of her brother whom she knew about, and where they could usually be found. Buffy didn't recognize any of the names, but that wasn't surprising. Until yesterday, she didn't even know Salma existed. She passed the list over to Willow, who sat in the chair next to her.

"I love your place," Buffy said as Willow read.

"Thank you," Salma replied graciously. "My parents did not want me to live in student housing. This building has security downstairs, and it's comfortable."

"I'll say."

So she doesn't want to talk about being rich, Buffy thought. *That's okay.* She let the subject drop.

Willow looked up from the paper. "No bells," she said.

"But it's a good starting point," Buffy added. "We'll talk to these people, see if we can get a line on Nicky."

"Just like detectives," Willow offered.

"Exactly like that," Buffy agreed. "Except, no badges."

Willow moved into helpful mode. "We could get badges."

Buffy wrinkled her nose. "I don't know that badges are strictly necessary."

"I'm only *saying,*" Willow insisted, "if we wanted badges, I know where we could get some."

"Let's do without the badges," Buffy said.

"Okay. Badgeless detectives for hire." Willow glanced

at Salma. "I mean, not really *hire*. We don't want to be paid or anything."

"Oh. I could—" Salma started to say. Buffy cut her off.

"Not necessary. We're doing this because you're a friend. Of Willow's, I mean. Strictly a favor. Okay?"

"Okay," Salma said. She smiled that nice smile again. She seemed a little more relaxed today, even though Nicky was still missing.

Probably because someone's finally going to make an effort.

Salma had described her trip to the police station to report her brother as a missing person. They hadn't sounded very encouraging, trying to sell her on the irresponsible teenager theory of his disappearance.

"Well, we'll get started on the list," Buffy said. "Call us if you think of anything else. Or if you hear from Nicky."

"I will," Salma agreed.

Everyone rose, and she walked them to the door. As they said good-bye, Buffy thought Salma's calm facade was slipping a little. Her lower lip might have trembled a bit.

When Salma closed the door behind them, she was pretty sure she heard the girl start crying.

"We have to help her."

Willow nodded. "We really, really do."

"I'll go check out the park," Riley said. To Giles, he added, "I'll let you know what the crime scene looks like."

He, Xander, Giles, and Anya had stayed at Giles's place after Buffy and Willow left to see Willow's friend Salma. They'd discussed their strategy and floated some theories as to what the shadow monster might really be. But none of the theories really rang true, and Riley ultimately decided that he had to check out a known location where the thing had been. Maybe there was some kind of physical evidence there, a footprint, a bit of skin. Anything would give them more to go on than they had now, which was a big fat goose egg.

"Right," Giles said. "We'll be here working."

"I'll keep you posted," Riley said. Part of him hoped he walked right into the thing, though he doubted it would be out in broad daylight, and it was still hours until dark.

"If you see anyone having sex in the park, you should warn them that it's not safe," Anya added.

Xander just closed his eyes.

"Got it," Riley said.

"Some people like to do it in public," she continued. "In fact, once Xander and I—"

"Ann," Xander interrupted wearily.

Riley chuckled and headed for the door.

Which was when Willow's girlfriend, Tara, walked in.

"Oh, Tara. Hi," he said, stepping back to let her in.

"Hello, Tara," Giles echoed.

Xander and Anya added their greetings.

Tara was a sweet girl, dressing up a bit more since she and Willow had started hanging out; also, some glittery new makeup. She had no cause for the shyness and insecurity she often exhibited, as far as Riley knew, but he was very new to the world of complex emotions and unspoken agendas. A soldier's life was black and white.

Or should be, he thought, bitterly remembering Maggie Walsh's exploitation of him.

"Hi," Tara said. She was wearing a long, feltlike skirt much like one Willow owned. She had a black jet choker around her neck and an Indian-print shirt with jet beads on the front.

She looped her hair around her ear. "Willow left a message. On my machine? She said something about a meeting . . ."

"Sort of," Riley said. "Broke up a while ago, really."

"What's up?" she asked, gazing at all the faces.

Riley wasn't sure how far he trusted Tara yet. Sure, she had proven to be an invaluable ally on that horrible last night of the Initiative. And her bond with Willow seemed very real. But she was still a bit new to the group, relatively unknown. And Maggie Walsh's motto, drilled into him throughout his Initiative training, was "Trust no one."

He wanted to trust her, for Willow's sake, if nothing else.

But it was something he'd have to work at.

"Giles can fill you in," he finally said, maintaining his pleasant tone. "I have to get going."

She ducked her head. "Okay, see you."

Riley left.

He doesn't trust me, Tara thought as he went out the door. *He thinks I can't tell. But I know he thinks I'm hiding something.*

Which I am. But anyway, that doesn't seem to bother anyone else.

Not that they know about it, but still . . .

"Something's going on?" she asked the room at large.

"Monsters," Anya reported, yawning. "Tearing people's guts out and spreading them around the park."

"Just another day in paradise," Xander said blithely.

"Y-yes, well, umm . . ." Giles gestured to the group as a whole. "Anya has summed it up rather succinctly, I think. In her own inimitable fashion."

Tara bobbed her head. "So you guys had a meeting about it."

"Right," Xander said. "At the crack of dawn."

Anya elbowed him. "It was noon. And that was hours ago."

"Well, it felt like dawn," he insisted.

"Then I guess you need to go to bed earlier at night."

And I was at the magick shop and missed the call, Tara thought. *Willow and I should work on our communication.*

"You're sad that you weren't home to get Willow's call," Anya announced. "And you feel like she should know how to reach you." Tara looked at her in surprise. She hadn't thought that reading minds was one of Anya's tricks, even when she had been a demon.

"No, I can't read your mind," Anya continued. "But it's all over your face."

"Anya, do we need to have the sensitivity talk again?" Xander asked.

"Well, look at her," Anya insisted. "Any idiot could see—"

"She's right," Tara said. "I think I can be of help, that's all."

"I'm sure you can, Tara," Giles said, looking contrite. "We've seen ample evidence of your abilities. I suspect we're just still not quite accustomed to including you when there's a general alert."

She felt a little better because of his assurances. She'd done all kinds of things with the gang—cleansed Riley's frat house, helped with the Gentlemen—but she still felt like she wasn't one of the in-Scoobs.

"I will try to do better," Giles promised, inclining his head. "Your assistance is truly valued."

"Thanks." She smiled at him. The others smiled at her. Much with the smiling.

"Anything I can do to help now?" she asked hopefully.

Giles thought a moment, his gaze cast toward the ceiling.

"Donuts?" Xander suggested. Tara looked at him. He looked away. "Never mind. Guess that's still my job."

"Riley is checking on the scene at Weatherly Park,"

Giles told her. "Buffy and Willow have gone to see if they can help find Salma's brother. Anya, Xander and I are going to do some reading, to see if we can determine what manner of creatures these are. You're welcome to join us."

"Salma?" Tara asked uneasily.

"She's not a friend like you," Anya assured her. "Not a shark-bait friend. She only started being friends with Willow to get her to help find her brother."

Tara flooded with embarrassment. She realized how jealous she had just sounded. Also, how petulant, like a little girl stamping her foot because she had not received an invitation to the party.

She would feel claustrophobic in here, right now, with these people, she knew. She needed to be outside, in the fresh air and the space.

"Maybe later," she said. "I think I'll have a look around town, see if I can l-learn anything."

"Be very careful," Giles warned. "We don't know what we're dealing with."

"I always am," Tara assured him. "Careful."

She glanced Anya's way. Anya said, "Shark-bait friend, because Giles was talking about wild dogs, or maybe sharks, and you and Willow——"

Xander cleared his throat.

Anya huffed. "I thought people in this country believed in speaking their minds."

"No, no. That's your rude countries," Xander said. "Here, we believe in liberty and politeness for all."

"I'm sure that's not true." Anya frowned. "Although it does sound familiar."

Tara bade them good-bye and headed out the door.

Chapter 3

Los Angeles

NIGHTFALL.

Angel could move around more freely. He and Wesley drove to the address Cordelia had given him. Crickets were scraping and in the distance, someone's stereo was up way too loud, the bass a heavy boom-boom-boom like thunder.

"How shall we approach it?" Wesley asked. "Good cop, bad cop? Starsky and Hutch? Crockett and Tubbs?"

"What about if we knock on the door?" Angel replied.

The house was a stucco bungalow with peeling green paint and a yard that had seen better days. The patches of grass were neatly mowed, but browning from insufficient water and the summer sun. A series of flagstones cut across the yard from the sidewalk out front to the three creaky steps leading to the front door; they gave under Angel's weight as he climbed them and looked for a bell.

The porch light glowed behind a cracked and foggy glass globe, which was nevertheless very clean.

He pulled open a torn screen and knocked on the door, then let the screen swing closed on rusty hinges. He waited. He glanced at Wesley, who shrugged. No one came to the door. He repeated the process. Stood, looking out at the quiet street. South Pembroke dead-ended at the end of this block, so there was no through traffic.

The houses all had a certain similarity—postwar construction, thrown up fast and cheap to meet the needs of the rapidly growing suburban population. Then the city grew, swallowing this neighborhood, so those who could afford it moved to different suburbs, farther out. It was the kind of neighborhood populated by people on their way up or on their way down, or simply stuck in houses they couldn't afford to get out of.

From somewhere in the bowels of the house he heard a loud crash, and a scream.

Angel yanked the screen open, tried the knob on the main door. Locked. He reared back and kicked it, right at the lock. It swung open.

And he stood there, unable to enter.

Wesley pushed past him. "I'll check it out," he said.

"Be careful," Angel called to Wesley's departing form. But if Wesley replied, he couldn't hear.

"Hello!" he called. "Anyone here?"

He waited again, straining to hear anything besides Wesley's footfalls in the quiet house. As he waited he studied the living room, visible from the doorway. Wesley had dashed through this room and out a door at the far end that Angel guessed would lead into a kitchen. He could see clean hardwood floors, a few chairs with lace doilies on the arms, a coffee table with a large family Bible on it. The walls were empty except for a crucifix on one of them, and an arrangement of family photos on another. Everything was spotless, well cared for.

After another couple of moments, a door opened and a woman appeared in the doorway with a laundry basket in her hands. She seemed startled to see Angel standing at the door.

"Hi," Angel said. "I heard a scream. And a crash. And my friend—"

Wesley returned from the kitchen just then. "Nothing in there," he started to say. But seeing the woman, he stopped in his tracks.

"What are you doing in here?" she demanded, face clouding with anger. "Who are you?"

"Well, we heard the noise," Wesley explained. "It sounded like, if you'll forgive the expression, all hell had broken loose."

"Oh, it was nothing," the woman replied, trying to sound casual and failing miserably. She looked exhausted, with ash-colored circles under her eyes. She was in her late thirties, maybe, black hair pulled into a short ponytail with escaping wisps, and large gold hoop earrings. A chain disappeared into the top of her T-shirt, but Angel could almost feel the crucifix dangling against her chest. Despite her haggard appearance, her arms, holding the laundry basket, looked strong, and though she was at least a foot shorter than he, she carried herself like someone who knew how to take care of herself, even around a tall, mysterious stranger.

Her dark eyes examined him carefully, her gaze alternating between him and Wesley. "I dropped something."

"We came to see Carlos Flores," Angel said, not believing her. "Are you his mother?"

She looked surprised all over again. "Yes, I am. Who are you?"

Wesley stepped forward. "His name's Angel," Wesley

explained. "I'm Wesley Wyndam-Pryce. We understand that he's in some kind of trouble. I know this is very odd, but Angel might be able to help. He's really very good at that kind of thing." He puffed himself up a bit. "And I'm not so bad myself."

She was cautious, suspicious. "I don't see how you could help. Are you lawyers? Or millionaires?"

"Well, no," Wesley replied.

"May I see Carlos?" Angel asked.

"Are you a social worker? Because he's been going to school, and we're fine." She lifted her chin. "We have nothing to be ashamed of."

She talked like a woman under siege, and Angel wished he was better at this part, trying to put people at ease, help them through the first initial, awkward meeting with him. It had been easier when Angel Investigations had an office, and he could wait—at least occasionally—for clients to come through his door. But Wesley seemed to have some skill at it, a nonthreatening persona he could project when necessary—or, most of the time, as it turned out.

"Mrs. Flores," Wesley said imploringly, "please believe me. We want to help your family."

She slumped. "We don't have money, if that's why you're doing this to us. We can't pay blackmail."

"We're not here to threaten you," he assured her.

Taking a breath, she added, "We're legal. We have green cards. We have a right to be in this country."

"We're not from the INS."

Tears welled and she averted her gaze, wiping them away.

"I can help you." Angel promised, his voice soft.

She nodded and opened the screen door. "I have no one to trust," she murmured, "and I have prayed day and night for help."

Still he hesitated. She almost smiled and gestured for him to enter. "Come in."

With the invitation made, Angel could cross the threshold. He stepped inside and offered his hand. The creaky screen door swung shut behind him. "I'm Angel," he said again. "I'm a private detective."

"And I'm, well, you already know that," Wesley said with a halfhearted chuckle. "Wesley."

Mrs. Flores put the laundry basket down on the clean floor. The clothes within it were worn but neatly folded. She took Angel's hand and gave it a firm shake, then followed suit with Wesley.

"Isabel Flores," she said. "You must be from Mr. Preston's office."

Angel remained silent, and let her think so. Wesley started to say something but he noticed Angel's silence and took the cue.

"Where is he? Carlos?" he prodded gently.

She turned back toward the door to the downstairs from which she had emerged. "He's been staying down there a lot," she said. "Since his father . . . well, you know."

"I'm afraid that there's a lot we don't know," Angel suggested.

She gave him a look that he couldn't quite read—an appraising stare, as if she were wondering just why she had allowed him into her house. But before she could speak, there was another loud noise from downstairs. Their eyes locked.

"You didn't drop *that*," Angel pointed out.

She pulled open the door and ran down the stairs, and he followed. At the bottom, she came to a sudden stop, taking in a sharp gasp of breath.

"Oh, my word," Wesley uttered.

The main room down here was a utility room. A furnace and an old washer and dryer hulked together in one corner. An ironing board stood nearby. On the other side of the room was a futon couch that faced a color television.

But what was remarkable about the room was that the iron had apparently abandoned the ironing board of its own free will. It flew around the space in a dizzyingly tight circle, its cord trailing behind it, narrowly missing the walls with each circuit.

Sitting on the floor, watching it with curiosity and what looked like barely contained terror, was a boy who could only be Carlos.

Poltergeist, Angel thought. He had some experience with the phenomenon—Cordelia, after all, shared her apartment with a ghost named Dennis, who had exhibited some of this same kind of behavior.

Usually, poltergeists were mischievous, not harmful. But if this one dropped or lost control of that iron, the boy sitting beneath it could be badly injured. Angel timed his move, outpacing the iron by a little, and snatched it.

As strong as he was, it still took everything he had to bring it under control.

It felt like a regular, mundane steam iron, but there was something—some force—propelling it around the room, and the force didn't want to let go of it.

Angel struggled with it, though, and wrestled it down. Once the force, whatever it was, let go of the thing, he was able to return the iron to the ironing board, coiling its cord around the handle as he did.

The boy and his mother had been silent through the whole ordeal.

But their silence was over. She ran to Carlos, dropped to her knees and scooped him into her arms. He regarded Angel over his mother's shoulder. He was trying hard not to cry, probably, Angel assumed, because there was a stranger present. But he was clearly terrified.

"Are you okay, *mi hijo?*" she asked him. She repeated it over and over, like a mantra. "Are you okay? Are you okay?"

"I'm fine, *Mama,*" the boy assured her. "I'm fine."

Angel watched from his position next to the ironing board. As Isabel Flores released her son, Carlos glanced at a door that seemed to lead into a small bathroom. The door slammed shut with a bang.

"Maybe you should tell us what's been going on here," Angel said.

They were back upstairs in the bungalow's compact kitchen/dining area. Isabel had given Angel a glass of water, brewed tea for Wesley, and poured the boy a Coke from a can. They sat around the dining table, a scarred veteran of thousands of meals, with their drinks on coasters. Isabel brewed a cup of strong Mexican coffee for herself, and puttered in the kitchen as they talked.

"This began about the time Carlos's father was arrested," she explained.

"Arrested for what?" Wesley asked.

"For murdering somebody," Carlos said. "But *Papa* didn't do it. I know he didn't."

"That's right, Carlos." She put a protective arm around her son. She looked at Angel. "He's right, he's not just saying that. Rojelio didn't kill anybody. He wouldn't. I don't know why he was picked, but the police saw him when he was out taking a walk, and they arrested him."

"Yes," Angel said. He hated to let her continue in her assumption that he worked for her husband's attorney, but he had to find out what was going on.

She shook her head, pinching the bridge of her nose as

if she had a terrible headache. Then she lowered her hand to the table. Her fist was clenched.

"Well, as you know, he's still in jail, waiting for his arraignment. I'm sure Mr. Preston is a good attorney, but you see, in our community, we often have problems with the public defenders not taking the time . . ." She swallowed and cleared her throat. "Not that I think your boss is a bad lawyer, but you see—"

"I understand," Angel said softly. "I'll see what I can do. But most of the lawyers I know, you wouldn't want on your side."

"My dad will be set free after his trial," Carlos insisted. "No one can prove he did something that he didn't do."

"You just keep on thinking that," Wesley said with a warm smile. "I'm sure your dad wants you to keep a sunny attitude and a—"

Angel interrupted Wesley's soliloquy. "So after your husband was taken, the poltergeist activity started? Things started moving by themselves?"

She looked very hesitant. "I haven't even told Father Alonzo, our priest. It sounds so crazy."

"It's not," Angel said firmly. "I've seen it before. It's real."

"When you came to the door, I thought . . ." She looked down at her hands. "I thought one of the neighbors had seen. Called someone . . . authorities. We have no place else to go."

"We'll try to help," Angel promised her. "I've worked with this kind of thing before."

"We certainly have," Wesley said, a little bit of emphasis on the "we."

"Are you a priest?" she asked, surveying Angel's dark clothing.

"No."

"Doors slamming. Books and toys flying around. Pictures coming off the walls . . ." she murmured, as if he really were a priest, and her kitchen was his confessional.

Carlos nodded, his dark brown eyes enormous and frightened.

His mother continued. "What you heard earlier today was a tray with Carlos's dinner on it. I had just taken it down for him, and set it in front of the sofa, when it flew up and hurled itself into the wall."

Carlos started to cry silently. His mother stroked his hair and pressed on, as if determined to get it all out.

"I picked up the pieces of his plate and glass, and the bits of his sandwich, and put them into the trash downstairs, then came up with the laundry to put away."

She looked drawn, exhausted.

She hasn't had anyone to confide in, Angel realized.

"Which is where I came in," he said.

She exhaled long and slow. "Yes."

"How long has this been going on?" Angel asked, trying to make connections out of the two sets of events. "When was your husband arrested?"

"Three weeks, now," Isabel answered sadly. "It's . . . I look at the calendar every morning and it seems like it's been forever."

Carlos snaked his little hand under his mother's, attempting to comfort her. Mother and son exchanged looks; the boy patted her wrist with his other hand. Angel was moved by the child's attempts to reassure his mother, when he was obviously as frightened as she was.

Angel thought back to the pictures he had seen in the living room. There had been a man in some of the family pictures, clean-cut and carefully groomed, with a neat mustache and thinning dark hair. His smile was wide and genuine, and in one picture, he was holding a child, definitely a younger Carlos, with obvious affection. He didn't look like a murderer to Angel, and this didn't look like a killer's house.

But then, if killers could be identified by the way they look or how they keep their houses, Angel knew, *the streets would be a whole lot safer.*

"You said you could help Carlos," Isabel reminded him. "How?"

"It might be difficult to explain," he answered.

She regarded him.

"Try."

Tad Barlowe thought of himself as a tough guy. He was a guard in the 77th Street Regional Police Headquarters jail, for one thing. That alone qualified him, as far as he was concerned. There were other ways one could be labeled tough, in his book. Running a class-five rapids solo, in a kayak. Skydiving. Climbing a peak higher than fourteen thousand feet. Going fifteen rounds with a prize fighter, or eight seconds on a bull. Those all counted.

But most of those were once-in-a-lifetime things. To Tad Barlowe, getting up and strapping on a Sam Browne belt and going to work in the jail was every day, except Sunday and Monday.

After work he went out drinking with some of the guys, or worked out at the gym, or both. Then he went home to his wife, Penny, who seemed always to be a little scared of what he did for a living. She was a timid sort. He sometimes found himself wondering what she saw in a guy like him. But she stuck around, and he guessed that was toughing it out, in her own way, and he respected that.

At work, on the block, the most important thing was to have confidence in himself, and to never show fear. If the inmates smelled fear on a guard, they'd never let go of it.

Tad had known more than one guard who let it be known that he was afraid, of a particular prisoner or of the whole situation. None of those men were still guards.

But Tad never backed down, never watched his back. The inmates—he wasn't allowed to call them convicts, since most of those incarcerated at the jail were awaiting trial, and he feared the day was coming when he'd be ordered to call them clients or customers—had learned that Tad was a guy they couldn't bully, couldn't terrorize.

It was a little after eight o'clock at night. The inmates were watching TV, or sharing private games of cards in their cells. A few literate ones were reading books checked out from the jail library, including several who planned to represent themselves and were studying law books.

Tad was in the block office working on some paperwork. From here, through thick, scratched windows, he could look up and see the rows of cells, and the people in those cells could see him. So even as he did his paper shuffling, he remained alert, kept his back straight. He didn't want to look like he was tired or weak.

But when the binder raised up from the desk in front of him, he dropped his pen.

When it shot up to the ceiling as if yanked there on invisible wires, he followed it with his gaze, craning his neck to look at it hovering there over his head.

When it suddenly plummeted straight at his face, he threw his hands up and batted it away.

Then the pen that he had dropped took flight, zipping around the office's perimeter, once, twice, three times. Tad felt the color drain from his face. He knew he looked frightened as he watched it, wide-eyed. He knew he looked helpless. He stood there next to the desk, trying to track the pen. But when it shot toward him like a bullet fired from a gun, it was moving too fast.

remembering Giles's tape of
w."
ed around, but saw nothing. I
ehind the building. I threw my
hen I turned to come back in."
e look on Salma's face, Buffy
he moment that had scared her so.
d and stroked Salma's hand. "It's
e now."
mile, but it was not a very convinc-

. Anyway, I turned, and I thought I
e shadows. Moving away from me,
But as I tried to see it, I realized it
s. It *was* the shadows."
an?" Buffy asked.
ep breath. She was way wigged, and
about her experience was going to

here are floodlights outside, mounted
here isn't one facing the Dumpster; it's
orner. So there is a shadow of the build-
e parking lot back there, in a straight line.
as I watched it, it moved. It wasn't a
as kind of humped, and huge, and then the
and whatever I had seen was gone. There
raight shadow of the building's corner."
ou do then?" Willow asked her.
e as fast as I could and locked all the doors."
seen anything else strange?" Buffy inquired.
oothed back her hair. "Isn't that enough for

uckled grimly. "You should hang with us—"
ke a look," Buffy quickly offered.

It impaled his left arm.

He let out a yelp, clapped his hand over it, tugged it out and threw it to the floor.

He was on the phone, screaming for backup and a medic, when the desk started to bounce.

He no longer cared how he looked to the prisoners on the block. He threw open the office door and ran.

Tough was tough, but some things were just too much to deal with.

Chapter 4

Sunnydale

"I CAN'T BELIEVE IT'S STILL SO HOT," WILLOW SAID, AS she and Buffy walked up to the entry of Salma's condo complex. "Maybe somebody left the Hellmouth open."

Buffy grimaced. "We'd know it. There'd be a whole lot more lurking around besides hot air. Not that air lurks." She looked at Willow. "Does air lurk?"

"Maybe dark air," Willow replied. She glanced around nervously.

Buffy and Willow had gone by the condo to check on Salma. Dark had fallen by the time they got there. The name of the complex was Sea-Vue, although one couldn't actually have a view of the sea from there. The ocean's tangy scent made it this far, as did the steady roar of surf, but the view from the building was of complexes across the street which actually did have ocean views.

Willow pushed the button next to Salma's name. Buffy

"Oh, yeah," Buffy said.
the police report. "We kno
"It bothered me. I look
went to the Dumpster, b
bag of trash into it. And
She stopped. From t
thought she was reliving
Willow leaned forwa
okay, Salma. We're he
Salma attempted a s
ing one.
"Thank you, Willo
saw something, in th
when I looked at it.
wasn't in the shadow
"What do you me
Salma took a de
apparently talking
help.
"The shadow.
up on the walls.
right around the
ing that falls in th
"Except that,
straight line. It v
shadow moved
was only the st
"What did
"I ran insid
"Have you
Salma sm
one night?"
Willow c
"I'll go t

T
out a
went
Saln
Wher
could tel
set into t
dark again.
"Salma?"
There was
When it op
"What's wr
"Salma?" She
and kept her atte
Salma simply
firmly behind thei
Once they were sa
onto a couch. Every
lit several candles as
"Salma?" Willow
chairs that faced the so
"I was outside," Sal
out some trash. It was j
someone was watching m

Salma touched Buffy's arm. "Be careful, Buffy. What if it is still there?"

"I'll cope." Buffy rose, heading for the door. "Lock it behind me," she said firmly. "Don't let anyone in but me."

"Don't worry," Salma said, looking small and very, very scared. "There's no chance of that."

The back parking lot was as Salma had described it. The side of the building was brightly lit with floodlights, mounted high on the pink stucco walls. But at the back of the building was a nook with a Dumpster, behind a large gate to keep it out of sight, and the only light there was what spilled over from the side. She saw the building's shadow Salma had described, knife-edge straight.

Buffy stood there for a few minutes, watching and listening. Not knowing exactly for what. *Shadows don't make noise, do they?*

But the things that cast them do.

So the Slayer kept still, and listened.

At first, there were only the usual night sounds. The rasp of crickets. The shush of passing cars on the road outside the complex. The distant boom of the surf. A TV, somewhere in the building. A closing door.

And, in those few moments when everything went silent at once, the quiet of a summer night.

Then there was something else, very faint. At first it didn't even register, but gradually it dawned on Buffy that although it was so silent as to be almost nonexistent, she could hear it simply because it was so . . . so wrong.

That is not a normal nighttime sound, she thought. *That would be one like . . .*

Well, I don't know. But this one's not right.

It sounded like the rustle of silk on soft flesh.

The sound a shadow makes?

Buffy was already at Slayer Def-Con Five; now she turbo-charged her senses, staring hard into the darkness.

There it is again.

She kept still, which had always been a hard thing for her to accomplish. In her book, slayage meant action. Research and killing time was for other people. Killing stuff . . . that was the Slayer's job.

All things come to those who wait: something moved, not creeping exactly, just kind of gliding, maybe forward, maybe backward; it was impossible to really tell.

"Who are you?" she asked. "What do you want?"

There was no reply. Where she had seen movement—just a shift of black on black, nothing she could really put her finger on—now there was nothing. She could see into the shadows, through them, to the wall of Salma's building. There was nothing there except the stucco and a couple of straggly foxtails.

And yet—as Salma had described—she felt she was being watched. The fine hairs on the back of her neck tingled.

"Come on out and face me," Buffy challenged.

Still no reply.

She called up her senses to see beyond, sense beyond. Standing as still as she could, she felt sorry for Salma, who had been frightened out of her wits by something she couldn't see, touch, smell or run from—when one's enemy was invisible, one was never certain if one had left it behind or it had followed one home.

For another couple of minutes, she stood poised for battle, watching, staring. Goose bumps traveled up her arms and her face prickled. Her body was reacting to a threat she could not otherwise detect. She was not loving this at all.

Frustrated and very much weirded out, she finally gave

up. It took a lot to turn her back and hoof it toward Salma's building.

Nothing tried to stop her.

The shadows were still.

Los Angeles

An odd hush hung over the main branch of the Los Angeles Public Library that night. It was almost, but not quite, as silent as a tomb.

A quiet library was nothing unusual, Cordelia knew. But this one felt different—not like people weren't speaking, moving, turning pages, shuffling—but like sound was being swallowed up, somehow, before it could travel any distance at all.

She found herself feeling uneasy, looking up from the terminal every few minutes as if expecting something to happen.

Angel had called her at home and asked her to come here, to L.A.'s central branch, to go through the newspaper records of the days surrounding Rojelio Flores's arrest. She was looking for anything strange, anything that might provide some hint as to what had really happened the day Flores was framed.

Of course, what really happened, she thought, *might be that he really committed the murder.*

But something in Angel's voice prevented her from expressing that thought. He seemed to believe in the man's innocence.

So she kept her opinion to herself—with some difficulty, as it wasn't her normal way of doing things—and went to the library.

Where she found absolutely nothing that looked like it might help. The *L.A. Times* website only seemed to have certain articles in its archive, or else she hadn't thought of the correct terms to look up; besides, what she was looking for might easily be a tiny mention of something that wouldn't make it there. So she paged through the library's microfilmed archives.

There had been a sale on pashmina at Nordstrom's that day, it turned out. Had she known about that she might have harangued Angel for something resembling a paycheck. But it was old news now, weeks old. She tried to ignore the ads and focus on the articles.

But she didn't know what she was looking for. There was a brief report in the crime section of four officers arresting Rojelio Flores for the murder of a Russian man named Mikhail Nokivov, who had been in the U.S. on a six-month visa for a little more than two years. Meaning that Nokivov had been in the country illegally for eighteen months. But that was all it said.

She decided she needed a break; also something to drink. The library was a dusty, musty place, and she had always harbored a suspicion that she was allergic to dust. Sighing, she pushed her chair away from the terminal, and stood, heading for the Library Café, out the main doors and down a walkway from the main library proper.

She pushed open the glass door to the café, and the smell of coffee wafted over her. A steamer was *cussshing* milk for somebody's latte, and the luscious fragrance of chocolate enticed her toward the order line.

She passed next to a table heaped with books. A young man sat there, poring over a big, thick volume and making notes. He was lean and young and looked like a college student, maybe trying to cobble together a term paper at the last minute. He picked at an order of fries as he worked. A soft drink cup was near his elbow, and beside that was a paper plate with a cheeseburger that he had unwrapped but not started on yet.

He rose to grab a refill on his drink at the same time Cordelia realized there was a variety of bottled water in the refrigerator compartment against the wall. She glanced through the clear glass door, trying to decide if she'd rather have something from it than a fountain drink.

Reflected in the glass, a thin girl in a baggy denim shirt got up from a nearby chair. She looked this way and that, but didn't seem to notice Cordelia watching her in the door. When she was convinced she was unnoticed, she swooped past the student's table, snatched the burger, then kept walking quickly out the exit.

At first, Cordelia was appalled. That poor guy was going to come back to his table to find his dinner gone and no clue where it went. But almost immediately, her feeling turned to concern. *If that girl is reduced to stealing food, how could she be surviving? And why is she stealing? That's just wrong.*

I'm not getting anything done here, she decided. She left the line, determined to find the girl, find out what her story was. *A person ought to be able to have a snack at the cafeteria without losing his food. Anyway, eating that stuff is terrible for her skin,* she thought.

She went back out of the café. The girl was already out of sight, but the door back into the main library building was just swinging shut. Cordelia ran, yanking it open just in time to see burger thief girl round a corner. Cordelia gave chase.

The girl had taken the turn to the right, which led to a long escalator down. Cordelia stopped at the top, looking down. The girl was just getting off at the bottom. Cordelia pushed past a patron and descended as well, losing track of her quarry but hey, dead end, right?

But when she got to the bottom, she saw that there was a door beneath the escalators with an AUTHORIZED PERSONNEL ONLY sign on it. Cordelia pulled it open.

Behind it was another corridor. The girl was out of sight, but there didn't seem to be many places she could have gone. Cordelia could see six doors from here, staggered on both sides along the wall. *This is a lot of effort,* she thought. *It must exhaust Angel to chase after evildoers all night long.*

She briefly considered giving up and just heading back to her apartment. But she had come this far, so she didn't want to turn back now. Besides, as unusual as this sort of behavior might be for her, she knew it was standard fare for Angel, and she kind of liked the crusading avenger bit. *As long as this basement doesn't get too grungy.*

She pushed open the door number one.

Whoah, Giles heaven.

It led into a room filled with shelves, and on the shelves were books. Old books, with ragged edges, broken spines, loose pages hanging out. This looked like where the books went to die. They were probably volumes that had come out of circulation and were waiting for their ultimate destination. The air was thick with the musty smell of them.

At the back of the silent room Cordelia heard a scraping noise. Moving swiftly but cautiously, she made her way to the back of the room, behind the shelves of doomed books.

A sheet of plywood, maybe three feet square, leaned against the wall. It looked like it had been there for decades. But Cordelia could see that, although it had once been nailed into the wall, the nails were not in line with the holes anymore. The wood was just standing there.

She took a deep breath and pulled it away from the wall. A dark hole had been cut into the wall itself, almost like a tunnel opening. Cordelia immediately regretted having come this far, because it made turning away now so much harder to do.

It's just a girl with a stolen cheeseburger, she thought. *No business of mine.*

But deep down, she knew she had already made it her business by witnessing the theft in the first place, and by following the girl. *First thing, when I get home,* she thought, *a loooong shower.* She quietly pushed the plywood aside, steeled herself, and ducked down, down, down into the rabbit hole.

The opening was ragged, and boards and nails tugged at her clothes. With her job, she kept up on her tetanus shots, but there was nothing she could take for cobwebs. There weren't many of those, however, just tatters—further evidence that the girl had taken this route as well.

Cordelia could barely see in front of her face. But there was air ahead, cooler air that she could feel on her cheeks. So the tunnel grew wider somewhere, not so close and stuffy. She took some comfort in that and kept going.

For the first fifteen steps she had to walk doubled over, one hand in front of her and the other measuring the ceiling height so she didn't bump her head.

But after that, she came into the open area. There was only the faintest light seeping in from the hole in the wall behind her, but it was enough to let her see that she was in another hallway much like the one she had been in before. This one was apparently in some part of the building long since walled off and unused. The age of it was apparent even in the dark—the style of the few doors she could see, the hardware, even the exposed electrical conduit and plumbing pipes running the length of the ceiling were outdated.

If she had been peering back the way she had come, instead of into the gloom before her, she might have seen the girls creeping up on her.

Suddenly there were four, no, six hands on her.

They clutched at her arms, her hips, clawed her cheek. She let out a yelp and tried to spin, batting at the grasping hands.

In the dim light she could see that they were all younger than her, all girls. Four of them. The one she had been following hung back, while the other three had come up on her in the dark.

"What are you doing?" Cordelia demanded, her heart hammering. She shook herself free of their grips. Why had she done this? She was no policewoman. That guy's dinner should have been his own concern. Now she was here in a dark tunnel, surrounded by who knew what kind of girls. Would they want her purse and what little money she owned? "You just about scared the life out of me!" she blustered.

"Why are you in here?" one of the girls responded. She was completely Gothed out, down to the black lipstick and nails. "You following us?"

"No!" Cordelia insisted. "Well, yes. I was following you." She pointed at the girl in the oversized blue shirt. The girl flushed. "I saw her steal someone's food."

"So," the blue-shirt girl asked. "You a cop? You're not library security, we know all them."

"No, I'm not the police," Cordelia replied. "I don't really know why I followed you. I just saw you doing something wrong, and thought someone should try to stop you."

"She's a good Samaritan," another girl snapped. She was the tallest of the lot, almost as tall as Cordelia, and probably thirty pounds heavier, solidly built. Her red hair was wild, uncombed, and matted. She wore a tight, ripped T-shirt, torn jeans, and heavy-soled Doc Martens. The glint in her eye looked like madness. In her fist was a sharp-edged kitchen knife. "But we got no problem cuttin' you up, Samaritan or no."

The other girls glowered at her and Cordelia felt a flash of panic. "I'd have a problem with that," Cordelia said sharply. *Ha, no joke.* "Look, I know when I'm not wanted. Although, to be perfectly honest, I don't have a lot of personal experience with the feeling."

The girl with the knife shifted her weight impatiently. Denim shirt ticked her glance at the girl beside her, who took a breath. She was nervous. That made Cordelia more nervous.

She kept that emotion to herself, however, and simply shrugged. "But I've made others feel that way often enough, so I've seen what it's like. And I can tell I'm not wanted here. So I'll just go back upstairs, and—"

"Wait," the girl in the denim shirt said, stepping forward. A couple of the other girls moved to let her through. "We could maybe use her."

"What for?" the bigger girl asked.

"I'm hungry," blue shirt said. "You're hungry. Maybe she's got money."

"Not much," Cordelia offered. She tried for a little smile. She had no idea if she got anywhere near one. Her voice was still sharp, and she was sorry about that. But she was having trouble controlling her tone of voice. Also, her desire to scream for help.

"Enough to buy us a meal?"

"How many are there?" Cordelia asked. "And we're not talking about Morton's or anything, right?" She allowed herself to relax, just a little. If they wanted her to buy them food, then chances were they weren't really planning to just steal her wallet and bury her corpse.

Maybe they were runaways or something, but perhaps not truly criminals.

Except when it comes to burgers.

The girl looked taken aback. So did a couple of the others. "You'd really buy us food, even after we scared you? I just don't think anyone has ever done anything like that for me."

"What about your parents?" Cordelia asked. "I'm sure they—"

"Don't be so sure," Big Red interrupted. "I had Kayley's parents right here right now, I'd slit both their throats in a heartbeat."

"How very . . . supportive of you," Cordelia managed faintly. "Kayley's lucky that she has a friend who's so levelheaded."

"You think we're all nuts?"

"I don't know you well enough to have an opinion," Cordelia replied. But inside, she was thinking, *Is there any doubt?* "My offer still stands, Kayley. If you're hungry, or if there's anything I can do to help you, let me know." She knew that, left on her own, she'd have a pretty hard time finding her way back out of this maze. But if they took her out to buy them a meal, she could learn the way. She didn't want to spend the rest of her life underground, and the whole pale, sallow look was really Angel's thing.

"We're all pretty much starving," Kayley said. She toyed with a gold choker around her neck with the letter K in the center of it. "I bagged that guy's burger but it wouldn't go very far split eight ways."

"There are eight of you down here?"

"Kayley," Big Red warned.

"But she said she'll feed us, Pat."

Pat looked Cordelia in the eye. She tucked the knife away someplace, pulling out a pack of cigarettes and a

eld it for a moment, looking for
set it back down in its original
. What's your new evidence?"
n't do it."

. "And you're a private investi-
nse through the mail from the

ox and picked up a slice, offering
. Angel demurred, and the guy

rms and leaned against a table,
ail as it threatened to tumble to the
uch to go on. But there are strange
house, and they make me believe
explain any better than that."
the piece of pizza and shut the lid.
Then I'm sorry I let you wake me
am, Angel. I was kicking Johnny
s."

like what?" the man said, wiping
er napkin. "Wife being threatened?
one speaks, then hangs up?"
said. He paused. "It might be posses-

s of the law," Preston said. When
he tried again. "Possession of what, a
ntraband?"
n," Angel replied.
el. "You're kidding. You woke me up
ed *The Exorcist* on the late show?
alling the cops."
id. "I lied to Mrs. Flores. Well, I didn't
t her think something that wasn't true."

66

matchbook. She struck the match, and in the dim light it
seemed to flare like the sun. "You'll really buy food for
all eight of us? And not try to make any trouble for us?"
She touched the match to the cigarette and inhaled, causing the end to glow.

Cordelia mentally added up the money she carried.
"Nothing fancy," she said. "But I could treat for burgers
and fries."

"Good enough for us," Pat said, blowing a stream of
smoke. "Let's go, guys. Dinner's on this chick."

Chapter 5

ROJELIO FLORES WAS HELD AT THE 77TH STREET RE-gional Police Headquarters, a low, sprawling structure facing Broadway, in the temporary detention facility there. He was being held without bail because of the nature of his crime and, according to Isabel, the incompetence of his court-appointed attorney.

Angel visited said attorney, whose name was Greg Preston, at his home on Glendale Boulevard. His house was a small adobe bungalow, nothing to write home about. *He may not be a good lawyer,* Angel thought, *but at least he's not getting rich by being a bad one.*

Angel rang Preston's doorbell until he came to the door. He opened it a crack and peered out. He was overweight and ruddy-faced, with stubbled cheeks and blond hair in disarray.

"Yeah?"

"Mr. Preston? I need to see you about one of your clients, Rojelio Flores. May I come in?" Angel asked.

picked up a pizza box and
another place to put it. He
spot. "Pretty open and shut

"His family says he di
Preston brayed a laugh
gator? You get your lice
back of a comic book?"

He opened the pizza b
the other slice to Ange
went to town.

Angel crossed his a
catching a pile of junk m
floor. "I know it's not m
things going on in that
his wife and son. I can'

Preston threw down
He faced his visitor. "
out of a pleasant dre
Cochran's butt on cro

"Look, Preston—"

"Strange goings-o
his mouth with a pap
Phone calls where n

"Stranger," Angel
sion."

"Being nine-tenth
Angel said nothing,
deadly weapon? Co

"Occult possessi

He stared at Ang
because you watc
Man, that's it. I'm

"Look," Angel s
lie, exactly, but I le

"Now you think this looks like a confession booth?"

"She thinks I work with you. She thinks you're finally taking some steps to get her husband freed."

Preston rubbed his eye sleepily with one fist. "Okay, and telling me that is supposed to make me trust you? Now I think you're insane and a liar."

"So you don't believe in possession?"

"I'm a rational man."

"How about poltergeists? Demons? Vampires?"

"Shouldn't you be writing for one of those supermarket tabloids?" Preston asked.

"I can think of one way to convince you," Angel said. "But you won't like it."

"Try me."

Angel stood in front of the lawyer and willed the change to come over him. His forehead became thick, his teeth lengthened, his eyes narrowed. He was unmistakably a vampire. He held it for a moment, and then changed back.

"This better?"

Preston stared at him for perhaps a full minute.

"Y-yeah, let's just k-keep it like that," Preston stammered. "Holy sh—"

"I'm not threatening you," Angel said. "I just don't think we have a lot of time to fix this, and I can't do it without you. Now, let's talk about possession."

"How'd you do that?" the attorney blurted. His face was chalk white and he was beginning to sway.

"It doesn't matter."

"Yeah, it does." Preston wiped his forehead with a trembling hand. "It matters a whole of a lot, excuse me very much."

"I'm a freak of nature. Let's leave it at that."

Preston looked like he wanted to say more, but maybe he wasn't sure what that would be.

"I can't deny that," Preston agreed. "I still don't see how it's going to help Mr. Flores any."

"I just have to get in to talk to him."

"Visiting hours are between ten and three tomorrow. Be my guest."

Angel pointed toward his teeth. "Jails are sort of on the high-security end of things," he explained. "If I could get in through tunnels, or even wearing a blanket, I could go during daylight. But jails, you pretty much have to be able to walk in the front door."

Preston blinked. *"Oh.* You're a . . . *oh."*

Angel nodded. "An oh."

The lawyer looked terrified. "I had hepatitis in college," he said in a rush. "I can't give blood."

"I figured you were pretty bloodless to start with," Angel said. When the man stared at him, he smiled. "Bad lawyer joke."

"Ha," he said tightly, "ha."

"It's got to be tonight," Angel persisted. "And I can't get in without his attorney walking me in."

"I know I'm going to regret this," Preston muttered. "But if it'll keep you from doing that thing with your face, then I'll do it."

"I promise."

Sunnydale

"Anything?" Willow asked when she came back inside.

Buffy had already decided to lie. She didn't want Salma to be any more terrified than she already was.

"I couldn't see anything," she replied, deadbolting the door, a very normal precaution to take. "Vast amounts of nothing. Nothingness as far as the eye can see."

"Which," Willow added, glancing out the window, "it's night."

"Right. So, visibility's not very far." She forced a little smile and walked into the room. Salma was sitting on her couch, and Willow was curled up like a cat in an over-stuffed chair with a throw over her lap.

"They could clean out that Dumpster a little more often, maybe." Buffy took a seat in a chair opposite Willow's, at right angles to Salma. There was a coffee table in the center, and two cups of tea were steaming there. Also, some fashion magazines in Spanish and a Sunnydale Yellow Pages.

"What's up in here?" she asked.

"Just talking," Willow replied, reaching forward and picking up her teacup. "Salma was telling me a little about her family."

"Would you care for some tea?" Salma asked.

"That'd be nice." Buffy was glad to give the nervous girl something to occupy herself.

Salma rose. "We're drinking peppermint. Is that all right?"

"Homegrown," Willow said, smiling, raising her eyebrows. "From her grandmother."

"Sure, thanks. Did you say your folks live in Los Angeles?" Buffy asked as Salma moved into the kitchen.

"That's right," Salma said, calling back to her.

Buffy looked at Willow and held out her hands in a helpless gesture: *Didn't find anything.*

Willow frowned and motioned to Buffy, holding an invisible stake her in hand: *vampires, maybe?*

Buffy shook her head. She made a face: *not a clue.* But whatever it was that had been out there was something she would want to talk to Giles about. Soonish.

"I used to live there. What part do you guys live in?" Buffy asked.

"Laurel Canyon," Salma said.

Buffy turned to Willow and mouthed *"rich."* "Nice up there in the hills."

"Yes," Salma said.

"Salma's grandfather made a lot of money in Mexico," Willow offered aloud.

The kettle whistled. Apparently Salma had kept the water simmering in case Buffy wanted to join the party.

"He owns some factories," Salma went on. There was a clink of china. "He pays very fair wages and employs many people. He is well-respected. But sometimes, in Mexico, the wealthy become the targets of kidnappers. He wanted to live in the United States, where it is safer."

"We have kidnappers here, too," Buffy observed.

"This is true. But not so many, I think."

"So the family moved to L.A.?" Even saying the city's initials gave Buffy an involuntary mental shudder—she had lived there until her parents split up, and she burned down the high school gym, so already unpleasant associations. Toss in Angel and his possessive claim over it, and the whole place was just a little too emotion-laden for comfort.

Salma saved her by returning to the living room with a tray. On it were gold-and-black cups with Buffy's tea, sugar, and creamer. Also, a small plate of chocolate-chip cookies and—*get out! yum!*—chocolate truffles.

"Yes, shortly after my brother was born." Salma set the tray down. "My father also grew up in Mexico, before my grandfather became so wealthy. I think my father was really responsible for the move, when he became a parent. He was always worried about us."

Buffy took her tea and tasted it. It was hot, and full of minty goodness. She spooned in some sugar and stirred. Then she set it down and picked up a truffle.

Total heaven.

t wanted you to understand what we're up
Buffy interjected, giving Willow a chance to
self. "This isn't going to be easy, Salma."
oesn't matter," Salma said, clenching her fists.
s, and freaked. But determined.
liked her a lot in that moment.
t want to know that Nicky's okay. I just want my
back."
ll work on that."
a's face brightened a little. "At least there's one
hing," she said. "I guess I don't have to worry that
mixed up with something supernatural."
ffy remembered the sound she had heard outside,
ilken scrape of shadow against stone. She remem-
seemed to move. And she

n't come with anything
embling a steady paycheck. So to them, she was
art of the establishment that they had turned their
acks on.
Unless there was a free meal in it.
They had exited the library through a tunnel that led
oss the street and into an abandoned storefront on the
side. From this building, they could go in and out of
brary without being seen. They led Cordelia out and
d the corner to a fast food restaurant on Hope Street.

"Do you think that's what you saw outside? Someone watching you, stalking you?"

Salma shook her head agitatedly as she sat back on the sofa. "No. What I saw was not human. No human can blend into the shadows like that. I do not know what it was, but I know what it wasn't."

"Okay," Buffy said, luxuriating in having her mouth completely stuffed with extremely delicious chocolate.

"Whatever it was, it seems to be gone now," Buffy told her. "But, just in case, how about if you stay inside at night for a few days? Give me a chance to try to clear this up."

Salma laughed. It was not a sound Buffy had heard often. "You don't have to worry about me," Salma said. "I don't think I'll come out from under my bed for a few days."

"Oh," Willow interrupted. "We were going to talk to Salma about the list."

"What about it?" Salma asked.

"I ran some of the names you gave me, of your brother's friends, through the computer," Willow explained. "I wanted to show you what came up."

"We can use mine," Salma offered. She got off the couch and led the way to a spare bedroom that she used as a study.

Let's bring the truffles, Buffy thought, but she suffered in silence.

In the study, there was a big wooden desk with a bright orange computer on top.

Willow sat down in front of it and started tapping at the keys. Salma and Buffy watched her work quietly for a few minutes. Then the tapping stopped and Willow gestured to Salma. "Come here," she said. "Look at this."

Salma went around to Willow's side of the desk. Buffy followed even though she had already seen this once.

"This guy is Enrique Almeida," Willow said. "Also

known as Ricky the Rocket. He was once arrested with a grenade launcher stolen from the Sunnydale Armory."

The man on the screen looked angry and dangerous. He was shirtless, and dark, illegible tattoos snaked across his chest and shoulders. His unshaven face was set into a scowl. Willow had explained that the Sunnydale Police Department's gang unit took Polaroids of suspected gang members when they were stopped on the streets, and that's what this was.

Salma put a hand over her mouth. "And he knows my brother?"

"According to that address book you found. And look at this . . ." Willow typed again, then stopped. The picture on the screen changed to a mug shot, face on and profile, of a man with a flat, broken nose and cruel, hard lips.

"Jorge Cota. Arrested seven times since he reached adulthood two years ago. Juvenile records are sealed, of course, so I can't get to them. But chances are, he's got one."

"Oh, Nicky," Salma said plaintively.

"One more." Willow bent to the keyboard again. Stopped. "Domingo Ribeiro. Or Deadly Dom. He once killed three clerks in a clothing store in order to steal a designer jacket."

Another mug shot loaded onto the screen. This man looked small, almost girlish. But his eyes were like a shark's, flat and dead-looking.

Salma's eyes were filling with tears.

"I think that's enough, Willow," Buffy suggested gently.

"I know that one," Salma said, pointing at the screen. "Domingo. He has been over to visit my brother. I saw him a week ago."

Buffy put a comforting hand on Salma's shoulder.

"I know this looks bad," she said. "It *is* bad. It looks like Nicky is involved with a gang. According to the po-

lice reports, these guys a called the Latin Cobras. Th

"What can I do?" Salma a

"You can sit tight," Buffy in usual area of expertise. But I'll Nicky down. If I can get him aw it'll be your job to convince him t he wants to live his life."

"These Cobras," Salma said. " gang?"

Buffy wanted to pull her punches, glossed over her experience outside in she didn't want Salma to think this wh problem-lite.

"Yes," Buffy said. "The
Sal

"We jus
against,"
collect he
"That
Scared y
Buffy
"I jus
brother
"We
Sal
good
he is
B
the s

upset but B
Willow complied.

"They're called the Echo Park Band. From wha they're kind of like the Crips and the Bloods r one, except without the niceness."

Tears rolled down Salma's cheeks.

"I don't mean to upset you," Willow said
Buffy felt sorry. It was occasionally ha how sheltered some people were—comp bies and she herself, anyway. But she had been blunt.

acr
othe
the
aroun

they're on the bad."

_alma looked like she was about to cry. Buffy glanced at Willow, and the redhead stepped up to the plate.

"The Cobras are associated with a gang in L.A. that's a *majorly* powerful gang." Willow took a breath. "One of the worst in the country, and they've sprouted offshoots all over the place."

"*Ay, Dios,*" Salma murmured, pressing her fingertips against her cheekbones. She closed her eyes. Willow looked upset, but Buffy gestured for her to keep going.

bered the way the shadow had

thought, *That isn't necessarily so* . . .

Los Angeles

Cordelia was somewhat insulted by the way they treated her, like she was some middle-aged mom or something. She really wasn't that much older than these girls were. But she was out of high school—graduated, not just dropped out, like these girls had—and had a job, albeit one that did

All eight girls ordered, and Cordelia covered the thirty-dollar tab with a mental wince.

They took over two tables in the rear of the dining area and chowed down greedily on flame-broiled burgers and fries. In between bites, they told Cordelia a little of their personal stories.

At sixteen, Pat was the oldest and biggest of the lot—the group's natural leader. Little Kayley was the youngest, and Pat felt very protective of her—a fact Cordelia had already learned, at the point of a knife. Kayley had just turned fourteen a few days before. She was barely over five feet tall, with close-cropped blond hair and huge blue eyes. Spread between them were Amanda and Holly, both Goth through and through with pitch-black, dyed locks, dark-rimmed eyes, and black lipstick; Jean, a petite black girl with narrow brown eyes that seemed to view the world with suspicion and distrust; Nicole, a blonde who was almost as tall as Pat and twice as loud; and Keri and Erin, a pair of identical Korean twins.

They were all runaways, of course. Keri and Erin, Nicole, and Pat told of abusive homes. Jean and Kayley weren't abused, but their parents had seemed disinterested, remote. Only Holly and Amanda came from families that seemed to have any substance at all. Their reasons for running away seemed less clear to Cordelia. Holly said something abstract about needing to explore new horizons, new ways of doing things. "I have nothing against my parents," she said, stuffing another couple of fries into her mouth. "But they're just, you know, not really my thing right now."

"What is your 'thing?'" Cordelia asked her.

She smiled wide, touching her right canine tooth with the tip of her finger. "Vampires."

Great, Cordelia thought. *I believe I'm befriending a group of needy runaways, and instead they're vampire wannabes?*

"They're not all they're cracked up to be," Cordelia said. "Kind of smelly, most of them, if you want to know the truth. I mean, they can be charming sometimes, but you try a regular diet of blood. It's hell on the breath.

"Not to mention your looks. Most vampires forget about their looks after a really short time. They can't see their reflections, so after a while the lipstick goes on crooked, and you never know if your mascara's streaking. And your hair?" She moved her hands, invoking the international gesture for bedhead.

"And shopping gets dicey," she added, on a roll, "so there goes being trendy. You wouldn't believe how many vampires Buff—*people*—spot because of their outdated outfits. It's really not pretty," she concluded, wrinkling her nose.

"Like you would know anything about real vampires," Pat said, grunting with contempt.

Cordelia raised her brows. "More than you'd believe."

Pat raised her chin. "How?"

"Well, I . . . I am not really at liberty to say. But I know what I'm talking about." She pulled a face. "Really."

"What I thought," Pat said, disgusted. "Just a poseur. *I* happen to know a vampire." She straightened her shoulders. "A real one."

"That's right," Kayley added proudly. "And he's going to turn *all* of us."

Ew.

"Have you really thought this through?" Cordelia asked, not loving the idea one single smidge. "You know, being dead is a big part of the whole vampire bit."

"Look at us," Jean said, gesturing to herself and the rest of her posse. "You think we really have anything to live for? Being dead can only be an improvement."

The others nodded wearily, and suddenly they all seemed terribly old and very pitiful.

"That's never true," Cordelia countered, realizing she was up against a lot. But she was willing to give it the ol' not-yet-been-to-college try. "You have all kinds of things to live for."

"Like what?" Amanda asked.

"Like . . . well, clothes." That didn't go over well. "Um, sunny days." She smiled brightly. "Puppy dogs. Playgrounds."

"Gag me," Erin said, and the others stared at Cordelia, completely unimpressed.

"Okay, that's a little simplistic, I know," Cordelia admitted. *And I think I stole it from* The Sound of Music. "But I'm sure if you think about it, there are plenty of reasons why it's better to stay alive than to become a vampire and have to go around in the dark all the time."

They were not impressed.

"That's how we live anyway," Kayley told her. "We're never out in the daytime. If we try, we just get hassled. So we sleep through the day and go out at night."

"What makes you think he'll even go through with it?" Cordelia asked. "I mean, he could just drain you all. It's just as easy for him, and I think maybe even more satisfying."

Pat smiled, but the smile looked out of place on her, like that of a child pretending to be a sophisticated adult. "Because I have something he wants," she said.

"What's that?"

"A never-ending source. I know where the runaways live, where they hang out, where they go when it gets dark. With me around, he'll never have to go hungry again."

Doesn't seem to be a problem for most vampires, Cordelia thought. But it didn't look like she'd get anywhere arguing that with Pat. She decided to go back to her other tack.

"Look, there are all kinds of reasons to live, you guys," Cordelia said again, practically pleading. "What about your families and friends? What about college, and careers, maybe having kids some day?"

"I don't think any of us have the background to be very good parents," Keri replied, her tone practical, detached. "Our families won't miss us, and we already are each other's best friends. So we'll still be together."

They all kind of clumped closer together at that. Pat and the Patlings. Cordelia felt a wistful longing for the other days when she had her own clique of groupies who wanted nothing more than to be seen agreeing with the lovely and popular Cordelia Chase.

"Look," she said, "I can't divulge sources, but I've been having . . . dealings—not dealing, not like drugs, just say no to drugs!—but I've been around vampires for a lot of years. There's nothing good about it. Really."

"She's lying," Pat said emphatically, keeping a real good grip on her kitchen knife, if not reality. "She doesn't know anything about vampires. *He* doesn't have bad breath and he looks great."

He. Great. This chick's probably all crushy on some dork who got changed last Tuesday.

Cordelia gazed levelly at her nemesis of today. "Okay, so who is this vampire that *you* know, Pat?"

Pat's eyes gleamed. *Crushy for sure.* "His name's Kostov," Pat said. "He's Transylvanian, just like Dracula was in the stories."

Cordelia nodded, trying to formulate a plan of attack. But if there was one thing she'd learned in high school, it was never to diss another girl's boyfriend, even if he was the most loathsome slime ever to walk the planet—by day *or* night. *Of course, there's preaching, and then there's practicing.*

"You've read that book?" she asked, keeping her voice neutral.

Pat yawned. She was not so great on the breath angle herself. "Tried to. Boring. I like Anne Rice better."

Why doesn't that surprise me? Cordelia thought. *She's so enchanted with the romance of vampirism that she doesn't understand what it's really like.*

The other girls nodded eagerly. One murmured, "Lestat," and another said, "Louis. He rocked."

Yikes, they've all got it bad.

"And how do you know this guy?" Cordelia pressed.

Pat waited a beat, waiting for everyone to give her their attention. They did; all eyes were focused on her, like little kids about to hear their favorite bedtime story. Or for the lead in the musical to burst into song.

Cordelia wondered if she bolted, she could outdistance Little Miss Kitchen Knife, but she discovered that her feet were rooted to the floor; she was too scared to run. Besides, she wanted one more chance to disabuse these girls of their vampires-in-velvet misconceptions. *Cordelia Chase always rises to a challenge.*

And boy, does that sound like something Wesley would say.

"I met him on the streets one night," Pat said in a low, hushed voice. One of the other girls sighed. "He had just taken a victim, so he wasn't hungry. Still had her blood dripping at the corners of his mouth."

And that was attractive? Cordelia thought, but held her tongue.

Pat lifted her chin, going somewhere no not-insane girl had gone before. "I convinced him that I didn't mean him any harm. I told him I was curious about him. We talked for hours."

The girl's face was rosy, almost shy. *Vampires are such users,* Cordelia thought with disgust. *Oh, sure, he'll promise to respect her in the morning after he sucks her dry, but he'll just roll over in his coffin and he won't ever even call.*

"We talked for hours," Pat repeated, maybe for dramatic effect, maybe because she was losing her mind along with her memory, "and then we made arrangements to meet after that. When I told these guys, everybody was excited about being turned, so we made a deal." She gestured as if to say, *And the rest is written in the stars, for me and my vamp.*

"Turning you all."

Pat nodded. The others followed suit. They looked like a bunch of wobbly-headed dolls, the kind people used to stick on their car dashboards.

"He offered to turn me right then, right there, but I asked him to turn all of us. That's how close we are." She smiled at her posse, who seemed so enthralled by her generosity that none of them felt like objecting to the fact that she was, in essence, delivering them to the slaughterhouse like a cowboy on a cattle drive.

Cordelia was not pleased. So very not. "When is he supposed to do this?"

"I'm not telling you that," Pat retorted, showing her teeth. "You'd probably try to stop it or something."

"It doesn't bother you that he's a killer?" Cordelia leaned forward, trying to make her point. "That you'll all become killers if you let this happen to you?"

"Those people out there?" Pat indicated the land past their plywood barrier—customers in the restaurant, families with kids, eating their dinners in peace. Teenagers checking out magazines and hanging with their friends. "They don't care about us. They'd just as soon we were dead. They're meat to me, nothing more." Her voice was incredibly bitter, and Cordelia could only fathom the depth of her emotional wounds.

"That includes me?" she asked, putting down her best

card—that she wasn't just meat, she was someone real, someone who had tried to extend a hand.

Pat looked at her with supreme contempt, as if sizing her up for a meal. "Meat," she said. "Don't think just because you bought us some greasy food that makes you our friend or anything."

"I don't want to be your friend," Cordelia replied, keeping her voice calm even if very little else of her was serene in the least. Being threatened with death tended to have that effect on her, no matter how often it happened.

"But I've done you a bigger favor than someone who wants to kill you is going to do you."

"Maybe the Red Cross will give you a medal," Jean said. Some of the others chuckled at her fine wit.

"I haven't asked you for anything in return," Cordelia said, looking around at the circle of faces. "A little gratitude would be nice, but obviously that's not coming my way. So forget about it. I tried to do something nice for you. I did it. It's over."

She gave Pat an equally contemptuous smile and clapped her hands. "Have a nice life. Death, I mean."

She stood up and started for the door. By the time she reached it, little Kayley was at her side.

"Cordelia," Kayley began, "I just want to thank you. For wanting to help me. No one's ever done anything like that before, I mean outside of Pat and the girls, you know?"

"It's nothing," Cordelia said. "It's just what people do for each other. You know, *living* people, not the undead ones."

Kayley's cheeks reddened. "Pat, she's real excited about this Kostov guy turning us. I guess we all are. But it's more Pat's deal than anything, you know?"

Cordelia tried to press her advantage. "You don't have to go along with it."

"It's what I want, too, don't get me wrong," Kayley

said quickly. "I'm just saying Pat is sort of the one pushing it hardest. She's all gung ho on the whole fang scene."

"I think she's an idiot then," Cordelia told her honestly. She grew as serious as she possibly could. *This might be my last chance with this girl.*

"Listen to me. It's not like those books. It's a hard existence. It's all about staying in the dark and looking for the next kill, hunting and being hunted. It's not pretty and it's not fun."

"You sound like you really know something about it," Kayley said, intrigued.

Cordelia lifted a hand to touch her shoulder, decided against it, and dropped her hand to her side. "Believe me, I do."

Kayley nodded slowly, not asking the questions on her face. "I do believe you. But you'll never convince Pat. And she's got the others wrapped around her little finger."

"There's still hope for you, Kayley. You can come with me right now. Just walk away from it."

Kayley looked back at her friends. They were watching, mostly with curiosity, though Pat's eyes burned with contempt.

"No. I can't. I'm with them."

Cordelia dug one of Angel's cards from a pocket and slipped it to Kayley. She had crossed Angel's address and phone number out and written her own in, after his office had been blown up. "If you change your mind, get in touch with me there."

"I won't," Kayley said. She pocketed the card anyway. "But, okay. And thanks."

Cordelia stepped out through the double glass doors into the night. Kayley stayed inside, with her friends.

Where the night would never end.

Chapter 6

Sunnydale

To most of society, the phrase "Night of the Long Knives" has two specific meanings. Historically, it's a reference to June 30, 1934, when Adolf Hitler cemented his power over the Nazi Party and Germany by ruthlessly and systematically assassinating a thousand people who might have opposed him.

As a result of that night, the phrase entered the popular vocabulary to refer to any kind of merciless consolidation of power, whether in politics or business or any other kind of human activity.

But in the context of magick, Nicolas de la Natividad knew it meant something else entirely.

It was the night that a warrior could not be hurt.

Tomorrow night would be Nicky's night.

Nicky knew that where he wanted to be was in the bosom of his family—his *real* family. Not the people to whom he was born, not the oversized, Anglicized house in which he had grown up. He didn't hate his family, but he felt that they had given up too much to be where they were. They had given up their heritage, turned their backs on their people. When his father and grandfather had associates over for dinner or a party, they were almost all wealthy and white. If any of them came from poverty, they had forgotten all about it.

Nicky had never known poverty in his life, but he knew that was where his roots were—with the peons, the poor farmers and laborers, not the rich owners. He felt that knowledge burning in him every day he spent within the confining walls of that big estate in Los Angeles.

The Latin Cobras. These were the people who cared for him. They looked out for him. There were *machos* and *mamas* in the crew who would give their lives for him without a moment's hesitation. He would do the same for them.

Give lives, or take lives. Whatever it took. They backed each other's plays.

Even though Nicky was the new guy, he felt secure with the Cobras. No one would give a Cobra any grief, not if they wanted to live through the night.

But there was one thing left for him to prove himself worthy of their trust. To become a full member of the gang, he had to volunteer for a dangerous assignment. Everyone did.

For most, it was doing a hit, pulling a drive-by, maybe knocking over a gun store to arm the membership.

But compared to what Nicky had run up against, that was child's play. Piece of cake.

Because Nicky had come into the family at the same time the family had gone up against Del DeSola.

DeSola was an oil magnate—one of the few Mexican-

Americans Nicky could think of who was richer than his own grandfather. He had started with a small oil operation in the Mexican interior, then parlayed that into some fields in the States as well. These days, he pumped oil wherever he could find it in the world, and shipped most of it into the States, to quench the insatiable thirst the Americans had for the black stuff.

Which meant he had a constant supply of ships moving in and out of American waters.

The Cobras wanted access to those ships. They had product of their own they moved into the U.S. Product for which there was an equally insatiable demand, but which the government did not want to allow across the border.

Heroin.

Poppies harvested in Mexico and farther south were distilled into pure heroin. The Cobras had the connections down there—this was not some nobody-street gang, but part of an association of people with roots as deep and extensive as any gang in America and most legitimate businesses, with arms reaching to the East Coast and all across the Midwest—and they had the distribution network in the States. It was only a matter of getting sufficient product into the country to meet the enormous demand, and they'd all be wealthy.

So they wanted DeSola's ships to carry a little of their product in addition to his.

They asked, and he refused.

They insisted. He continued to refuse.

So they were going to make their case in a more forceful way.

Nicky was alone.

The Latin Cobras kept a headquarters in a little house on the edge of town, a quiet suburban neighborhood where no one really bothered them. They had another spot where they gathered for meetings and parties and general hanging out, behind a pool hall on the highway. There would be, on any given night, a few of them crashing at the house, maybe two or three more sleeping on or under the pool tables. But each member had his or her own place, or shared a crib with other Cobras.

Now that he was one of them, semiofficially, Nicky had moved out of his sister's place. She would not have approved of the Cobras, and she would definitely not have approved of Nicky's immediate plan—a plan which had been in motion for a week.

One of the Cobras, Rosalie, had a studio apartment, a tiny stucco bungalow on a little gravel courtyard in a place that had once been a motel, back when Sunnydale had had a tourist trade to speak of. This is where he'd been staying.

Tourists seldom came to town these days. The place didn't have a welcoming reputation anymore; that had dwindled with the decades, until daytrippers didn't even think of going there for fun. Sunbathers who wanted to enjoy southern California's beaches went elsewhere. The scenery was unspectacular and the weather no different than anywhere else in southern California.

As for "attractions," there really weren't any. The zoo was mediocre and the museum, though occasionally offering an outstanding collection, was not enough of a draw in itself to entice many out-of-town visitors.

But what it came down to, ultimately, was the wrongness of the town. There was nothing about Sunnydale that looked out of kilter, but it certainly felt wrong—at a subliminal level. Tourists just didn't feel like going there, or so they told themselves. If asked, they would realize that something kept them on the highway, heading for the next exit after Sunnydale.

But they were rarely asked; Sunnydale was simply below the radar of most people's conversations.

Tonight—as for the past five nights—Rosalie had gone off with the Cobras somewhere. Nicky had barely seen her in days, and he had not left the apartment in as long. He needed the solitude to prepare for his Night of the Long Knives. It was a complicated spell—he had been working on it, learning the procedures and rituals inside out, gathering the ingredients, preparing himself mentally and physically—for more than a month. He worked out every day, lifted four times a week, meditated for at least an hour every morning to clear his mind and cleanse his spirit.

Now, he watched the fire.

He had a pot cooking on her little two-burner gas stove. A selection of herbs, some obtained from the magick shop in town, some lifted from his grandmother's kitchen, some stolen from appropriate spots in town, simmered in an inch of water. The mixture stank, but then the apartment wasn't exactly daisy-fresh to begin with. Four cats shared it with Rosalie, and when Nicky first walked in the ammonia stench had almost knocked him over. She had no air conditioning, and he couldn't risk leaving any windows open, so the place felt like the inside of an oven set to "high."

But this was the last night of preparations. The next night would be the real thing. He could take it for that long. He shook his head, sucked it up, ignored the smell and the feverish heat.

He dumped the contents of his paper bag onto the tiny tiled countertop. Herbs. Paint he had made himself, following an ancient recipe he had found, from graveyard clay and stolen holy water and some crushed berries. A talisman he had boosted from his grandmother, a round amulet about two inches in diameter with a sun engraved on it. This he had strung on a strip of leather that had been tanned from the skin of a murder victim, though the guy at the shop hadn't been able to guarantee that the victim was human.

Nicky was positive it didn't matter. As with a gift, he knew, it was the thought that counted.

Magick was all about representation. The microcosm, that which one could control, represented the macrocosm, the greater world outside. The actual type of being the leather strip came from only mattered in that it represented the flesh of humanity.

It could as easily have come from one of Rosalie's cats.

Nicky checked the faded floral curtains once more, drawing them fully over the windows, rattled the doorknob to make sure it was locked, and took off his clothes. He was tall and muscular, with shoulders as wide as an ax handle and a deep chest. He had chopped off his thick black hair close to the scalp. He breathed through his open mouth as he worked in the torrid kitchen, and a sheen of sweat glossed his form.

He opened the plastic container of paint he had made, and, breathing in the rank odor of the bubbling stew, he began to paint himself. A line from his hairline to the top of his nose, across his third eye. Another line from his lower lip to his chin. A third line from the hollow of his throat to his navel. Then he smeared the paint over his hands and made five semiparallel lines across his chest, around his ribs, at the small of his back. Tomorrow night he would have to repeat this entire ritual, but he had been doing it for days and it was becoming second nature. As he dabbed himself he spoke the required words under his breath.

He capped the paint and turned to the talisman. Lifted it by the strap and held it over the simmering broth. He kissed it once, then dipped it into the pot. He held it there for five minutes, inside the gently boiling mixture.

Then he drew it out, held it over his head, slipped it around his neck and let the amulet fall against his chest.

His skin sizzled.

He leaned forward so that the amulet fell away from his chest. There was a red mark on his flesh, where the thing had burned him. The previous nights' efforts had done the same thing. The scar, he knew, would remain with him—a reminder of his night of power and a badge of honor.

He let it fall back against him, back to the burned spot. Left it alone.

Rosalie's sink was piled high with dirty dishes. Nicky found a chipped coffee mug with a cartoon cow on it. He rinsed it out, dumped the water, and filled it from the simmering pot. Before the liquid cooled he threw his head back and poured the contents of the cup down his throat. It burned, like swallowing flame.

Then the pain was gone. He felt nothing. He touched the amulet on his naked chest, moved it aside. The red mark was already starting to fade.

Tomorrow, it would be real. He was ready for it.

The Night of the Long Knives.

Tara sat alone in the Bronze, letting the music wash over her.

She had wandered Sunnydale all evening, hoping to find Willow. So far, she had not succeeded. She had come here thinking that Willow and Buffy might drop in. While seemingly every other teenager in Sunnydale had passed through the doors during the space of the evening, Willow had not.

Tara was on her third cup of chamomile tea. She knew she couldn't sit here much longer, watching everyone else paired off and having fun. But when she left here, there was no place else to go, nowhere she could think of to look that she hadn't already tried. So she'd have to head to the apartment she'd been renting all summer, and she'd be alone there, too.

Only with the four walls around her, she would feel much more alone than she did here.

One more cup, she thought. *Another half hour. If she hasn't shown by then, I'll go home and get some sleep.*

If Willow hasn't called me, then she's involved in something really important.

And anyway, I haven't been at home for her to call.

She had periodically checked her answering machine, but there had been no messages. Logically, Tara knew that if Willow was running around with Buffy, helping out in some kind of emergency, she wouldn't have time to leave a message anyway.

Tara sipped her tea and twirled her hair around two fingers of her right hand. She sat and watched the dancers and partiers as the bass thrummed up through the floor, through her stool, and into her bones. The Bronze was one of the few places people under twenty-one could go to listen to music, hang out, drink coffee.

Willow had told Tara that she, Buffy, and their friends had hung out at the Bronze almost every night. "Sometimes we were too broke to buy anything, so we asked for hot water and snuck in our own tea bags," Willow had added, chuckling to herself. Tara hadn't known if that was some kind of inside joke or not, but she'd smiled anyway.

However, the Bronze wasn't the hangout now it had been then. Since Willow and the others had started at UC Sunnydale, they'd spent less time here. Willow said it wasn't as close to campus, and what with classes and homework and fighting evil, time seemed to be more precious for everyone.

Tara knew the feeling. Her own high school life seemed far away now, and its pursuits less important and meaningful than they had been. She'd been shy and awkward, a total outcast, and it hadn't been until she'd met Willow that she'd felt truly accepted by another person.

Friendships, studies, even Wicca . . . everything was more serious in college. Tara hadn't known Willow and the gang then, but it was true for her and she believed it to be for them as well.

She smiled to herself. A lot had changed since high school. Just leaving home, going to college, did that.

Most especially, finding Willow changed her.

They had met in a Wiccan group, but the other girls—except Willow—were more concerned with talking the talk than walking the walk. Willow had seemed very different, somehow—more real, more attuned to the forces that turned the world around. Tara found herself drawn to Willow, and was delighted when the opposite turned out to be true as well.

And they had found, by working together, that their powers were increased when they combined them. Separately, each girl was gifted. But together, they were really a force to be reckoned with.

Tara had never felt as good about herself in her life. Willow gave her that gift.

And another gift. Tara couldn't quite bring herself to call it love.

Not yet.

But there was time.

Speaking of time, her self-imposed half-hour deadline had come and gone, as had her last cup of tea.

She slipped off the stool and threaded her way through the crowd, out the door. As it closed behind her she heard the thump of the bass fading away.

It doesn't matter, really, if I don't see Willow tonight, she knew. Willow was in her life, for keeps. That was what mattered.

Feeling slightly reassured, she decided to head back to the apartment. It was only a few blocks away, upstairs over a hardware store.

The streetlights pierced blooms of shadows that spilled over the curbs and alleys; things skittered in the darkness that might be cats or rats, or something evil that could suck off your face. Despite the quiet, the air thrummed with menace. Death whispered on the night breezes, as it always did in Sunnydale.

Most of the citizenry had no idea that their deceptively pleasant little town was situated on a Hellmouth; nor had they any conscious awareness of all the steps they took to avoid being outside alone at night. People in Sunnydale were nervous after dark, and the tension was like the emanations from the power lines over by the substation: low-grade enough to ignore, but strong enough to affect their behavior.

Tara, new to the place, and more acutely focused on her feelings and emotions because of her interest in the arcane, felt the wrongness. It was as if the angles and lines of the buildings and streets didn't quite add up; as if everything was askew and there was no hope of its ever being put right. Sunnydale kept people nervous. They went to places like the Bronze, where there was always a crowd.

But they didn't wander the streets after dark. They didn't like to be out alone.

At some deep level, they *knew.*

Tara almost envied them their surface-level denial. She knew what kinds of things lurked in the shadows—everything they were afraid of, and then some. It was hard to carry on a day-to-day life once you realized that every nightmare you've ever had couldn't compare with the reality of the evils that walked at night.

The street was unusually dark. There were lights on in a few windows in the two-and-three-storied buildings on either side, as well as the standard set of street lamps lighting the sidewalk. But the shadows seemed more dense than usual, impenetrable.

She was still more than a block from her place when the shadows came alive.

And came toward her.

A black shape seemed to rise from the center of a shadow, up against some storefronts. It reared up in front of her and then struck. She sensed a breeze, heard a faint rustling sound, and then felt something like a claw scrape against her cheek. She threw her arms up in self-defense, and took a step backward.

The shadow came at her again.

This time, it landed solidly in her midsection, knocking the wind out of her. She fell backward, landing painfully on the sidewalk.

She rolled to her feet just in time for the next assault. This time the shadowy claw came at her face again. Tara sensed it, and dodged. It swept past her, the rush of its passing very tangible indeed. But when she batted at it with one fist, her hand passed right through it.

She didn't know what she was fighting, but she knew it wasn't a fight she could win with her hands.

She didn't need to. Something else Willow had given her was confidence in her other skills. She retreated, halfway down the block, then stopped and turned to face the shadow being, racking her brain for some kind of spell she could use against it.

As it came toward her, advancing and pulling back like

liquid flowing down a gentle slope, she came up with one.

"Dark of soul, dark of night," she spoke loudly, struggling to keep her stammer at bay. As she said the words, she projected her will toward the shadows, visualizing golden ropes wrapping around the formless black. "By Hecate and the Green Man, I bind you in chains. By the power of the Goddess, I hold you fast."

The spell seemed to work. The shadow still bulged toward her, but the black tendrils ceased in their advance. The thing made no more attempts to strike at her, writhing instead as if to escape invisible bonds.

Tara allowed herself a faint smile.

That was when it broke free and came at her again. It splashed to the ground and bounced up at her, catching her under the chin with the shadow equivalent of a boxer's fist. Her head flew back and she lost her balance, sprawling on the sidewalk again.

And something else came up from behind her, another shadow—but with a form to follow.

"Leave her alone!" it shouted, stepping over her. When it was clearly framed against the shadow, between it and her, she recognized him.

Riley Finn. Buffy's boyfriend. He stood tall, facing the shadow thing with only his fists.

"Riley!" Tara called. "Be careful!"

He glanced over his shoulder at her, tossed her a devil-may-care grin. "Always."

As she watched, the shadow monster attacked him. A tendril shot toward Riley but he dodged it, leaping high into the air as it passed harmlessly beneath him. When it sent a second one, Riley turned and twisted, kicked and chopped the air, and though his hands and feet didn't connect with anything substantial, the shadow seemed to withdraw from his advance.

Tara attempted a different spell. "B-beast of shadow . . ." She hesitated, not remembering the words. Her panic was getting the better of her.

She tried again. "Beast of shadow, fiend forlorn, show yourself in solid form!" she shouted. "Mass and weight you have now found, binding you to solid ground!"

As she spoke the words, the thing seemed to shrink in on itself and to coalesce. Its shape was still amorphous, its outlines vague. But this time, when Riley kicked and punched at it, she could hear the impact of his blows. It tried to take a swing at Riley, but he avoided its attempt and trapped its blobby arm, wrenching it forward into the light. Riley looked as though he was battling the tar baby of the stories, except that he wasn't becoming covered in it. He was winning.

But the creature got in one good shot that sent Riley sailing. Tara rushed to his side. By the time she reached him, he was already scrambling for balance, ready to face the thing again. Blood trickled from his mouth and nose, and his forehead was scraped.

Something changed in his eyes. Tara looked away from him, down the street.

The shadow monster was gone.

The street was normal again, all the shadows where they belonged.

"The one that got away," Riley said.

"That's okay," Tara told him. "If your f-face got any more banged up Buffy would give me such hell."

"You were great," Riley said, favoring her with one of his radiant smiles. "But those spells of yours—they always have to rhyme like that?"

She grimaced. "Sucked, huh. I couldn't remember the words. I feel like Sabrina. On TV."

"I'm just kidding you, Tara," Riley said reassuringly.

"You were great. I couldn't figure out any way to fight the thing."

"I managed to bind it for a minute, before you came along." She rubbed her upper arms. "But it's hard to bind something with no solidity, I guess."

"I think that's the thing that's been attacking people all over town," Riley told her. She nodded. "We'll have to come up with some way to battle it. Probably making it take solid shape is the best first step, like you did there. But then, once it's solid it has to be defeated or confined quickly."

"Probably I should have reversed the order of the spells," Tara said, thinking aloud. "S-solidified it first, and then bound it."

"Could be," Riley agreed. He smiled at her. "We'll try that next time."

She was confused. "Next time?"

"We're a good team against that thing. We should go back to Giles's place, report on it, and see if he can figure out what it is. Then we should get back out on the street and see if we can find it again."

"Anyone ever tell you you're a glutton for punishment?" she asked him, flattered beyond words for being included in the plan.

"Hey, if I wasn't, would I be dating a Slayer?" he joked. "Come on. We don't have all night."

Chapter 7

Los Angeles

AT DINNER, CORDELIA HAD PROMISED KAYLEY AND THE
other girls that she wouldn't tell a single living soul about
their plans.

Which, of course, didn't rule out Angel.

And she knew where to find him—at her apartment in
Silver Lake, most likely. He and Wesley had been spending most of their time there since Angel's apartment and
office had been converted into yet more smog.

Being Angel Investigations HQ was only a problem
when she wanted to do something personal like, say,
sleep. The dating thing wasn't really working out this
summer, so no interference *there*.

She went straight home after her meeting with the
girls. True to form, Wesley was asleep on her couch, with
his Argyle socked-feet up and a big book over his face.

"At least you took your shoes off," Cordelia announced. "Thank goodness for those British manners." She dropped her bag on her coffee table for emphasis.

Wesley stirred, then suddenly started and sat upright, yanking the book away from his face. "I'm sorry," he said quickly. "I was doing some research and just thought I should rest my eyes a bit and . . ."

His voice trailed off as he studied Cordelia's face. "All right, I confess. I went to sleep. It is late, after all."

She was miffed. "Oh, yes. It's . . . wow, eight-thirty. I'm out working, and Angel is . . ." She looked around. "Where is Angel, anyway?"

"Out working," Wesley admitted sheepishly.

"And you're here minding the fort with those ridiculous socks on my furniture and your face buried in demonic literature."

"Yes, that's right," he replied, on the defensive now. He gestured toward the big book. "Angel and I helped Isabel and Carlos move from their house to a motel. Dreadfully seedy place called the Flamingo, but it looked clean enough, and not too expensive. Angel said it was the kind of place where they didn't even want to know anyone's real name. They should be safe there while we find out what's haunting their house."

"So you're fine for fighting demons, but carrying a few suitcases tuckers you out?" Cordelia jibed.

"You'd be surprised how much some people feel like they have to carry with them," he replied. "Especially the boy. Each and every toy he owns seemed to be his favorite." He glanced down at the stack of books next to him. "Besides, some of these Renaissance authors are dreadfully long-winded, you know? This one went on and on about the grooming habits of certain Bavarian demons, which could easily be described as nonexistent, I should think, and I found that I just couldn't keep my eyes open."

"Why are you reading about them, then? Nonexistent demons?" She smiled faintly to let him know she was teasing him. *A little.*

"Angel wanted me to brush up on poltergeist activity," Wesley replied. "These particular demons were quite adept at mimicking poltergeists, causing people to have their houses cleansed and even exorcised, when the actual culprits were on the outside laughing, in some cases literally, their tails off." He smiled back, equally faintly.

British humor is where you find it, I guess. Cordelia had always suspected that English people actually knew they weren't funny most of the time, and tried to cover up their shortfall in the ha-ha department by pretending their sense of humor was exotic and therefore incomprehensible to non-English people. Which didn't work with Americans, because, hello, speaking tons of English?

"Think that has anything to do with the case he's working on now? I mean, we're in Los Angeles, not Bavaria, right?"

"It's a global village, Cordelia. Demons certainly don't respect national borders any longer."

"Did they ever?"

"There's no evidence that they did, no."

She sat down next to him on the couch. "So do we know where he is? Or when he's coming back?"

"No, and no," Wesley answered. "Why? What have you been up to?"

"Can't say," Cordelia told him.

"Why not?" He raised his brows.

She moved her shoulders and raised hers back. "Promised."

"Very well. A promise is a promise." He inclined his head. "Good for you."

She turned to face him. "Oh, Wesley, there are these girls, and they've offered themselves up to this Transylvanian Dracula movie extra named Kostov, and they've run away from home and they're living under the Los Angeles main library and I just don't know what to do about them. They're just kids, like fourteen- and fifteen- and sixteen-years-old and they don't have the slightest idea of what they're getting into.

"But I don't really know how to tell them that life can be any better than it is for them, and . . . oops. Guess I told." She covered her mouth with her fingertips and mugged a look of extreme guilt.

"Hmmm," he pondered in his hmming British way. He kind of reminded her of Winnie the Pooh at times. "Unless there's more to it than that. But that certainly sounds like plenty. Can we take it a step at a time?"

"Well, cat's out of the bag now, so we might as well pour it some milk, right?" she asked, feeling chipper.

He yawned. "Is that some kind of metaphor, or another part of the story?"

"Metaphor, Wesley. You are one muzzy guy."

"Being startled out of a very deep sleep does that to one." He harrumphed. "Very well, then. Now, these girls. They're living in the library?"

"Underneath it. In these closed-off sections."

"And they've all run away from home."

"That's right. Some of them from abusive parents, others from neglectful parents. It doesn't sound like any of them really have a lot of reason to want to go back home."

He looked skeptical. "And their only alternative is offering themselves up as vampire refreshments?"

"That's what they seem to think. They want to be turned. They have all these romantic ideas about what it's like." She made the "ew" face.

He took that in. "Yes, well, they're not alone there."

"I know. That's why it's so hard to convince them what a mistake they're making. I mean, even if Angel went to see them . . ." She trailed off meaningfully.

"Yes, Angel, young girls, I see what you're getting at. The whole billowing coat thing, redux. No, what we need is an ugly old vampire with a skin condition. And possibly a hump."

She looked pleased. "That might do it. Know any?"

"Sorry, no." He shook his head. "What about this Kostov? Have you ever heard of him?"

"No. He's apparently made friends with the leader of these Lost Girls, Pat. He's promised to come by and turn all of them. I don't know when. Pretty soon, I think."

"But not tonight?" Wesley framed his question in the form of a question.

"No, not tonight. They made me take them out for dinner. If you can call it that. Burgers at a fast food joint." She patted the epicenter of her heartburn. "Better than blood, but not by much. They wouldn't have left the library if it was tonight."

"So we have a little time. We should tell Angel about it, and see if he has any ideas. Have you tried calling him?"

Cordelia smiled ruefully. "I tried his cell phone. It's turned off."

"Well, no surprise there," Wesley sighed. "In the meantime, we can do some research." He sighed and raised his book from his lap. "See what we can find on Kostov, for one thing. And I'm intrigued by their hiding place." He cocked his head. "Why the library?"

"Bookworms?" she guessed. "I don't know, Wesley."

"I just find it odd."

"So that's it? The answer is, wait till Angel gets home? Why did you make me tell you, then?" She scowled at him as he began to scan his book some more. "I broke my promise for nothing."

"So sorry I twisted your arm," Wesley said. He looked up from the page. "And that's also a metaphor."

Wesley watched Cordelia pore over some vampire texts, looking for anything she could find on Kostov. The poor girl was clearly exhausted and ready for bed, but something about these girls had gotten to her. She seemed unwilling to let herself sleep until she'd figured out something that could be done to help them.

For his part, Wesley felt much the same, even though he hadn't met them. He had been a Watcher, and Watchers were trained specifically to work with teenage girls, direct their activities, and keep them safe from harm, when possible.

Of course, the girls a Watcher worked with were Slayers, and he had not, to be brutally frank with himself, been the most effective Watcher ever. How many Watchers had not one, but two Slayers reject his services at once? No, that had to be a record that would stand for ages in the history of the Watcher's Council.

He'd been fired from the Council, after that. Buffy and Faith had continued on their respective paths, and he wanted to be around to help them, even on an unofficial basis. Now Faith was in jail, here in Los Angeles, and Buffy was still in Sunnydale.

But the battle went on, the struggle against evil, and he was here too, helping Angel where he could. Buffy, after all, had Giles, but Angel had no one. And if Faith ever got out and needed him, he'd be close by for her.

Not that I can ever imagine her admitting that she needs me.

He signed on to the Internet and began researching the

Los Angeles Public Library, hoping to find some reason that the girls might have chosen that particular place, out of all the places in the city where they might have camped out, to stay.

He didn't have to look for long.

"Cordy," he called. "Cordelia."

She put her book down and came to stand beside him.

"Listen to this," he said. "You said your young friends lived underneath the library, in a closed-off section, right?"

"That's right."

"Are you sure it was actually part of the library?"

"What?" She looked off into the distance, as if revisiting the library in her mind's eye. "It looked like it to me. Same basic architecture and everything. But it was dark. Why?"

He indicated the screen with his head. "It says here that, according to legend, there was once an entire city underneath the library. Stretching all the way from there to Dodger Stadium. It was inhabited by 'Lizard People,' who vanished from there five thousand years ago."

Cordelia leaned over his shoulder, scanning the screen. Her fragrance was an interesting mixture of raw onions, perfume, and the microwave popcorn they'd shared about half an hour before.

"I didn't see any lizards down there," she said. "Some dust bunnies, maybe."

He tapped the screen for emphasis. "This is supposed to have been a lost race who built underground cities all up and down the coast, thousands of years ago. Then they vanished. Nobody knows why or where. The cities held about a thousand inhabitants each, with all their supplies and stores of food. Various people have searched for the city, but they've never found it."

"So what makes you think it exists?" she asked, turning to look at him.

He clicked to the next page. "I don't necessarily think it does. I just find it interesting that this is the place your would-be vampires chose to hide out. Really, how many runaways can you think of who would hide out underneath a library?"

"Not many, I guess."

"Exactly." He went to the next screen. "I wonder if these girls know something about the legend. Or if they were drawn to that place by the lost race, or something."

Cordelia shook her head. "I really think you're reaching here, Wesley. I think they picked the library because they found the passageways underneath, and because it's warm and dry and open to the public."

"You may very well be right, Cordelia. I simply think it's a fascinating coincidence." He tapped the keys with his fingertips, frustrated that he'd found nothing more about the Lizard People.

At least, at this website.

"Okay, great. Fascinating," Cordy said bluntly. "I'll go back to my highly thrilling reading now." She picked up something thick and dusty. "Why don't they have indexes in these books? Do you know how many pages *without* the name Kostov on them there are in one of those texts alone?"

"I'm sure it's a substantial figure, Cordelia," he said gently.

"You got that right." She went back to the book and resumed paging through it.

Sunnydale

Ruben Velasco had worked for the de la Natividad family for years. He had been with the old man in Mexico, beginning as a security guard for one of his factories there, and eventually joining the household security staff as well.

Within a few years, he was the family's head of security. He supported the move to the U.S.—he knew that security would be easier there, for one thing. And he wanted to be able to bring his own children over, which he would be able to do once his citizenship was established.

He was getting on in years now—at forty-one, he was twice as old as some of the guards who worked for him. But he still put the family's interests first, and when there were missions of special sensitivity, he made sure he was personally involved.

This mission was one of those.

Salma, Armando and Carolina's daughter, had gone to college in Sunnydale. The coastal city wasn't that far away from Los Angeles, but it was far enough to make Ruben nervous. And the fact that she had refused to have a bodyguard there made him more so. But she had seemed fine, even happy to be out on her own.

Until tonight.

Earlier in the evening, her parents had received a phone call from Salma. She had been on the edge of hysteria, saying something about a shadow that seemed to be watching her, outside her own condominium building. As they spoke, she calmed down, eventually to the point of telling her parents that she had overreacted, that she had some friends coming over and would be fine. Carolina had called her again a couple of hours later, and the friends were just leaving. Salma was settled by then, insisting that she had simply panicked for no good reason and was not in any danger.

But Carolina de la Natividad did not believe her daughter. She called for Ruben, and explained the situation to him. Salma must be brought home, she declared. With her brother Nicky missing, the family had to be together. Carolina would not sleep until Salma was safe on the family estate.

So Ruben climbed into a powerful Lincoln Navigator and hurtled to Sunnydale in the middle of the night. The smooth engine purred as bright headlights split the dark empty freeway. At the correct exit he pulled off the highway and headed toward the Pacific.

As he closed in on Salma's neighborhood, he thought he glimpsed something in the Lincoln's rearview mirror. He turned to look behind him but could see nothing back there but the empty road and dark buildings. He kept one eye on the mirror and made a turn, then another, then a third, in rapid succession. If there was anyone following him, he would know about it.

He was looking into the mirror when his windshield exploded.

Glass sprayed over him like the water from a breaking wave. It was safety glass, but something cut him, blinding him. He threw his hands up and the big sport utility swerved, slamming into a telephone pole.

Ruben clutched at the door handle and wrenched open the door, spilling himself out of the vehicle onto the street. With one hand he clawed at his eyes, blinking and brushing the glass from them. He could see out of only one, and everything was blurry, but he thought he could see well enough to figure out what had happened to the car.

But he must have been wrong, because what he saw was impossible—a dark shadow moving through the night, coming toward him. When it reached him it had the solidity of a brick wall—tendrils of shadow, like a dozen fists, pummeled him. He took hits to the face, the head, the solar plexus. He tried to fight back, but there was nothing to fight. He went down.

Chapter 8

Los Angeles

AN HOUR LATER ANGEL AND GREG PRESTON SAT IN THE clean, modern room of the recently remodeled jail called the "inmate visitation area." It was a well-lit facility, looking very little like Angel thought it would. The colors were cool and soothing, not the institutional green or gray he had expected.

Getting in had not been a problem, with Preston's credentials and a hacked-together license for Angel that Preston made himself. Preston simply told the administrators that Angel was in the employ of his office, and he was admitted under the same rule that allowed lawyers and their clients to consult at any hour. Flores was no happier about being dragged out of bed than Preston had been, but he was less vocal about it.

A uniformed guard walked Flores into the visitation area, stood next to him as he sat down in one of the molded plastic chairs across a table from Preston and Angel, and then crossed to the far side of the room and sat, keeping an eye out but trying not to listen to their conversation.

Rojelio Flores was bleary-eyed, and he moved with the slow, relaxed manner of someone who has been deeply asleep. He wore a dark blue shirt over a white T-shirt, and baggy pants, almost like a doctor's scrubs, but with L.A. JAIL printed on the shirt in big white letters.

"Sorry to wake you, Rojelio," Preston began.

"You got good news for me, I don't mind," Flores said with a wan smile.

"No news," Angel said. "Just some questions."

"Questions that couldn't wait until daytime?"

"Afraid not."

"Don't look at me," Preston said. "Angel woke me up, too."

"I'm a private investigator," Angel explained. "I've been out to your house. Do you know what's going on there?"

The man looked extremely worried. "What do you mean, what's going on?" He looked at Preston. "Is my family all right?"

"It's not like that," Preston assured him. He looked expectantly at Angel. Angel knew that most people either didn't see, or chose not to see, a whole range of existence. Things that fell outside the mainstream, things that couldn't be easily explained by science, occurred on a kind of invisible plane that most average folks turned away from as if acknowledging them would somehow threaten their lives, or at least their sanity. Maybe they were right, but Angel had been walking that plane for so long, he sometimes couldn't understand why people looked away. *Wouldn't they be better off knowing what's out there?* he wondered occasionally. *Aren't they at more risk from the unseen than from the everyday?*

Obviously, Rojelio Flores fell into this category, so Angel decided he had to get specific.

"Poltergeist activity," he said. "Things flying around. Loud noises."

Prisoner and attorney stared at him. The only sound was the creaking of Rojelio's chair as he sat back in it. He glanced at Preston, who made a "don't ask me" gesture, and then at Angel.

"Sounds like crazy talk to me," Flores said.

"So Isabel and Carlos haven't told you about this?" Angel queried. "Or you aren't talking to me because you don't trust me?"

Rojelio Flores sat with his arms crossed over his chest, saying nothing.

"Isabel and Carlos trust me," Angel told him.

"You can say that, but I don't know it's true. They aren't here for me to ask, are they?"

"And they can't be until tomorrow morning. I don't know when it'll be too late for them. I think they might be in danger from this phenomenon, and I want to try to bring it under control. Since it started when you were arrested, I think it might have something to do with you."

Rojelio dropped the act. "You really think they could get hurt?"

"Even if by accident. Heavy objects flying around the house could hurt anyone."

He considered. "I guess that's true, isn't it?"

"So if you know anything about this, then—"

"Hey!"

Angel was cut off by a shout from the guard on the other side of the room. The three men looked over.

The guard was on his feet, chasing his own clipboard,

which hovered about eight feet up in the air—just out of his reach. He jumped for it.

After a moment, it dropped as if released by an invisible hand. The guard caught it before it hit the floor.

Preston rubbed his florid face with one meaty hand. He looked at Angel. "You said . . ."

Angel shrugged. "I said I wouldn't make the face. I didn't have anything to do with that."

He turned back to Rojelio Flores. "Your lawyer is not a fan of the supernatural, Rojelio. Maybe you should start talking."

Sunnydale

Salma de la Natividad was sleeping uneasily when the doorbell rang. She picked up the phone—it was connected to the building's security system—and punched the nine. "Yes?" she mumbled.

"Miss de la Natividad?"

"Yes."

"I'm a police officer, ma'am. My name is Jeff Jacobs. May I come upstairs?"

Her heart skipped a beat. *Trouble. Oh, Nicky.* "What's it about?"

"I'd rather tell you in person if that's all right. There's a video camera system here, right? You can take a look at my badge on that if you're concerned."

"Okay, just a minute." She went to the tiny monitor on the wall by her front door, and flipped the switch that turned it on. He looked like a cop, and he was holding a badge up to the camera. She jotted down the badge number and then pressed the button that unlocked the door.

A few moments later, he knocked on her front door.

She had taken the time to pull on a robe and pour herself a glass of water.

"Yes?" she said again as she opened the door.

"I'm very sorry to disturb you at this hour," Officer Jacobs said.

Salma stepped back and invited him inside. He came in, but remained standing formally before the door, which he left open. "What is going on?" she asked.

"You know a Ruben Velasco," Jacobs said. It wasn't a question.

"Yes, I know him." Her heart skipped a beat. "Has something happened to him?"

"He was involved in an accident. A very severe one. He may have been attacked, as well. He has wounds that don't seem to be consistent with the accident, and he was found well away from his vehicle."

Oh, Dios, mio. She reeled, holding onto the door. "Where? Here in Sunnydale?"

"Yes ma'am," Jacobs said. "Just a few blocks from here."

"What happened?" Salma demanded. She felt tears welling in her eyes, fought to keep them down. She had cried enough lately; it wouldn't help Ruben to start again. "Is he okay?"

"He's still unconscious, ma'am. He's at the Sunnydale Medical Center. They're doing everything they can for him. As for what happened, well, we're still trying to piece that together, ma'am. I was hoping maybe you could help."

"I didn't even know he was in Sunnydale. Can I see him?"

"I'd give it until the morning. Let the doctors do their thing. May I have a glass of water?" Jacobs asked.

Salma nodded and went to get it. Her hands trembled as she got the glass and turned on the faucet.

Jacobs continued. "I was one of the first people on the

scene. Someone heard the crash and called 911. We got there about the same time the paramedics did. There was no sign of anyone else. If he had been attacked, we don't know by whom. I checked his identification, found a business card with a Los Angeles number on it. I called the number."

"He works for my family."

"That's what I was told. And I was told he was coming to Sunnydale to bring you home to Los Angeles."

She blinked. "No one told me that."

"I was told that, too. They were afraid you would refuse to come home. But if Mr. Velasco was here to get you . . . well, I was given to understand that he could be very persuasive."

"You make it sound like he would torture me," she snapped, then reminded herself that this man was only trying to help. "Yes, Ruben could have persuaded me, but not in a bad way. He has nothing but love for me and my family. I would have gone with him, if he had insisted it was for my safety."

Jacobs considered. "So he didn't call ahead because he wanted to convince you in person."

"That is what it sounds like," Salma agreed. "And this must be why my family didn't call me to tell me about Ruben—because they wanted you to be able to take me to them."

"I'm not a delivery service," Jacobs said. "*Are* you in any danger?" he asked, narrowing his eyes. His interest was clearly piqued.

She swallowed down her reaction and tried to keep her face from betraying her. "Not that I know of."

"Would you tell me if you were?"

Maybe she was not convincing.

"Do I have any reason not to? I didn't know he was

coming, so I don't know why he was coming. He didn't say anything to you?"

The police officer drank the rest of the water. "Like I said, he hasn't regained consciousness."

"I'll call my family and find out from them, then. Thank you for coming to tell me about it."

She took his glass and held it with both hands. She was afraid she would crush it, she was clutching it so tightly.

"Will you be okay, ma'am? Do you need me to get a policewoman out here to stay with you for a while?"

"No, thank you, Officer Jacobs. I will be fine."

Officer Jacobs said good-bye and left. Salma went straight to the telephone and called Willow.

Ruben Velasco could barely focus on Salma when they went to see him at the hospital. He was full of painkillers, the doctor had said, but he forced himself to open his eyes and carry on a conversation that was almost intelligible. He had a tube running into his nose, which Buffy always thought looked like the very definition of uncomfortable. His face and hands were cut. Some of the cuts were bandaged, others had some kind of purple ointment smeared over them. His lips were bruised and swollen, and one eye was almost shut from the swelling under it. Buffy was glad her Slayer powers included healing ability—she rarely had to worry about the cosmetic realities of combat.

In a mixture of English, which Buffy mostly understood in spite of his accent and his injuries, and Spanish, which, well, she understood the English part, Ruben explained to Salma what had happened to him—and his fear that she was in mortal danger from the same thing that had attacked him. Salma had promised to be very careful and had held his hand as his eyes had drooped shut and he had fallen asleep again. Then they had retreated to Salma's apartment to discuss the next step.

"I don't know what it is or why, Salma, but I think, somehow, this is about you," Buffy was saying. She was happy to be away from the antiseptic smell of the hospital and back in Salma's kitchen. Salma brewed a pot of coffee. Riley, Willow, and Tara sat around the tile-topped kitchen table. Everyone looked tired. The sun was beginning to lighten the sky, out the kitchen window.

"What do you mean?" Salma asked, as the water dripped through the grounds. The coffeemaker began to make noises.

"This, this shadow monster or whatever we want to call it. It threatened Tara and Riley. Either the same thing that got Mr. Velasco, or something very much like it." Tara and Riley nodded in unison and Willow looked upset. Since the attack, she had looked upset every single time the words "monster" and "Tara" had occurred in the same sentence. "And we know it's been hanging around you. There's just too much there to call it coincidence. I think it's been watching you, maybe waiting for a good opportunity to attack you."

Buffy watched as Salma got the now-familiar black-and-gold coffee cups out of her dishwasher. She was hoping for more chocolate truffles.

"Or maybe it was trying to make sure you weren't attacked—like it's trying to protect you in some way. And then, when someone tried to come into town to take you away, it attacked him," Willow offered.

Salma looked skeptical. Buffy took the first cup of steaming hot coffee as Salma poured it and handed it to her.

"Maybe it has to do with your brother instead of you," Buffy suggested. It seems like this all started around the time that he disappeared. Maybe it's just coincidence, but it doesn't feel that way to me."

"Are you saying that it's Nicky, somehow?" Salma's brown eyes widened and she sloshed coffee over the rim of the second cup. "He would never attack Ruben!"

"I'm not saying the monster is Nicky," Buffy soothed. She looked at Willow for assistance. "Just that the timing of its arrival seems awfully coincidental."

Riley jumped in. "We still don't know what Nicky's into, except we think it has to do with that gang his friends are in."

Salma touched her forehead. "But—"

"But you found those books, and you were afraid he was fooling around with the supernatural," Buffy continued. She set down her coffee. "What if he was? What if he somehow summoned that shadow creature and couldn't send it back?"

"That could have happened," Willow volunteered. "I've done some experimenting in that area. Sometimes you call up things you didn't expect."

Tara gave Salma a sympathetic smile. "It doesn't mean your brother is a bad person or anything."

"Anything is possible, when it comes to my brother," Salma admitted, cleaning up the spill with a pink sponge.

"We're not trying to accuse him of anything. We want to help him," Willow added.

"And that includes keeping him from hurting anyone else," Riley added. His features clouded. "Sometimes good people do things because they want to help other people, but they lose control of what they're doing."

Buffy saw the flicker of pain on his face and knew he was thinking of Maggie Walsh. She couldn't help her own hurt; Riley still mourned the disintegration of the once-great scientist, but that woman had tried to kill her.

"If he had any control over the thing, it would never have attacked Ruben Velasco," Salma said, looking even more upset. "Nicky loves Ruben as much as if he were a blood relative."

Buffy nodded. "There's still too much we don't know about it," she said. "But it's obvious that your family wants you at home. And my guess is that you'll be safer there, away from Sunnydale."

"But it doesn't look like travel is especially safe, Buffy," Willow pointed out. "At least, not for Salma and her family."

Salma looked straight at Buffy. Buffy thought to herself, *Anybody can go with her. It doesn't have to be me.*

"Please, would you mind, Buffy?" Salma asked in a small voice.

Willow looked at her hopefully as well. Buffy hesitated. Then she thought about Ruben Velasco lying in the Sunnydale Medical Center, and whatever put him there. If it was following Salma, she'd need some good protection.

"I can go with her," Riley offered.

Salma kept looking at Buffy, and the Slayer realized, hopefully before Riley did, that Salma preferred Buffy. So she said quickly, "Actually, I'd like to go with her. Check up on my old buds in L.A."

She turned back to Riley. "I'll make sure she gets to L.A. safely. Then I'll work on locating Nicky so we can try to figure this out once and for all."

Salma exhaled, relieved. Buffy kept her attention focused on Riley.

"You'll have to patrol, make sure the shadow thing doesn't hurt anyone else. It's already afraid of you."

"Me and Tara together." He grinned faintly at Tara, who shifted in her chair. She looked totally exhausted, yet pleased.

"Good," Buffy said. She looked at Tara. "You guys keep an eye out for it."

"For all we know, there could be more than one," Riley added. "The one Tara and I ran into might be a baby."

"Oh, great," Willow murmured.

"We're going alone?" Salma asked uneasily.

Buffy put some sugar in her coffee. "The thing isn't attacking anyone in Los Angeles; we'd have heard about it if it was."

"From Angel?" Riley asked, his voice calm and level.

Buffy fixed him with a steady gaze, trying to read him. He knew that Angel was in Los Angeles, and that if she went there she might see him. *Correction, would see him.* They had been very close, and there was also the matter of "professional courtesy"—if whatever was stalking Salma followed them to Los Angeles, then she owed it to Angel to let him know that she had played a part in bringing it to town, and she'd have to share what little she knew about it. What Riley worried about, though, the romantic aspect of her past association with Angel, wouldn't happen. That part of her life was over, to everyone but Riley. He was the only one who couldn't see that any attraction there might once have been was long gone. Angel was a guy—strike that, a vampire—she had once known. That was all.

And that's definitely the truth, she told herself. *Riley is my guy. I love him.*

"Does that sound okay to you, Salma?" Buffy asked.

Salma looked at her, then at Riley, and finally at Willow.

"Yes," she said, her voice small. "But may I ask for Willow to come with us?"

Willow looked startled. Then she nodded. "That makes sense, Buffy," she said. "Salma knows me the best out of all of us, and she'll probably be more comfortable if I'm along. Anyway, if something does come up you could probably use an extra set of hands, or, you know, spells or something."

"Okay, Will. You come along. You, me, and Salma make the trip. We'll stay just long enough to make sure Salma's safe at home and the shadow monster hasn't followed her.

"Riley and Tara, you guys will stay here and keep a lookout for any more activity in Sunnydale. Giles is still trying to figure out what the thing is, but last time I talked to him he hadn't come up with anything definite."

"It's hard to reach any solid conclusions when you're dealing with a shadow," Willow pointed out.

Standing across from Willow in the kitchen, Tara looked stricken.

Twenty minutes later, Salma had packed a couple of bags and was standing by the doorway with them. Tara and Willow sat together on Salma's couch.

"Be careful, Willow," Tara said, taking Willow's hand in hers. She looked into her friend's sea-green eyes, touched her cheek tenderly. Willow's red hair brushed against the backs of her fingers. "Do a warding spell for the car."

"I will," Willow replied softly. "You be careful, too, Tara. We don't know what this is. If anything happened to you . . ." She trailed off, and Tara's answering smile was sweet and shy.

Riley and Buffy stood in a corner, having an intense moment of their own. Their faces were separated by mere inches. Tara couldn't hear what they were saying, but the meaning was clear. Not only would they miss one another, but there was an undercurrent of something else going on that she could only guess at—but that, if forced to guess, she would say had something to do with Angel, Buffy's vampire ex-boyfriend who lived in the city Buffy was headed for.

Then Riley and Buffy stopped talking and brought their lips together in a passionate kiss. Tara looked away, giving them their privacy. She noticed that Salma was looking at her own shoes.

And Willow was looking right at her. Which meant no one else was looking at them.

She kissed Willow good-bye.

Chapter 9

Los Angeles

W HEN ANGEL GOT BACK TO CORDELIA'S APARTMENT, just before sunrise, the place was empty. "Cordy?" he called out. "Wesley?" No answer.

On the refrigerator, a magnet shaped like a Hollywood clapboard shoved itself to one side, and the note stuck underneath it fluttered through the air toward him. Angel took it when it came close enough.

"Thanks, Dennis," he said. Cordelia's phantom roommate had taken a liking to Angel, and did him any number of small favors.

The note was in Cordelia's handwriting. It said, "Angel, we're at the main library to talk some girls out of becoming vampires. Turn on your phone! C. & W."

He tugged his cell from his pocket. Sure enough, it was off. He'd had to turn it off going into the jail, by law, and then had forgotten to switch it back on again. Something about his two-hundred-forty-plus-year-old mind and cell phones just didn't mesh sometimes. He turned it on now.

He looked at the note again. *Would the library be open at dawn?* He didn't think so. But she hadn't asked for help, and if he spent his life trying to understand Cordelia Chase, he wouldn't have time for anything else. So he let it go.

He helped himself to a container of pig's blood from the refrigerator and sat down with it and a couple of books. From the stacks Wesley had made next to the coffee table, it was obvious that he'd been reading up on poltergeist phenomena.

That was probably a good thing, since Flores had been unable to shed any light on the strange forces that seemed to surround him. Angel pulled some books from the bottom of the stack, ones Wesley hadn't made it through yet, and began flipping pages. After doing that for a few minutes, he decided he was too sleepy to focus on the words just now. He kicked his shoes off, put his feet up, and went to sleep.

In his dreams, Dennis the ghost was rearranging furniture.

Like an indecisive person in a new house, he put a chair against one wall and then took it away again, carrying it over to the opposite side of the room. He turned a table this way and that. He removed pictures from the walls, switched them around, then switched them again.

But at some point during the dream, he realized that Dennis was standing to one side watching all this. It wasn't Dennis moving the furniture at all. Angel was moving it himself, with his mind.

He woke up. *Of course!* He and Wesley had been looking up the wrong kind of phenomenon. He grabbed an encyclopedia of psychic phenomena from the supply of books that Wesley had brought over when they'd decided to make Cordy's apartment their temporary headquarters, and rifled through the pages.

He stopped when he got to "telekinesis." The definition given was very simple: "The movement of objects without visible or perceptible cause; the mental ability to move objects in space."

Bingo.

He'd been looking at it all wrong. He had been trying to find a reason for the Flores house to be "haunted" by a poltergeist, when all along it was haunted by one of the Flores family.

Probably Carlos, the boy, he realized. Seeing the same thing happen at the jail should have tipped him off. The chances that the husband and wife would share the same ability was slim to none, but father and son? That could happen. And, as seemed to be the case, if the father was unaware of his own power, then the boy would be, as well. It was probably the stressful event of being framed for murder that set off the power in the first place.

He had to go back to Isabel and Carlos. Moving to a motel wouldn't do any good—it was not the house that was haunted, it was one of them.

He went to the window and looked outside. He'd only slept for a short while, and the sun was just rising through the morning haze. It was overcast; not dark enough to make going outside a good idea, though he could do it. He thought about calling, but didn't want to panic the family. Better to test the boy himself, in person, and be there to help him deal with what he would discover about himself.

"Are you sure this is a good idea, Cordelia?" Wesley whispered. "What if this is someone's home we're breaking into?"

"Have I ever steered you wrong, Wesley? Don't answer

that. I'm sure, all right? It's an empty store. No one lives here." She looked at the door again, then took a few steps back, and leaned out to look at the storefront next door. They were both boarded over. "Or was it that one? They look so much alike, and it was dark, after all."

"We're both going to jail," Wesley complained.

"No we aren't. If we pick the wrong store, then we'll just say we made a mistake."

"Yes, officer, we're sorry, we meant to break into the place next door. That will go over well in court."

"Will you relax, Wesley?" Cordelia hissed. "I'm ninety percent sure this is the one." She rattled the door. "Well, eighty. I don't remember the door being locked."

"Why can't we just go in through the library?" Wesley asked.

Cordelia looked at the gray early-morning sky. "It's not open yet," she explained.

"Just what is it we're supposed to accomplish, anyway?"

"You're supposed to use your expertise to talk the girls out of becoming vampires."

"My expertise? If you couldn't do it, then what makes you think they'll listen to me?"

I haven't the faintest idea why anyone would, Cordelia thought. But she said, "You can tell them all about the Watchers Council and everything. I still don't really understand that whole business."

"Yes, well, I can be rather persuasive at times," Wesley admitted. "When I set my mind to it."

"You go," Cordelia encouraged him.

"I still think waiting for Angel would have been the better course of action," Wesley insisted.

"But we don't know if we have time to wait for him. Who knows when he'll decide to drop by? He didn't come home last night."

"I know that, but the sun is up, he may well be there by now. I just think that rather than breaking into a store that may well be the wrong store, in order to try to talk some teenage girls out of a course they've fixed their sights on, we should let the actual vampire have a go at it."

"Just open the door, Wesley," Cordelia said. "Before someone sees us—"

"What are you doing there, Cordelia?" a voice behind them asked.

Cordelia spun around. "Kayley. Shouldn't you be hanging upside down from the rafters somewhere?"

"Not quite yet," Kayley replied. "I thought I'd take your advice. See what the world looked like with the sun on it."

"Not much sun yet," Wesley observed.

"One step at a time," Kayley said, warily eyeing him. "If I can deal with sunrise, maybe I can make it through the day."

"We were, uhh, we were just coming to see you," Cordelia told her.

"What for? Going to buy me breakfast this time?"

"Are you hungry?" Cordelia asked her.

Kayley gave her a smirk. "What do you think?"

They took her to a nearby coffee shop. On the way, Cordelia introduced Kayley and Wesley. "This is Wesley," she said. "He knows more about vampires than anyone who hasn't been one."

"Do you know Kostov?" Kayley asked.

"Well, no, I haven't had the pleasure," Wesley replied.

"Have you read Anne Rice's books? Or Laurell Hamilton's?"

"Er, there's a lot more to this than . . . what's found in books, Kayley," Wesley said. Before he could elaborate, though, a waitress came and took their breakfast orders. Tiny Kayley surprised Cordelia by ordering scrambled eggs, bacon, hash browns, toast, and oatmeal. The waitress poured coffee and brought a pot of tea for Wesley.

"Look, if you haven't even read the basic books I don't see how you can claim to be an expert," Kayley said.

"I never said I was an expert," Wesley rejoined. "But neither are those authors. They're making up stories. The reality is very different."

"I've never really been sure there is a reality," Kayley admitted. She sipped from a cup of coffee that seemed nearly as big around as her head. "I know Pat believes, and she's convinced that this Kostov guy is the real thing, you know? But so far, he hasn't met the rest of us. I'm not totally convinced."

"I wouldn't tell you this if Cordelia and I weren't worried about you," Wesley said. "But we are. And it is. Real, I mean. I don't know if Kostov is. We haven't been able to find any mention of him in the literature. But vampires are certainly real, and they're nothing to play around with."

"You sound like my dad talking to me about booze or something. Next thing, you'll go to the bar and make yourself a martini."

Cordelia laughed. "I know he comes off that way sometimes," she said. "I think it's the British thing. But he's right. Vampires aren't a game. They're out there, and their life is nothing you'd want for yourself."

"How do you know what I want? You don't really know me, Cordy."

Cordelia looked at her, so small and fragile-looking in the restaurant booth. She saw a bit of herself there. Not that she had ever been a shrinking violet or anything. She had always been beautiful and well-loved, the apple of her father's eye. She had skated through school, gaining acceptance to several top colleges and universities— which she couldn't afford to go to, after her father got in trouble with the IRS—yet masking her scholarly ability sufficiently to win the popularity game hands down.

But there were times in any girl's life when she felt like she suspected Kayley did now. When she first heard that Xander Harris and Willow Rosenberg had formed the "I Hate Cordelia" club, in grade school, for instance. She didn't really care at the time what Xander and Willow thought of her, but the idea that anyone would think so badly of her to make it the basis of a club hurt.

She believed that Kayley was carrying around some of those kinds of feelings. She was cast out, neglected by those around her, unwanted. Whether it was real or all in her head didn't really matter.

"I think I know you better than you think, Kayley."

"Right," Kayley scoffed. "Now you sound like my mom. Or my mom's shrink. Or both."

"You don't have to be here if you don't want to be, Kayley," Wesley offered. "But if you're going to sit here and eat our food, you might as well listen to what we have to say with a relatively open mind. You might actually hear something useful."

"Okay, sorry." Kayley stopped talking as the waitress came back with their food and spread it around the table. When she was gone, Kayley continued. "I'll stop being so judgmental. Or try to be. It's just, you both sound a little nuts, you know?"

"I'm sure we do," Wesley said with a chuckle. "Perhaps we are. But then, perhaps we also know what we're talking about. Do you really want to take the chance that we don't?"

"Okay, then, start talking," Kayley said. "So there are real vampires. And their lives suck."

"So to speak," Cordelia added.

"Not lives, per se," Wesley clarified. "Since they're not

alive, but rather undead. Which means, first they have to die. An unpleasant activity for anyone."

"It's not the sexy, exciting thing you've seen in the movies," Cordelia said. "It isn't this great-looking vampire guy tenderly piercing your throat with his teeth and then sensuously drawing your blood out of you with his incredible suction powers."

"That's right," Wesley continued. "What's really happening, when a human is turned, is that he or she is killed, and then the human body becomes the host for a demon to inhabit. There's very little of you left in you, mostly the demon who has taken over your lifeless corpse."

"So you might think it's all good, gooey fun, at first. But when it's over you're not home anymore, and there's some ancient evil nastiness walking around inside what used to be Kayley."

The girl shivered inside her oversized denim shirt. She hugged her own arms.

"Not a pleasant image, is it?" Cordelia asked.

"You know, I'm not so sure I want these eggs anymore," she said. "I'm thinking about going vegan, you know?"

"You'd get over that quickly, once you'd been turned," Wesley told her. "Of course, it wouldn't really be you. But there might be just a trace of you still inside there— just enough to be appalled at yourself whenever you took another victim. Most of the victims of vampires don't turn themselves, they just die, the blood drained from their bodies. None of that rising in three days nonsense. That's a fairy tale."

Kayley looked at both of them, in turn. "This is for real? You guys aren't making this up to creep me out?"

"We are telling it to you to creep you out," Cordelia confessed. "But we're not making it up. And we have way more experience with it than we'd care to."

"Listen, I think I should go. I gotta think about some stuff, you know? Maybe talk it over with some of the other girls. I don't think Pat would even listen, but Erin and Keri might, and maybe Amanda or Jean."

"If they want to talk to us, you know how to reach us," Cordelia said. "And please, don't do anything without giving me a chance to talk to you again first."

"Okay," Kayley agreed.

"Cross your heart?"

Kayley made an X over her chest. "And hope to die."

Angel couldn't wait any longer.

The day was still overcast, but that could burn off at any time. He had to take the chance while there was no direct sunlight. He threw one of Cordelia's blankets over himself and made a dash for his car. He leaped into the GTX, glad the roof was up, and stepped on it, racing across town toward the Flamingo.

When he arrived there, he pulled into the parking lot and pulled the blanket over himself again. The Flamingo was an old L.A. motor court, a collection of log cabin-style cottages arranged in rows around a cracked and weedy drive. A pool between the rows had long since been emptied, and some of the growth inside it was tall enough to be seen over the rim. The car to the door of cottage C was only a few steps, and the sun was still shrouded by clouds, so he made it without damage, the blanket only smoldering a little. Knocking once, he pushed open the door and hurried inside, glad a vampire only had to be invited over any given threshold once.

Inside the room, Carlos stood trembling, tears running down his narrow cheeks, next to an upside-down bed. When he saw Angel he pointed at it, sobbing.

"Isabel?" Angel asked.

A muffled shout came from underneath.

"She's under there?" Angel asked. The boy nodded.

"Hang on, Isabel," Angel said. He went to her side, bent over, and lifted the heavy motel bed high enough for her to slide out.

"Are you okay?"

"I-I think so," she said. Angel helped her to her feet.

"I was taking a nap," she said. "I thought I heard the door, but it was like part of my dream. Then the next thing I knew, my bed was spinning over, and I was on the floor, and then the whole thing landed on me."

Carlos went to his mother and threw his thin arms around her hips. "She's okay," Angel told him. He turned the bed over and put it back in place, lining its feet with the indentations in the worn blue carpet.

"What are you doing here, anyway?" Isabel asked, sitting on the bed. "I mean, I'm glad you came by. But why? Have you seen Rojelio?"

"I've seen him."

"How is he?"

"He'll be better once he's out of jail."

"Do you think you can get him out?"

"I don't know. I really came to see Carlos. To try an experiment."

"What? What do you want to do with him?"

"Just watch," Angel said. He knelt next to Carlos. "You know what?" he said softly. "I think you and your dad both have a pretty incredible ability. But I don't think either of you knows how to control it. Controlling it comes with practice, and you haven't practiced because you didn't know you had it. Does that make sense?"

Carlos nodded silently.

"Here's what I want you to do. Move that pillow."

He pointed to a pillow that had been tossed to the floor

when the bed turned upside down. Carlos started to walk toward it. Angel held him fast.

"No. From here. Just with your mind. Think about the pillow moving. Imagine it moving. See it move, in your mind."

Carlos shook his head, looked at his mother. His eyes were full of tears.

"I'm afraid," he said.

"Angel," Isabel said. "I don't think—"

"It's important," Angel insisted. "It can help your father. Just move the pillow. It's not heavy. It's not hard. It's just a pillow."

"But . . ."

"Move it."

Carlos stared at the pillow. Angel could feel the boy's whole body tense. His small fists were clenched. His lips pressed tightly together.

The pillow moved.

Almost imperceptibly at first, scooting less than an inch along the wall, away from Carlos. Then, as if building up steam, it slid another couple of inches, and then it sped the last couple of feet to the far wall.

Carlos was sweating. And smiling.

"You did it," Angel said, clapping the boy on his bony back.

"Carlos," Isabel said. "That was amazing!" She turned to Angel. "Does that mean . . . ?"

"It's been him all along? Yes, I think it has. Only, like I said, he didn't know he could do it, so he's had no control over it. The stress of his father being arrested and jailed has been tearing him up inside, and his emotions manifested themselves in this way."

"Creating chaos in the household to match the chaos in his heart," Isabel said softly.

"That's right."

She fell to her knees and wrapped her arms around her son. "I am so sorry this has happened, Carlos," she said, beginning to weep.

"It's not your fault," Angel told her. "Or your husband's, I think. But we'll make it right."

"Thank you, Angel," she said. "For this. And everything else."

Angel smiled. He knew what he came to find out. On his way to the door, he scooped up Cordy's blanket.

Chapter 10

THE TRIP TO L.A. WAS UNEVENTFUL, WHICH WAS FINE with Willow. She'd had enough of events; as far as she was concerned, the rest of her life could fall into the uneventful category and she'd be happy.

There were no unexplained shadows, no assaults on the car. A couple of hours after they left, they pulled onto the grounds of a palatial estate in the hills off Laurel Canyon. There was a security gate at the road. Salma entered a password into an electronic box, the gate swung open, and they found themselves driving up a thickly forested road. A quarter mile later, they caught their first glimpse of the house. It rose high into the air, three stories tall, built in the Mediterranean style so popular in southern California.

"Wow," Willow said. "That's beautiful." She continued to admire it as they closed in on it. The acre or so leading up to it was carefully trimmed, rich green lawn. "Did I say 'Wow?' "

"It's quite a house," Buffy agreed.

"Thank you," Salma said offhandedly. The car came to a stop in a cobblestoned courtyard surrounded by two outthrust wings of the house. The walls were pure white stucco, broken by wood-framed windows and balconies. Numerous chimneys poked up from the red tile roofs.

"What's it like to be so rich?" Willow asked. "Do you like it?"

"It's kind of a pain sometimes, but it's nice, too," Salma replied. "It means more to my parents than it does to me, I guess. They enjoy having lovely things."

"That's a hobby I wouldn't mind taking up," Buffy said. "If, um, I wasn't so busy doing other things."

By the time they were out of the car there were three servants there to get their bags. They each greeted Salma with hugs and kisses.

Willow pressed herself close to Buffy and whispered in her ear. "Too bad they don't like her."

"Yeah," Buffy said dryly. "The lack of love is palpable."

With the greetings over and their suitcases carried into the house, Salma turned back to Willow and Buffy. "I think you'll like my grandmother, Willow," she said. "Doña Pilar. She's a *bruja.*"

"A what-ha?" Buffy asked.

"It's like a witch," Willow explained. "Mexican folk magic."

"Because this looks so much like an old cabin somewhere in the Mexican outback, or whatever it's called," Buffy said.

"My grandfather made a lot of money in industry," Salma told them. "But he and my grandmother both come from very poor families. My grandmother lived in a village deep in the interior. Her mother was the town's *bruja* before her, and passed down her skills."

"I can't wait to meet her," Willow said cheerfully.

"I'll introduce you. She's probably in the kitchen. She nearly always is."

After an hour of meeting relatives and sitting down to a gigantic lunch, Buffy excused herself and went to the room that had been offered to her. She was tired and just wanted to veg out for a while before dark. That was when she would be needed, if she was at all.

The room was as gorgeous as the rest of the house. The furnishings, Salma explained, were all antiques from the Spanish colonial period, shipped up from Mexico. They had belonged to the wealthiest Spaniards in the country, rich landowners. Buffy lay back on the bed and closed her eyes for a while, slightly troubled by how much history this bed, and that armoire, and the rest of the furniture in the room, must have seen.

It all reminded her of Angel. He had also seen a lot of history.

Which, although she didn't really think of herself as "history," included her.

She was painfully aware that she was in his town now. And no matter how awkward it might feel, she had to see him, as soon as she had an opportunity.

When it became clear that sleep wasn't likely, she decided to get up and check out the house. Salma had impressed upon them that nothing was off limits, that they should make themselves feel completely at home. While Buffy knew that she would never be really at home in a palace like this, she thought it was worth making the effort.

Besides, maybe there was something she could learn about Nicky. Something that would help her track him down. He had lived most of his life here, and maybe the things that had started him down—well, whatever path he was on—had left some traces here. Giles had always told her not to overlook someone's past if she needed to predict their future. She left her room and went out into the vast adobe-walled, wood-beamed hallway.

She felt like the house was a place where she could be lost and never found again. It was castlelike in that respect—there seemed to be whole wings that went unused, although they were furnished and spotlessly clean. As she passed from one wide corridor into another, through heavy wooden doors that were at least nine feet tall, she felt as if she were passing into some foreign land from which return was not guaranteed.

It was here, looking for Nicky's room, or suite, or wing, or whatever he had, that she found the library. The room must have been fifty feet long and almost as wide. The walls were lined with shelves that reached twenty feet high. Partway up was a brass rail that a tall ladder slid along to make the higher shelves reachable. In the center of one end wall there was a big stone fireplace, tall enough for Buffy to stand up in. The only wall that wasn't covered in bookshelves was the outside wall, which was broken by gigantic casement windows, easily a dozen feet high, some of which were open to catch the day's breeze. Leather chairs were spaced randomly around the room, each one with its own reading light and small chair-side table.

Giles would love this room, Buffy thought. She roamed the room, scanning the shelves as she went. The books seemed to be a diverse mix—fairly recent bestsellers shelved alongside complete leatherbound editions of Shakespeare, Dickens, and other classics. One entire wall was nonfiction, including everything from literary biographies to cookbooks to treatises on how to survive in the wilderness.

"Miss Summers?"

The voice startled her. She turned to the door. A young

man, mid-twenties, maybe, had come in. He wore a maroon polo shirt, the sleeves of which were straining to hold in his biceps, with khaki pants. His thick black hair was pulled back into a ponytail. His handsome face was placid and open, with well-defined features and a strong jaw. He smiled at Buffy and extended a hand as he walked toward her.

"I wanted to introduce myself. I'm Elfredo," he said. "I work for the de la Natividad family."

"Buffy," Buffy replied. "But I guess you already knew that."

"Yes," he said. He shook her hand firmly. "I work in the security department. Ruben Velasco is my boss."

"I'm so sorry about what happened to him."

"We all are. We've heard from Sunnydale today, though. He's awake. It looks like he'll pull through okay. He's a tough old guy."

"That's good."

"Don Francisco, who is Miss de La Natividad's grandfather, has asked me to stay close to you, as long as you are a guest of the family. I'm certain that you are safe in this house, but since we don't know what's going on, we don't want to take any chances."

"I don't really need a bodyguard," Buffy protested.

"I'm sure you don't. According to Salma, you are the bodyguard. But Don Francisco insists that I be at your disposal."

She took another look at him. He was a very good-looking man, and at other times in her life, to have him "at her disposal" would have sounded promising indeed. But she was not in one of those times. She had Riley—and she was in the city of Angel's. More complications of the heart, even ones that only occurred in her mind, were not what she needed.

"That's very kind of him."

The man inclined his head. "The comfort and safety of his guests is paramount for him. I won't be in your way, and you have the full run of the house and grounds. But I'll be there if you should need anything. In the meantime, perhaps I can show you around. As I said, I highly doubt that we are in any danger here. But on the off chance that we are, you should know your way."

Buffy believed him. The elder Mr. de la Natividad had shown at lunch that he was a good host. He was a handsome, silver-haired gentleman who had come to the table in a fine suit and tie. He and his wife, the *bruja,* Doña Pilar, had made sure that Buffy and Willow were comfortable and well-fed. And apparently safe.

Doña Pilar was a tiny woman, gray and shriveled and barely taller than the massive table on which they had dined. But her eyes shone and she sparkled with life and energy, and throughout the big lunch she had kept up a running commentary that left everyone in stitches, despite the solemn nature of the gathering. Salma's mother, Carolina, a serious and elegant woman in her mid-forties, had joined them at lunch, but Salma's father was in the city on business and hadn't been able to get home.

"That would be great," Buffy said. "Bodyguarding is a little outside my usual range of activities, so maybe you can give me some tips."

"I will do my best," Elfredo promised. "You've seen the library. Shall we start with the grounds?" When she nodded, he took her elbow and led her from the room.

"I'm afraid you'll be bored hanging around with me," Buffy said as they traveled the long corridor toward a side door. "I don't expect to be in any danger."

"That's when I like my job the most," Elfredo replied. "When there's no danger."

You and me both, Buffy thought. *But on the bright side, maybe I can use him.* "Do you know Nicky?" she asked.

"Of course. I have been with the family for six years. I know them all."

"What do you think of the idea that he might have gotten involved in some kind of gang? A rich kid like him? Why would he do that?"

Elfredo unlocked the door and pushed it open. Buffy watched the way his arms bulged as he did. He shook his head sadly. "Unfortunately, it is not uncommon," he said. "Many wealthy Mexican kids here in the States find themselves drawn to criminal gangs, street gangs. I'm not sure why. Are they bored? Are they looking for some kind of national identity that they're not getting at home?"

They stepped out into a side yard. Rows of herbs grew in patches near the house, and farther away, a flower garden bloomed in a riotous profusion of reds, pinks, yellows, greens, violets, and whites. Buffy gasped at the beauty of it.

"Doña Pilar's herbs," Elfredo explained. "The de la Natividads try very hard to live like Mexicans, but there's no escaping the fact that they are here in *Norteamerica,* not at home. So maybe it's a way for these kids to reconnect with their homeland, to band together with other Mexicans in a way that is at odds with their own family life."

"You'd think with all the advantages a kid like Nicky would have, he wouldn't be sucked into that kind of thing," Buffy offered, hoping for more insight.

The man hesitated. Buffy understood that he was being discreet for the sake of his employers . . . *and his employment, probably.*

"For Nicky, that would be so," Elfredo said blandly. He led Buffy through the flower garden, toward a wall that rose up a hundred yards from the house. "I'm sure for some of them, perhaps most, it's a matter of survival on hard streets.

But not for all of them. Wealthy boys don't have to steal to feed their families. They don't have to sell drugs, or shake down merchants. If . . . someone close to Don Francisco's grandson has become involved in these kinds of activities . . . and I truly hope no one has . . . I can't imagine Nicky de la Natividad remaining friends with him."

Buffy took that in, but she wasn't taken in by it. *This guy's just spouting the Party line.*

"Nicky is a wonderful boy. He has shown every sign of growing up to be a fine young man," Elfredo continued.

They stopped near the wall. It was ten feet tall. At the top of it, two rows of wire were stretched between posts that jutted up every six feet. "The top wire is barbed, as you can see," Elfredo said. "The one below that is electrified. The surface of the wall's top is inset with ground glass. No one would come over that wall happily, or in one piece. This is the environment in which Nicky grew up. Safe, but possibly feeling confined."

"Poor little rich boy," Buffy mused aloud, hoping to draw the man out. "Don Francisco casts a long shadow. It might be hard to make one's own mark with a grandfather like him."

"Perhaps. Perhaps not," Elfredo said loyally. His face was a mask. "Nicky is a resourceful, clever young man."

That's exactly what I'm worried about, Buffy thought.

Tad Barlowe was beyond tense, and it took a lot to freak Tad Barlowe out. He was a uniformed cop who guarded the prisoners at the 77th Street Police building, and he'd seen a lot of bad stuff, including a guy who had hanged himself in his own cell.

But this was worse.

Part of the 77th was a temporary detention facility, a holding area for people awaiting trial. As such, it was not

Casa de Hardened Criminals particularly; most of the guys inside quickly figured out that it didn't make a lot of sense to act up, because it would just make things go worse in court.

Two days ago, his own pen had gone berserk and stabbed him in the arm. Just flew up from the desk, spun around like that kid's head in the movie, and stabbed him. He had tried on all sorts of explanations for size, and none had fit.

So he'd told himself that it was an isolated incident, a one-time freak of physics. That didn't freak him out much less, but it was something to hang onto. Just one of those weirdo things that happens in life.

But then it turned out not to be so isolated after all. In fact, weirdo things were happening all over the cell block. Not in the rest of the building—so the cops in other sections of the 77th didn't quite understand why those in the jail were so on edge. Last night in a bar, a couple of them had tied a string around a pencil and tossed it onto the table of some jail guards, then had made it dance around the table, hooting with laughter.

One of them ended the evening with a broken jaw, and three cops were on suspension today for fighting in public.

Tad almost called in sick. He could have done it—the wound in his arm would have given him a good enough excuse for a day or two. But as bad as going into the 77th was, it still wasn't quite as bad as staying home, with his wife, Penny, hovering over him as if he were on his deathbed. So he pulled on his uniform and went in.

Only to find that the mood today was, if anything, worse than it had been the day before. Not only were the guards on edge, so were the inmates.

"Stuff's been flyin' around all day," Henry Murson told him. Henry was getting off shift just as Tad was coming on. "A cot pinned one guy up against the wall of his own cell. Clothes, pillows, shoes. Everybody's so uptight, it's like the entire population's standin' on the edge of a razor blade waitin' for someone else to slip."

Great, Tad thought. *A recipe for disaster. Should've stayed home after all.* Murson went on to tell him that tempers were frayed, that if he looked sideways at someone—officer or prisoner—he was likely to find himself in a shouting match, or worse.

"All I can say, buddy, is I'm glad I'm headin' home," Murson continued. "Better you than me, at this point."

"Yeah," Tad responded. "I'll be thinking about you, safe and warm in a bed somewhere."

"Seriously, Tad," Murson said. "Don't let your guard down for a second. There's some major bad stuff goin' down here today."

"Thanks, Henry." He clapped Murson on the shoulder and watched him head out of the building. On the way to someplace more sane, which today was just about anywhere in the city of Los Angeles.

There had been times when it was reversed. When the city was inflamed, on edge, insane, and coming into a building where everyone knew their place, where the only people with weapons were the ones in charge, was a comfort.

There had been times when the city burned, and on those occasions Tad was always glad he was inside the jail with those who were already in custody, rather than on the line in riot gear, a transparent plexi shield all that stood between him and stones or bricks or bullets.

He hoped those days were over for good.

With a last look at sunset over the quiet city, he went inside.

Into the madness.

Chapter 11

THERE WAS MORE THAN ONE KITCHEN IN THIS HOUSE, IT turned out. Doña Pilar showed Willow through the main kitchen, the one where two cooks had prepared the big lunch, and then they passed into another, smaller kitchen.

This one was much less formal and high tech. It was a tiny room, by comparison to the rest of the house, not much more than a closet, really. In the center stood an ancient, scarred pine table, one leg of which had a folded bit of cardboard under it to steady it. Glass jars and canisters covered the countertops, each one carefully labeled in a precise though cramped handwriting.

There were no doors on the cabinets, so all of the contents could be seen at a glance. An old white gas stove with four burners leaned against one wall. A variety of pots and pans hung from hooks near it. A double-basin sink on four wooden legs sat underneath the window. The whole room looked like it had been brought here as a piece from some smaller, poorer house.

"This is where I am most at home," Doña Pilar told Willow, in a thick accent. "This looks just like my kitchen back in Oaxaca."

"This is where you do your spells?" Willow asked her.

"Yes, this is the place." Doña Pilar turned to Willow and took the girl's fingers in her own gnarled hands. Her skin was scaly but soft, and her touch was gentle. "I sense great power in you, Willow Rosenberg," she said. "Great potential."

Willow smiled shyly. "Thanks," she said. "I mean, I try, you know? I can do a few things. Comes in handy sometimes."

"Do not underestimate yourself, Willow," Doña Pilar insisted, releasing Willow's hands. "Your abilities are a gift, but it is up to you to use them wisely, to cultivate them, like a tall tree that you want to grow from the smallest seedling. If you care for them, they will never let you down."

Willow followed her as she walked slowly toward the table. The room smelled wonderful, of lavender and rosemary, beeswax candles and sandalwood incense. Dried herbs hung from wooden dowels along the soffit. Willow took in all the sights and smells, hungry for knowledge.

"Have you always known about your power?" she asked the older woman.

Doña Pilar gestured to a small, sepia-toned photograph framed in ornate, sparkling silver. It showed a lovely young woman wearing a tortoiseshell comb and lace *mantilla* over a plain cotton dress. On her lap was a very small girl with dark eyes and two long black braids, also in simple clothes.

"Since I was a young girl. Twelve, thirteen. *Mi madre*, she taught me. She was a *bruja* also."

Willow stood beside her and together they admired the photo. "Have you taught your children some magick? Or your grandchildren?"

The other woman sighed and turned from the picture. "My son? No. When he was young, it was not at all acceptable to practice openly. Our priest was very opposed to it, so Francisco made me promise not to."

She fingered the crucifix around her neck. "And my grandkids are interested only in the modern world, I'm afraid. The magic of computers and the stock market." She smiled sadly. "I tried to show Nicky and Salma a little, but they weren't interested."

At least, not interested at the time, Willow thought, recalling Salma's concern about the books she'd found in Nicky's room.

"What kinds of things can you do?" Willow asked her, trying to change the subject to something a little cheerier.

"Easier to say what I cannot do, my child," Doña Pilar replied, with no small measure of pride in her voice. "Or what I will not do." She held up her right hand and counted on her fingers. "I will not hurt others. I will not create wealth or property. I will not make someone love another. I could do all of those things, but I believe that is a misuse of my abilities."

I want to stay here for weeks, Willow thought. *Months. Tara and I could learn so much.*

"Sounds like a reasonable set of limitations," Willow said, mentally making note of them for herself.

With evident fondness for her new student, Doña Pilar tilted her head and folded her hands. She reminded Willow of the statues of saints in Catholic churches, posed in serenity and radiating goodness.

"Each person must decide on her own limits," Doña Pilar replied. "Those are mine."

Willow moved toward the table. Her hand hovered over a small stone bowl; Doña Pilar nodded and Willow picked it up. It was dark, shiny black, and quite heavy.

"Have you been trying to locate your grandson?" Willow asked.

Doña Pilar shook her head sadly as she came up beside Willow. "That bowl was given to me by a Navajo shaman," she said. "He said it was for carrying good wishes."

Willow handed the bowl to her and the woman thoughtfully set it down.

"I would have searched for Nicky, certainly," she mused. "But some of the necessary herbs and a very precious talisman for a finder's spell have been taken from me. They have been missing for more than a week now. I have been trying to replace them, but so far, no luck."

Taken? "Do you think they were stolen?"

Doña Pilar threw up her hands in an exaggerated shrug. "Who knows? But they were in this room, and now they are not. What do you think that means?"

"Sounds stolen to me."

She looked pained. "I cannot believe that a member of my family would do such a thing. Or a member of our staff, either one."

"Has anyone else had access?" Willow asked gently, not wanting to state the obvious: *"Missing" sounding very much like a synonym for "stolen" to me.*

"No. There are visitors from time to time. But no one comes in here." Doña Pilar looked slightly puzzled. "Why would they?"

"Do you think any of the family's guests know that you're a *bruja*?" Willow asked.

The lady's lined face scrunched as she thought about the question. "It's not a secret. But it's not something I talk about with just anyone."

"Well, then I'm honored you told me," Willow said.

"My granddaughter told you. But only because she

knew I would anyway. You would have known, as soon as we spoke."

"I guess that's true. The 'takes one to know one' thing, right?"

Doña Pilar's laugh was a cackle that sounded to Willow like the "witchiest" laugh she'd ever heard. Her own face broke into a wide smile at the sound.

"Yes, child, that's right. But let's not talk of mysteries we cannot solve, and problems that weigh on my heart. I have been working on healing elixirs." She moved over to the stove, where a closed copper pot was simmering gently. She lifted the lid, dipped a wooden spoon into it, and drew out a small amount of a thick brownish fluid. "This will close cuts and prevent bruising," she said.

"Sounds like something we could use in Sunnydale."

Almost as if on cue, there was a knock at the door, and Buffy poked her head in. "Will, can I talk to you for a second?"

"Sure, Buffy," Willow said. She turned back to Doña Pilar. "Excuse me. I'll be right back." She followed Buffy out into the main kitchen, which was deserted.

"What's up?"

"I was talking to one of the security guys, Elfredo," Buffy said, a little dreamily. "Great arms." She snapped back to the present. "But anyway, he said that lots of rich Mexican guys in the U.S. get involved in these street gangs."

"Great," Willow murmured, feeling protective of the worried old lady. "Doña Pilar can't even track him down magickally, because someone's stolen the herbs and a talisman she needs for that spell."

Buffy blinked at this revelation. "She have three guesses who?"

"You think it was Nicky?" Willow asked, not surprised.

"He takes off with exactly what she would need to track him down. Coincidence much?"

"Nope," Willow agreed.

"So what I'm thinking," Buffy continued, "is what's really going on with Nicky is a combination of what we think and what Salma was worried about. He's in with a gang, but he's using magick in some way, too. Maybe he's responsible for the shadow monsters. Maybe he learned a little too much at Grandma's knees."

Willow sighed and ran her fingers through her hair. She was tired, and the sorrow in the house was preying on her, wearing her down. "She said he never seemed interested."

Buffy gave her a look. "How many boys can you think of who would admit to being interested in their grandmother's hobbies?"

Willow nodded. "True." She added, "And yet, how many boys can you think of who would give up a chance to learn something that might someday allow them to turn invisible and visit the girls' locker room?"

They shared a moment, and Buffy said, "Are you thinking of Xander?"

Willow grinned back at her.

Buffy said, "See what you two can figure out. Maybe there's some other kind of finder's spell she can perform. Whatever we do, we gotta keep moving forward."

"Wish us luck," Willow told her, and went back to Doña Pilar.

Buffy watched Willow disappear back into the small room off the kitchen. She hadn't been invited in, but she understood why. Willow was perfectly willing to use her Wiccan abilities on Buffy's behalf, but Buffy had never really expressed any curiosity about trying any of that stuff herself. Her approach was much more basic—punch, kick, stake, dust.

So she wandered back out of the big kitchen, through the formal dining room with its dark wood table that would seat two dozen easily and the ancient tapestry hanging on the wall over the huge sideboard, back through the elegant main entryway. She reached the main doorway at the same time that Elfredo arrived there. She smiled at him.

"Upstairs safe?"

"No worries," he said.

"That's where I'll be, then," she said. "If you're wondering."

"Thanks."

She headed up, then made the right turn toward her room. Arriving there, she sat on the edge of the massive antique bed and looked at the telephone on her nightstand. She knew she had to make a call. She was in Angel's town, and there was the possibility that she had brought something with her, something that liked to crack people open like walnuts and eat the insides. Well, maybe that was an exaggeration—there had been no eating that she was aware of. Anyway, she knew he was right—she didn't know her way around L.A. anymore, not in the ways that mattered. With any luck, whatever had been stalking Salma had remained back in Sunnydale, and wouldn't even be an issue here. But if it became an issue, she'd need Angel on her side.

She picked up the phone, hands trembling just a little, and dialed the number of Angel's office. The line rang once, and then was picked up. Buffy's heart felt large in her throat.

"The number you are calling has been changed," a computerized voice told her. "The new number is—" Buffy scrambled for a pencil and paper, both conveniently provided in the nightstand's top drawer. *Just like a hotel,* she thought. She scrawled out the number the voice had given her and hung up the phone.

Looking at the number, she thought it seemed familiar. She stared at it for a few moments before she realized why. It was Cordelia's number. That was strange. *Angel and Cordelia? No, couldn't be . . .*

She picked the phone up again and dialed Angel's cell phone number. After a few rings, she got the message saying that he either had the phone turned off or was not answering. She put the phone down again. Looked around her at the lovely room, paintings on the walls that would look great in her mother's gallery, carpet so rich and thick someone could sleep on it.

The de la Natividad family owned a big house. There were many people in it.

So why do I feel so lonely here? she wondered.

No easy answer came to her.

Angel squealed to a stop outside the 77th Street Police building. Greg Preston threw his door open and climbed out, ashen-faced. "You always drive like that, Angel? Keep my card handy, you might need me to get you out of some tickets." The attorney straightened his threadbare tweed jacket and tugged on his tie. The collar and cuffs of his white shirt were frayed, but it was clean.

Angel looked at him with a wry smile, but said nothing. Preston wiped his brow with one hand and led the way inside.

Angel wanted to see Rojelio Flores again now that he had a better idea of what was really going on. If Flores was telekinetic, he had to know about it so he could control his abilities as long as he was stuck in here. Angel could try to prove he was innocent of the murder he'd been charged with—but not if the man didn't survive his incarceration. And if he was as out of control here as Carlos had been at home, there was every chance that he might not.

So he'd picked Preston up at his office and brought him to the jail so that he could bypass normal visiting hours again. He had called Cordelia's apartment while en route, and she had filled him in briefly on the library situation. She stressed that there didn't seem to be any rush, and he knew that the Flores case had a certain amount of urgency. Satisfied that she and Wesley were fine, he had turned his phone off again so he could take it into the jail.

As soon as they entered the building, Angel could sense that there was something different in the air this time. He practically had to wade through the tension in hip boots. The guard who signed them in—the same guy who had been chatty with Preston before—didn't say two words to them. His lips were clamped together, his jaw set. A vein in his temple twitched. He held his pen with fingers so rigid his knuckles were white.

They were escorted into the visitation area by a different guard, who kept glancing this way and that as if expecting a sudden attack. Someone else was dispatched to bring Rojelio Flores down.

When they were more or less alone, Preston turned to Angel. "What's up in here tonight?" he whispered. "Everybody's as jumpy as my cat in a room full of combat boots."

Angel didn't answer, but the tension had crept inside him like a bad smell. An electricity jittered in the air. His tongue tasted like copper. The taste threw his mind back for a moment to his evil days, hunting and drinking for sport. Hunting humans.

He shook off the memory, but not the sense of impending disaster. This place wasn't right, today. He had to fight the urge to leave, by telling himself that if he could get to Flores maybe he could forestall whatever was about to go wrong.

But he was too late.

This time of the evening, there were inmates in the activity areas. They played cards, argued over TV shows, immersed themselves in books. Others were still finishing dinner. No one was in a big hurry to get back to their cells, but they all knew it was coming.

The 77th Street Headquarters jail was only a temporary detention center, not a full-scale prison. The inmates here were believed to be guilty of a variety of crimes, but had not yet been convicted of their charges. A small percentage were people who had been convicted of misdemeanors, and would serve their short sentences at the jail rather than being transferred to a prison. So while security was tight, it was not as rigid as they would experience after conviction and sentencing.

Rojelio Flores sat in one of the activity areas, flipping the pages of a book that Isabel had sent him. He couldn't focus on the words. He gritted his teeth and massaged his jaw and neck, trying to relax.

On TV, a woman was trying to become a millionaire by answering a series of questions that proved only that she possessed a wide range of trivial knowledge.

Rojelio glanced at the screen for a moment, then moved his gaze away from the television and toward the book in his hand.

At that instant, the TV—which was bolted to the wall, wired for cable, and contained within a heavy screened cage—ripped itself from its bolted moorings. Television and cage both erupted away from the wall as if torn by some monstrous force.

They landed on the floor in between two rows of plastic chairs. On impact, the TV exploded, shards of glass flying everywhere. Several inmates were cut by flying glass, with more injured by the sudden crush of people moving to avoid it.

Rojelio moved away, shocked, and was swept into a mob of frightened, angry men. The fury and terror surrounding him was itself nearly overwhelming; added to that the stress of being imprisoned for a crime of which he was innocent, and it was almost too much for him to bear. He began to shake, and bile rose from his stomach into his throat. He began to see black spots, and his legs buckled.

I can't fall, he thought. *If I collapse, I'll be trampled.*

With a feeling of despair, he thought of his wife and son, and prayed to God to spare him, if not for his own sake, then for his family's.

Sunnydale

Everybody knew it was a suicide mission.

There was only one way to get Del DeSola's attention in any meaningful fashion. The man had no family he cared about. He didn't have any employees that he seemed to particularly value.

He loved oil.

And the things it could buy him.

To reach Del DeSola, one had to hit him where it hurt.

He had a couple of oil fields on the outskirts of Sunnydale. Derricks pumped day in and day out like shorebirds pecking at the sand for insects. The smell of the raw oil was thick and the air felt greasy.

The Cobras pulled up in two black SUVs and a Cadillac Eldorado, maroon with white trim.

Nicky de la Natividad got out of the Cad. The others looked at him like he was a crazy man. He was painted like some kind of ancient warrior. Lines on his face and his shirtless chest. He wore baggy black jeans, but his feet were bare. A gold disk lay against his chest, hanging on a leather thong.

He hadn't spoken on the way over.

The others had been loud and boisterous. This was a big night, a night that was going to have consequences for all of them for a long time to come. They were excited, nervous, scared, happy. They laughed and joked, traded insults and quips.

Nicky sat through it all, staring straight ahead. He was already somewhere else.

The oil field was surrounded by a high chain-link fence. It covered several acres of dusty flatland. Up against the fence were tall weeds and taller stalks that would be revealed in the morning light—if they were still there, come morning—to be sunflowers. There was no full-time guard there, just a patrol that came by on a semi-regular schedule, every couple of hours. There was really nothing there that anyone was likely to steal.

But the Cobras weren't there to steal.

Los Angeles

One of the inmates, a man named Arthur Berndes, clapped a hand over his neck where a long shard of glass had lacerated him. Blood oozed between his fingers. He bent down and picked the hunk of glass up from the floor. He turned it over in his hands. There was one broad end, two inches wide. It tapered at the other end to a narrow point. He jabbed it into his sleeve, tearing the fabric. When he had succeeded in freeing a rectangular piece of fabric about eight inches long, he wrapped it a couple of times around the wide end of the glass.

As soon as the TV fell, guards came rushing into the activity area. They warned everyone away from it while they brought in a broom and a trash can to sweep up the mess. Instinctively they seemed to know no inmate had done this to the TV, but they wanted to avoid precisely what was happening.

Arthur Berndes was in jail, basically, because he was a terrible driver. He racked up ticket after ticket. Speeding, reckless driving, endangerment. He shoved the tickets into his glove compartment and forgot about them. When he'd been stopped again for making a right turn from a left turn lane, cutting off two other lanes of traffic and causing a fender bender, the officer who detained him ran his license, discovered all the outstanding tickets, and brought him in.

He'd been in for three days. He hadn't slept more than thirty minutes in that time. He had barely eaten. He was scared, exhausted, hungry. In the dormitory-style cell he shared with sixteen other men, things had been moving around by themselves. Arthur Berndes, whose paranoia bordered on the psychotic, believed that he alone was the target of this strange activity.

Arthur wanted out.

Over the past week, the bizarre phenomena had made most of the other prisoners feel the same way. No one was eating or sleeping right. Everyone was tense, on edge.

Everyone was ready to explode with the violence of a picture tube striking concrete.

Arthur stepped close to one of the guards, who was bending over with a dustpan to pick up bits of glass and plastic, and he buried the pointed end of his glass knife in the man's ribs.

The guard let out a scream.

The other four guards in the room went for their guns. Someone threw a chair.

Inmates pressed in on the guards, wielding furniture, pieces of glass, fists and feet.

Two shots rang out, almost drowned out by the yelling, the din of motion and fear. One inmate fell.

Then the guards were overwhelmed, their guns taken away. The prisoners were armed.

Throughout the facility, Klaxons wailed.

Chapter 12

ANGEL AND PRESTON FOUND THEMSELVES ALONE.

All the cops in sight were grabbing weapons and rushing off toward the detention facility. One remained visible, monitoring the doors electronically. He looked nervous.

"What's going on?" Preston asked.

"Breakout," Angel offered. "Riot, maybe."

"Should we be here?"

Angel nodded toward the rest of the building. "You'd rather be in there?"

Preston looked around. He could only see the one cop from where he was. There were no inmates, no immediate danger. "I guess this is as good a place as any."

"You stay here, then," Angel said. "I have to get to Flores."

"Angel, you can't—"

But Angel was already out the door.

There was only one guard in sight, and he was busy with the doors. Angel assumed he was trying to make sure that no one in the central detention facility could get out. But he also wanted to keep the doors open for officers going in.

Six hundred police officers worked in the Headquarters complex. When it became apparent that the jail had erupted in a full-scale riot, many of those on duty armed themselves, strapped on body armor, donned helmets, and went to help restore order.

Angel moved in with them. On the way, he saw a guard station where an LAPD windbreaker hung on a hook. He snagged the jacket and tugged it on. Sufficiently disguised, he continued.

Flores is the key to this, he was sure. *His telekinesis has finally pushed everybody over the edge. But this is only likely to make it worse, and if it gets worse, the chances of him surviving the night are slim.*

Angel was afraid that someone would pinpoint Rojelio Flores as the source of the commotion. Someone would finally see that things only happened when he was within a certain distance, a given radius. Someone would decide that the only way to bring it to a stop was to take him out.

That was, if he even survived the attempts to bring the riot under control. Angel believed that Flores was probably in the thick of things, which put him in the line of fire.

He had promised Isabel and Carlos Flores that he would help Rojelio.

To do that, he had to keep the man alive.

Inside the detention facility, things happened fast.

The newly-armed inmates took the guards in the activity area hostage. Some of them began immediately to work on a list of demands, in exchange for which they would release their prisoners. Others went out to liberate their fellow inmates, carrying weapons and, in one case, dragging along a bound guard as a guarantee.

Inmates started fires in wastebaskets.

They flooded into one guard office, emptied the contents of filing cabinets and desks onto the floor, and lit the paper.

Smoke filled the corridors.

Ceiling-mounted sprinklers kicked in, dousing some of the fires but soaking everyone.

The omnipresent sirens were deafening.

Blinded, wet, rattled by noise, even inmates who wanted nothing to do with the riot were shaken, scared.

In the office, there were more guns and riot gear. Prisoners outfitted themselves.

None of them, if asked, could have said why they were rioting. Conditions weren't as squalid as they were in the state prison system. This was no San Quentin. The building was new and modern. The restrictions on the inmates were minor. It was just the weeks of fear and tension, bubbling over into madness. Mass hysteria.

And once started, not easily stopped.

Angel pushed through a heavy glass door. He hoped no one would notice that he wasn't carrying a gun. He wanted to get Rojelio Flores to safety, not shoot anybody.

There were several helmeted guards coming down the smoky hallway toward him. The acrid smoke didn't hurt Angel's eyes, and he could see them quite clearly, see their grim determination and smell their fear and anger. He ducked into a doorway to let them pass.

As they did, he eyed them. They looked official. They carried shotguns. They had Kevlar vests strapped over their uniforms.

But, as they passed by, he realized their uniforms were prison blues.

They weren't cops. They were inmates.

And they were heading straight for Greg Preston.

Angel was torn. He needed to get to Flores, to keep him alive.

But he had brought Preston here. Left him alone in a vulnerable situation. Put him in harm's way.

Flores or Preston?

Angel made his decision and ran.

Sunnydale

Nicky looked through the fence at the rigs bobbing up and down in the moonlight. He felt a moment's hesitation. *What if this doesn't work? What if I do something wrong?* But then he remembered the talisman, the burn mark that had completely disappeared by now, the boiling liquid he had swallowed like it was ice water.

He had found all that he needed to know in an old book inside the false bottom of a trunk in the attic of his parents' home. His *abuelita,* Doña Pilar, had once told him and Salma that the trunk had belonged to her mother. Apparently, she had never realized the trunk had a false bottom, nor had she realized her mother had catalogued some spells handed down from the Aztecs . . . including this one.

And now, this was Nicky's Night of the Long Knives. He was untouchable.

The guys came over to him. Enrique, Paco, Dom, Jose and Luis and Mace, Shotgun and Little King, Jorge and CG. They each spoke a word or two, slapped his cheeks, punched his arm. Then the ladies, Luisa first, followed by Cissy and Sally and DeeCee. They hugged him, kissed his painted cheeks. He knew they were saying good-bye.

"Don't worry," he said a dozen times. "Don't worry

about me, man. I'm cool. I'm fine. This is my night, you know? Chill."

Finally, Rosalie came to him. She kissed his cheeks, his lips. She held his hands in her own.

"You don't have to do this," she said.

"Yeah, I do."

"You're new, Nicky. Everybody expects you to make your mark. But not this way."

"I already said I would."

"That doesn't matter. Not a single person would call you a coward if you backed out now. None of them would do this."

"I would feel like a coward, Rosalie," Nicky said. He worked one hand loose from her grip, pointed to himself with his thumb. "I'm doing it. Don't worry, I'll be fine."

"I think I'm starting to like you, Nicky," she said with a smile. "Don't screw it up by dying."

"I wouldn't do that," he replied. "Not a chance."

She kissed him again, and he returned her kiss hungrily. She unhooked one of the long necklaces around her neck and handed it to him. A large gold crucifix dangled from the braided gold chain.

"For luck," she said. "Give it back when you're finished, okay?"

"Gracias, mi amor," he said, looping it over his head. She kissed him again, hard. Then she broke free of him, turned away, and walked to Enrique's SUV without a backward glance.

Nicky went through the fence.

Little King had clipped a space with a bolt cutter for him. He pushed through the heavy wire. A stray strand of it bit his bare shoulder, drew blood.

Nicky saw the blood, tensed.

That isn't right, he thought.

He wanted to turn around, to back out. *This isn't worth it,* he thought. *All this, for what? To send a statement to some rich* cabron?

But even as he watched, the drip of blood dried up. The wound closed. In a moment, it wasn't there at all. No sign that he had ever been cut.

He took a last look at his friends, his family, gathered on the other side of the fence. Some of them were already walking back to the cars. They couldn't be here when it went down. They'd come back later, to see the end results.

Nicky gathered up the gear that had been passed through the fence to him and started hiking toward the nearest derrick.

When the cars had gone, the night was quiet except for the steady *chunk-clank* of the machinery, the distant song of night birds, the whir of crickets in the fields. Nicky ignored the sounds and went to work.

At the base of the first derrick, he set down the canvas gym bag he carried and withdrew four long bars of a white, puttylike substance wrapped in olive drab paper. He packed the military issue C-4 plastic explosive around the base of the derrick, and tied a knot in a length of detonating cord. He then trailed the detonating cord out thirty feet away from the derrick and left the end on the dirt. That done, he walked past a couple of other derricks to one he had already picked out. Dom had scored enough of the explosives for five derricks, and Nicky had to hope that would do.

But everything about this operation was efficient. He picked the derricks he would target right off the bat, and worked out the most economical way to get to them all. It took a little over an hour. Nicky worked quietly and with great care, making sure the explosives were packed in tight. C-4 could be handled and molded without much danger as long as it wasn't treated too roughly. Setting it on fire, Dom had told him, wasn't a problem as long as he didn't try to stamp it out.

When he was finished setting the explosives, he took his spool of detonating cord and ran out a long line down the length of the field. To this, he connected the other five shorter lines he had buried inside the C-4 charges. This would be his trunk line. At one end, he attached an electric blasting cap. Short wires led from the blasting cap to a battery.

Nicky wasn't concerned for his own safety, but he didn't want to accidentally detonate anything before he had placed everything the way he wanted it.

At the end of the hour he was sweating in spite of the nighttime chill. He looked back over the line of fuse, catching the faintest bit of moonlight and reflecting back at him like strands of webbing.

He didn't feel anything about it in particular. He wanted to make a big bang. He wanted Del DeSola to understand that turning down the Cobras was a bad idea. He didn't really think about the fact that people's livelihoods might be at stake here. He thought briefly that firefighters might be dispatched to quench the flames, and that they might be injured. But that thought passed quickly. *Anyone who would go into a burning oil field to fight a fire deserves what they get,* Nicky thought. *The Cobras are making a statement here.*

He took one last look around. No one was watching. No one was nearby, but the security patrol might be along anytime.

He attached the wires to the battery terminals.

The blasting cap exploded.

The explosion there set off the explosive ingredient PETN.

The PETN rapidly ignited throughout the detonating cord.

So close as to be virtually simultaneous, the five oil rigs exploded.

The noise was deafening.

There was a brilliant flash of pure white light.

Nicky's pants ignited and vanished. All the hair on Nicky's body seared off at the same moment.

As the wells caught and blew great jets of flame into the night air, Nicky walked between them like a celebrant on the Fourth of July admiring a line of Roman candles. It was as bright as day inside the fence. Nicky felt a hot rush, like sticking his face next to a roaring fire. But he didn't feel his flesh bubble and peel, or his blood boil and evaporate, although he should have.

It was his Night of the Long Knives.

Flaming cinders streaked the sky, danced off his head, his body.

Nicky walked through it, calm and collected.

Los Angeles

Angel really had no choice.

Greg Preston, he knew, was still alive—and in trouble because Angel had made him come down here.

He turned and followed the armed prisoners. If they were headed for freedom, they had to walk right past Preston and the single guard who still remained back near the visitors' area. Maybe they'd assume that Preston would be fooled by their stolen helmets and jackets.

But maybe not.

Inside the glass-enclosed visitation area, Preston was backed up against a wall. The four inmates had him surrounded. One of them pointed a shotgun at Preston's belly.

Angel kicked his way through the door, not because it was locked but because he wanted a dramatic entrance. It worked. Three of the four prisoners spun around, one of them bringing up his shotgun at the same time.

Angel charged them, and the inmate pulled his trigger. A bullet would not kill him, but it could slow him down; he leaped over the blast, and behind him, glass shattered as one of the walls blew out.

Angel turned over in midair and when he came down, he was close to the inmates. He wrenched the gun from the hands of the one who had fired at him and flung it across the room. Then he kicked the guy, twice in the chest and head. The inmate dropped like a stone.

Another began to raise his shotgun. Angel stepped in close to him, lashed out with a quick right jab to the prisoner's throat. The man hit the floor, gasping for breath. Angel pushed past him, reaching for the one who still held a gun trained on Preston. He could see the man's finger tightening on the trigger. Angel clamped a hand down on the guy's shoulder.

At the same time, the fourth guy, still holding his shotgun, shoved it up against the side of Angel's head.

"Time's up," the gunman muttered.

"Angel . . ." Preston began.

Angel turned his face slightly toward the gunman—as much as the gun barrel would allow—and let his vampire nature come to the fore. His face changed.

Only the gunman and Preston could see it, and Preston had seen it before.

"Time's up for you," Angel replied, seeing the terror in the man's eyes. He reached up and batted away the gun barrel. The prisoner released the gun and backed away, hands up as if to ward Angel off, face crumpling. "I . . . I didn't mean nothing . . ." he sobbed.

"Take off," Angel directed. The inmate turned and ran.

"Angel . . ."

Angel restored his human appearance and turned to Preston. He'd been interrupted, and the guy holding a gun on the lawyer still had it there. He had moved a little, so he could watch both Preston and Angel.

"One more step and Tubby gets it," he said.

"You want him dead, why haven't you already killed him?" Angel asked.

"I want a hostage," the inmate replied. "He looks like a good one."

"What about me?"

"One's plenty for me," the guy said. "You're too much trouble. Tubby here's nice and easy."

"Don't underestimate him," Angel said. "That's not fat, it's all muscle."

The inmate prodded at Preston's soft belly with the gun barrel. "Don't think so," he said.

Angel glanced around at the inmate who had run away, and the two who were still on the ground.

"Too bad about your friends," Angel said.

"I don't need them," the prisoner replied, not taking his eyes off Angel.

"Everybody needs friends."

"Listen," the prisoner said with an angry scowl. "Just shut up. Tubby and I are leaving, but if I hear one more word outta you I'm just gonna shoot him."

Angel backed away a step, both hands in the air as if surrendering. He kept his mouth closed.

"Angel, you can't let him do this," Preston said, his voice quivering with terror.

Angel simply mimed pulling a zipper across his lips and took another step back.

"Let's go, Tubby," the inmate said. He cocked his head toward the door and pulled the shotgun out of Preston's gut far enough for the attorney to move.

Which was when Angel acted. He swept one of the plastic chairs up with his foot and kicked it at the inmate. The guy squeezed the trigger and the blast blew most of the plastic to shreds, but the metal framework of the chair slammed into him, entangling his gun. Angel followed the chair. He piled into the prisoner and they both went down to the ground.

Angel punched the guy, hard, three times. When the vampire stood up again, the human stayed down.

Preston stared at him, openmouthed. He was still shaking.

"Thanks, Angel," he said. "Where'd you learn to fight like that?"

"You pick things up here and there," Angel said simply. Preston let the subject drop.

"Get out of here," Angel told him. "This place must be swarming with cops outside. Go out there. I've got to make sure Flores is okay."

Preston nodded. "Just be careful, Angel. It's deadly around here."

But Angel was already on his way back into the depths.

Sunnydale

"Look at that burn, man," Enrique said. He had pulled his SUV as close as he dared. Rosalie sat in the passenger seat, illuminated by the flames. She chewed on her lower lip, nervous.

"No way he can survive that," she said.

"He said he has some way. Some trick."

"What kind of trick you think he's got going to make him fireproof?" she asked. "Hope this is worth it, cause Nicky's a dead man."

"It's worth it," Enrique assured her. "DeSola ain't going to forget the Latin Cobras."

A flaming bit of debris arced down out of the sky, slamming to the ground in a shower of sparks right in front of the vehicle. Enrique cranked the ignition. "I'm getting outta here—"

"No, wait!" Rosalie grabbed his arm, but he wrenched it free.

"Wait for what?"

Rosalie didn't answer. He looked at her, and she was pointing, awestruck, toward the oil field fence.

All Enrique could see was the conflagration, blinding to look at.

But then, as he peered into the flames, he saw a dark form silhouetted against them.

It was hard to tell which side of the fence the form was on. Enrique watched, and it became more clear, taking shape as it approached the SUV.

He was naked and charred, covered in soot and grime.

Her cross was around his neck.

There was a smile on his face.

Nicky.

Chapter 13

Sunnydale

As an explosion rocked the double-wide, Spike looked up from the female neck he was sucking on and said, "Bloody hell. What was that?"

"Who cares? It's just somethin' human," said the object of his foreplay. "Keep goin', hon. You're rockin' my world."

With razor-sharp acrylic nails, Spike's, ah, paramour guided his mouth back to her spotless white neck. The sheets were splattered with blood, all that remained of her tasty snack . . . except for the body, which they'd stashed under her bed. He'd made the mistake of coming to the door selling something, maybe encyclopedias, Spike thought. Cheryce didn't have much use for door-to-door solicitors, except as snacks. They'd washed the blood down with a six-pack of Coors long-necks, which she loved. He'd contented himself with butcher's blood, though he joined her in the Coors.

She was six feet tall, and the word for her was not lithesome. She was Cheryce, and she was a vampire. In her past life, she'd been a Vegas showgirl, and Spike had not been able to keep straight all the details about how she had come, as a vampire, to live in the Sunnydale Mobile Home Park. Suffice it to say the story involved a bad man and a worse vampire; and now she was here, and she loved his English accent.

And if he had thought the one true love of his vampiric existence, Dru, had had a gift for kink, he had never actually known the meaning of the word until now.

Chains, whips, manacles, brands—yes, all the usual kit—but it was astonishing how much other stuff this paragon of depravity managed to store in her portable home. It was like visiting the dungeon exhibition under the docks back home in London. Speaking of which, Cheryce was saving up for a rack with the same relish that shopgirls tuck a bit away for a new dinette set. She pored over the catalogs with fervor. Mahogany, teak, or should she spring for the steel model?

He resumed sucking, but his concentration had been thrown off by the explosion. A black velvet painting of Elvis as a vampire smiled at Spike as the undead Brit raised his eyes, still listening. Beside Elvis hung Cheryce's framed master of science in microbiology degree from Southern Methodist University. She had, she said, been pre-med, but had given up the academic life.

And that was what the real attraction was.

Certainly he enjoyed the dalliance. A good time was always, well, a good time, and Spike never liked to turn that down. But what had started as simple physical relief had turned to a quest for relief of another kind.

For, in one of the conversations that some people, and vampires, feel ought to follow the main event, Cheryce had mentioned one of her professors there. One Dr. Lionel Woodring. And Spike had overheard Maggie Walsh, in the Initiative, talking about someone named Lionel Woodring, under whom she had worked as a research fellow.

If Cheryce could get to Woodring, and Woodring had taught Walsh, then there was a chance that Woodring would know how to get the bloody chip out of him.

So far, though, she had resisted his subtle hints and even his not-so-subtle ones. He was hesitant to push it, because she was not the most predictable creature he'd ever encountered, and if he managed to drive her away, he'd lose what might be his best shot at a normal unlife.

Now sirens screamed outside, the familiar children of Sunnydale nights.

"Bite me," she whispered, undulating beneath him. "As hard as you can. Just rip me up, sugar."

Spike sighed. *You know how to make it happen,* he thought. *Take me to Woodring.* But he'd already brought up the name once, less than twenty minutes ago. She'd responded by rolling her eyes. Too soon to try again.

Lifting from his knees, he crossed over to the window and drew the curtain.

The sky was on fire. Oranges and crimsons flickered across the horizon like one's sweetest dream of Hell.

"Wow," Cheryce murmured appreciatively.

"It's that place with all the oil wells," Spike said. "The whole bloody thing is going up. What say we mosey down there and join in the fun, eh?"

When he got no answer, he turned around to look at her.

Completely disinterested, Cheryce was lying on her back in her red satin ruffled bed, checking her white-blond hair for split ends. One long, lovely leg was hooked over the other. She wore black spiked heels with scarlet caribou across the toes.

"Cheryce, look," he said. He found a pack of smokes and a lighter. He lit one of the cigarettes and let the lighter burn, staring into its controlled flame. "Fire and destruction. It's positively delightful."

"Baby, it's nothing to do with us," she insisted, pulling out a strand of hair and letting it drop to the black-carpeted floor. She vamped out, which was even more beautiful to behold than her human visage, and held out her arms. "I'm bored."

Spike glanced back through the window. "Fancy some barbecue?" he asked her.

She chuckled appreciatively. Then she cooed, "C'mon, Spike. You know what I want. Playing with you is all well and good, but I want to hunt with you."

"And you know I can't give that to you."

She thrust forward her lower lip, no small feat with her fangs in the way. "Are you sure you don't have a soul? Is that really why you can't bite them?"

He sighed again. *This bird really knows how to hurt a guy.* "Cheryce, I told you, I've got a bleedin' chip in me head. If I try to bite a human, it will cause me excruciating pain. Which is not something I enjoy doing to myself."

"Then you'd better figure out how to get it out of your head," she drawled. She rolled over on her stomach and bent her legs at the knees, crossing her ankles and resting her chin on her hands. "Or don't you like me, Spike?"

"You know I do, baby," he said. "Maybe your friend Woodring would know something about it."

"Spikie, I know you don't want me to think you just love me for the people I know."

Spike glared out the window, biting his tongue. The flames in the oil field rose higher and higher. A fun time would be had by anyone who loved chaos.

Dru would have wanted to go, he thought gloomily.

Right, mate. And she would no more have put up with a man who couldn't hunt with her than Cheryce will.

"C'mon, lover," she whispered, drawing him in with her long, red nails. "Come on over here."

Spike complied. Velvet vampire Elvis grinned at him.

Right bastard.

Cheryce opened her mouth invitingly and rolled out of Spike's reach. Understanding the game, he navigated his bare-assed way across the fluffy bed, which was not only slippery, but mined with a vast field of "devices" of a shattering array of shapes, sizes, and colors. Spike was amazed not only by the sheer number of them, but by how much Cheryce must have to spend on batteries to keep them all operational.

Playfully, she grabbed his ear between her teeth and tore.

More sirens screamed down the street.

After a while, Spike joined them.

Los Angeles

Rojelio Flores was terrified by the riot. Smoke and screams, the occasional report of a gun, the sirens—all of it added up to a huge disaster in the making, and one he wanted no part of. He still absently clutched the book he'd been reading as he tried to make his way back to his cell. He would be safest there, he figured—his fellow inmates wouldn't be looking to come into people's cells, they'd be trying to get out of them. And waiting in a cell would assure the guards that he was not part of the problem.

He hoped.

The smoke stung his eyes and nose, blinding him. He kept one hand on the wall as he traversed the corridor to the cells, counting doors as he passed them.

Two doors to go. He took a careful step, casting about

with his foot in case there was anything in his path, as he had done all the way from the recreation area.

Feeling nothing, he set his foot down.

And it slipped out from under him.

Flores went down in a heap. He reached back, touching the floor to see what had made him slip. Some kind of spilled liquid. It was sticky to the touch, tacky.

He brought his hand up before him, smelled it.

Blood. A pool of it.

He shuddered, forced himself to his feet, and kept going, his feet sticking to the floor with every step, his prison pants glued to his legs where he had landed in it.

One more door.

Tad Barlowe had had enough—not only were the inmates armed, but they'd set the whole place on fire. Everything was going up, adding to the terror and the mayhem.

Somehow, it all centers around Flores.

He couldn't even say why he believed that. It was a theory he'd been developing for the last several days. He had taken a look at where the inexplicable incidents were happening, and drawn a mental arc connecting them. They all seemed to be within a specific radius of a certain point, and that point was the cell Flores shared with three cell mates—smaller than the dorm cells because Flores and his bunkbuddies were all accused of major felonies.

But in the time these things had been happening, the other three people in the cell had rotated in and out. Flores was the only constant there.

It had to be him.

Barlowe couldn't guess how or why. Stuff like that was beyond him. He wouldn't classify himself as a nonbeliever, or even a skeptic. His Uncle James had seen a ghost once. His wife Penny was constantly going on about UFOs, and some of the articles she showed him made sense. The government seemed very concerned with covering up the facts in several cases. Roswell, Area 51 . . . the list was a long one.

And if that stuff could be real, then why not whatever it was that Flores was up to? Barlowe still had a scab on his arm that proved *something* was happening here.

So the way to put an end to the chaos was clear. Put an end to Flores.

He headed for Flores's cell.

There was a metal door in his way. He touched it, and it was hot on his hand. He ripped part of his shirt off, wrapped it around his palm, tried again.

When he pushed the door open, smoke billowed out. He took a deep breath and strode into it.

Before he had taken six steps into the dark, smoke-filled corridor, someone ran into him. An inmate, stumbling and coughing. The man had a long knife in his hand, and he swung it blindly at Barlowe. Barlowe kicked the guy's hand and the knife hit the wall, slid to the floor. Then Barlowe grabbed the prisoner's shoulders and slammed him into the wall. The guy struggled for a moment, but Barlowe put a hand under his chin and drove his head back, again and again.

The man was still.

Barlowe let him go, and felt around for the knife.

Better to use on Flores than my service weapon.

He continued through the smoke.

All around him he heard sirens and screams. He'd never been involved in a full-scale prison riot before. It wasn't quite what he'd expected. It was chaos. He thought it would be a bunch of prisoners holding a bunch of guards hostage, negotiating demands.

This was nothing like that. No one was organized

enough to issue a demand. No one, as far as he could tell, had hostages. This was every man for himself. There was so much smoke obscuring the hallways that he believed the greatest danger to anyone would probably come from the building burning down.

In spite of it all, he made his way to Flores's cell without seeing a living soul.

Flores, happily, was inside, huddled on his bunk, terrified.

Barlowe smiled.

This would be easy.

Angel burst through the smoke only to see a police officer swinging a knife at Rojelio Flores.

"You're a devil! You're a devil!" the man shouted. "You did it all! You're going to Hell!"

Everyone's gone insane, he thought as he threw himself through the air.

He rammed into the cop, landing hard. The officer let out an "Ooof" as the wind rushed out of him. Angel grabbed his knife-arm, yanked it across his leg, heard the snap as the arm broke. The knife clattered on the floor.

The man shrieked and Angel realized he had vamped out. Crazed, the cop pointed at Angel and shouted, "Devil! Two of you! Straight from Hell!"

Keeping his back to Flores, Angel knocked the cop out with two hard punches.

He lowered the unconscious form down on Rojelio's bed. Flores looked at the cop, blinking.

"That's Barlowe," he said with a low-grade hysterical laugh. "He was always cool. Nice guy, you know?"

"Not so nice anymore," Angel replied, feeling his face revert to human form. "We need to talk, Rojelio."

Chapter 14

Irrenhaus, Buffy thought, and grunted to herself. About three weeks ago, Xander had told her that the word was German for "nerve-house," and it meant insane asylum. Buffy had wanted to tell Riley about it because there'd been a student in intro psych last year whose name was Ernenhaus, and he'd been a nervous wreck. She'd thought Riley would get a kick out the similarity.

But by the time she'd seen him, she'd forgotten the word. Now it popped full-blown into her mind, when her mind was definitely on something else . . . well, kind of. Because the de la Natividad homestead was kind of like an *irrenhaus* at the moment. Maybe fear was colorless and odorless to the casual observer, but Slayers could practically taste it when it was as thick as it was tonight.

She walked to the window of her room and looked out. It was dark, but the darkness had seemed to fall more quickly at the de la Natividad house than it should have. One moment, the sun was out there, and the next, night seemed to have swirled around the house and settled there.

Hard to know, though. I've been preoccupied.

Buffy had taken to glancing at a clock and then the windows. *No reason it shouldn't be dark out,* she thought. *But should the darkness be so impenetrable? Shouldn't there be stars?*

Then the window imploded, spraying her with shards as she dove to the floor and covered her head.

Somewhere else in the house, a woman screamed.

Buffy scrambled to her feet and flew out the door. She was taking the steps three at a time; by the fourth stair, the screaming had stopped.

Uh-oh, she thought.

She got to the foyer, to discover one of the maids lying on the floor. A window had imploded in this room as well, and the poor woman bled from a dozen cuts. The good news was that she was breathing. *Probably fainted,* Buffy decided. She crossed to the ruined window and looked outside.

Meanwhile, Don Francisco and Salma and Nicky's mother also hurried down the stairs, and Armando, their father, appeared from the kitchen, drinking a glass of red wine. He had a piece of garlic toast in his other hand.

"What happened?" he shouted.

Through the window, Buffy saw a velvety, unrelenting darkness. It was like looking off the edge of the world.

"Elfredo, go outside," Armando said. "See what's happened."

"*Sí, señor,*" Elfredo said. Without a moment's hesitation, he opened the front door and shut it behind himself.

At that moment, another guard led Doña Pilar and Willow into the foyer. Both women hurried to the fallen maid.

Doña Pilar said to her husband, "She needs a doctor."

Willow looked frightened. She said to Buffy, "What's going on?"

But Buffy was already halfway out the door herself.

Elfredo was standing on the porch with a gun in his hand. He saw her and frowned, saying, "Miss Summers, please go back inside."

She shook her head. "I can help you."

"I'm really better off without having to worry about you," he told her.

"I can take care of myself," she said. "And then some."

"Please, miss, I'm responsible for your safety," he insisted.

"No, you're really not."

She tried to say it politely, but there really wasn't time for the niceties. She took a few steps away from the house, into the thick blackness outside.

She glanced back at Elfredo, but he had disappeared.

As had the house.

She was surrounded by darkness.

"Miss Summers!" she heard Elfredo call. He sounded like he was a mile away, though, instead of only a few feet.

Okay, I think it's safe to say that this is definitely not normal, she thought.

Downright creep city, in fact. It was not like the shadow monster she had seen, or sensed, at Salma's place. That had been a localized spot of shadow, but this was overwhelming, impenetrable blackness. This didn't feel like an entity, but . . . something else. Something she couldn't classify.

She turned to go back to the house.

But had she turned in the right direction? She couldn't see anything, could no longer hear Elfredo.

"Elfredo!" she called.

His answer was distant and muffled. She couldn't get a fix on his location.

She took a few steps, straight ahead.

Nothing.

She waved her arms before her. When she fully extended one arm, the hand at the end of it was invisible, lost in the thick black air.

She kept walking, fighting off increasing certainty that she was heading in the wrong direction, that she had somehow become turned around and was going farther and farther away from anything.

She forced the growing panic into a box and kept going.

A few steps later she *felt,* rather than heard or saw, a—something—a presence, maybe, swoop over her head.

Then she heard another window shatter.

She heard Elfredo call out. Closer, this time. She pushed forward, and ran right into him. He was still standing by the door, useless weapon in his fist.

"Get inside," she said. The house was visible again.

They both ran inside, slammed the door, bolted it.

Another window crashed.

Buffy found Willow and Doña Pilar coming out of the kitchen toward her.

"What's going on?" Willow asked, fear in her tone.

"I don't know, Will," Buffy told her. "Something, that's for sure. Outside, it's like pea soup—only, black pea soup. Black bean soup. And there's something in the darkness that's attacking the house. I can't tell if it's trying to get in, or if it's just causing trouble. It might be like a vampire, something that can't get in without an invitation. But it's not really a vampire, that's for sure."

"What do you think it is?"

"I don't have any idea," Buffy replied. "That's more of a Giles question. I don't usually catalogue 'em, I just beat 'em up."

"Right," Willow said.

"I have an idea," Doña Pilar said. She drew Buffy and Willow to one side, away from the glowering Elfredo, and spoke in hushed tones.

"What is it?" Willow asked her.

"Just a feeling I have," she went on. "Although, at my age, and with my experience, my feelings are always to be trusted. I have been trying to find Nicky, even without the correct ingredients for my locating spell. And I have been encountering something . . . some kind of resistance. So I pulled back. But I think . . ." She lowered her voice even more. Buffy had to incline her head just to catch the woman's quiet words. "I think it *followed* me."

"How?" Willow asked.

"I don't understand it myself," Doña Pilar said. "It is as if I left a mystical trail somehow, like Hansel and Gretel with their breadcrumbs. And it has come home to us."

"Whatever 'it' is," Buffy added.

"That's right," Doña Pilar said. "Whatever 'it' is."

"If it's magick, there must be a way to fight it magickally," Willow said.

Doña Pilar nodded enthusiastically. "Shall we go to work on that?"

"Bad idea," Buffy offered. "If it followed your magick here, then doing more might bring reinforcements or something, right?"

"I do not know," Doña Pilar said. "Possibly. But I don't believe so."

"I'd rather just find a way to kick its tail."

"Maybe there's a way we can both attack it with our strengths," Willow said.

Buffy knew what Willow meant. Willow's best way was with spells and enchantments.

Buffy's best way was more direct.

If it was out there, she could punch it.

Sunnydale

Riley pulled to the shoulder and stopped the car. He and Tara blinked at the fireball that rose above the pine trees. It was followed by several others. Then thick smoke roiled up, blanketing the sky.

"Wow," Tara murmured.

"That's gotta be some explosion," Riley said. "Big freeway pileup, maybe." He looked at Tara. "I think we should check it out."

"Yeah."

It had gotten chilly out, and just like anybody who lived in southern California, they had dressed in layers. The colder it got, the more one put on. Tara had started the day in a long skirt and a short-sleeved T-shirt. They were up to sweats, Tara in navy blue sweatpants and a puffy coat with faux fur at the cuffs and collar, and Riley, in a black hooded sweatshirt that matched his pants. The hood was down, and he wore a black knitted cap over his hair. He had been giving her a ride home from Giles's, where she'd been research girl, when they saw the fireball. He had detoured to see what was happening, feeling a responsibility to keep a close eye on Sunnydale while Buffy was out of town. "I think maybe I should check it out."

"Do you think it's related to the shadow monsters?" she asked, puzzled, watching the incredible amount of smoke.

"Tara, in this town, you never know." He flashed her a wry grin. "You want me to drop you off first?"

She shook her head. "No time," she said. "You should get there as soon as you can, just in case."

He reached into the back and handed her a cross, which she stowed in her pocket. He had packed holy water and stakes, too. *Never without.*

Between Tara's feet sat a black backpack, which was a

standard Wicca emergency kit consisting of a concise spell book, some herbs, a mirror, and a few other necessities.

Riley drove toward the red glow that painted the night sky.

"My God, that's huge," he said, half to himself. Explosions he'd seen in his Initiative days, both in person and on film, came to mind. He amended his earlier guess. "That's no traffic accident."

Tara closed her eyes and intoned a healing spell for anyone who had gotten injured. She also did a chant for protection for her and Riley. *And Willow,* she thought. *I hope she's okay.*

Riley glanced from the wheel and scrutinized her.

"You all right?" he asked Tara kindly.

She nodded.

"Sure you wouldn't rather I drop you off? This is probably going to be bad."

She shook her head again and watched the red glow. It was probably something magick, something evil. In this town, it usually was.

Sunnydale. Come for the education, stay for the exciting, demon-packed summer.

They drove for five, maybe ten more minutes, going out past the abandoned Sunnydale Drive-In, cresting the most minor of hills, when both of them craned their necks and stared at the fire looming directly in front of them.

It was the oil field on the outskirts of town. Greasy black smoke choked the scene; even with the windows rolled up, Tara could smell it. All the derricks were ablaze, parked vehicles, work shacks, everything. The perimeter fence had been knocked down and fire trucks driven over the collapsed chain-link. Overhead, helicopters circled, their searchlights trained on the ground.

Camera crews swarmed after a few individuals, trailed by police, who gestured to yellow police-line tape and made the press corps move their butts to safer ground.

As close to the madding crowd as possible, Riley instructed Tara to stay back, out of danger, and climbed out of his car. He remembered a time, not that long ago, when he had had the authority to commandeer any situation in Sunnydale, underscore any. As a government special operative, he had outranked all local civilian law enforcement as well as FBI agents. Now he was simply Riley Finn, no rank, no serial number . . . and no legal rights to do half the things he did before.

Still, old habits died hard; as he strode toward the front lines, the first two police officers he approached recognized him and took on a deferential stance, answering all his questions. Not that useful: neither had the slightest idea what had happened.

Next he approached the fire captain on the scene, a rotund old boy who resembled Police Chief Wiggins from the *Simpsons,* down to his porcine features. How a man could retain a position as a firefighter when he was as heavy as this man gave Riley pause, but he didn't spare much time worrying about it.

"I see you've deployed your units in a flying-V formation," Riley said. "Good call."

The captain tossed him a quick, working-here smile and looked away.

"Any idea of a cause?" Riley pressed.

"We're thinking arson," the fire captain told him, after giving him the now-familiar I-know-who-you-are-but-I-can't-quite-place-you look. "The way she went up, the way she's burning . . ."

The captain shrugged knowledgeably, allowing a supposed peer to fill in the blanks.

"But who'd set an entire oil field on fire?" Riley asked skeptically. "And why?"

"I'm thinking environmental whackos," the captain replied, looping his thumbs over his belt. "Those solar-power types. Greenpeace, one of them, you know?"

Riley—who was a card-carrying member of not one, but several, environmental groups—raised his brows. "Why bother with an oil field in a small town like Sunnydale?" He crossed his arms, unconsciously moving into questioning mode. "Isn't this field owned by a private individual? Could someone have something against him, not his oil?"

The captain loved the idea. "Class envy? Of course. Del DeSola owns all this. He's an okay guy, though. Paid for the new softball diamond after the last one collapsed. Sinkhole."

Doubtful, Riley thought, seeing the work of the city council's PR team all over what must've been something demonic. *Have to remember to ask Buffy about that one. I wonder how they'll spin this. Stray cigarette butt tossed from a car?*

The captain shook his head. "But I'm still thinking somebody with a 'cause.' " He uttered the word as if it were a juicy, dirty swearword.

Tara sidled up and joined the conversation. "Why?"

"This was a suicide mission, guaranteed." The captain watched the blaze with a proprietary air. Teams of fire-fighters stood by, hoses at the ready, watering down the surrounding landscape to keep the blaze contained. An oil field fire, Riley knew, required special equipment and techniques, and sometimes they just needed to burn themselves out. They'd be bringing in specialists for this one. "No way anybody could survive that."

Tara and Riley traded glances. Supernatural forces could have survived, Riley knew. There was still no indication that anything like that was at play here, but in Sunnydale it was safest not to assume that they weren't. Riley was beginning to wish he had a face mask—his lungs were starting to burn from inhaling the thick, acrid smoke.

"Have any bodies been located?" Riley asked.

Just then a firefighter in full gear—protective suit, hood, and breathing apparatus—approached the captain. The captain waved at the figure and moved toward it. Over his shoulder, he said, "Not so far. There was a rent-a-cop, but he's been accounted for. Thing is, that fire's so hot, I doubt there'd be much of anything left. We'd be lucky to find dental work."

"Right." Riley held up his hand in a gesture of appreciation for the time. Then he noticed that Tara had wandered off while the two men were talking. She was crouching over something, her hands gathered into her sweatshirt. As Riley grew near, she looked up, then gestured with her hand.

"The glint caught my eye," she told him. "I didn't know if it was okay to pick it up. It was a little hot."

It was a gold cross on a chain. Riley picked it up, only to discover that a portion of the chain had melted away.

"What we may have here," Riley said, imitating Strother Martin in *Cool Hand Luke,* "is a piece of evidence." He pointed to an engraving on the back. A crude rendition of a cobra, rearing up as if to bite someone, with the initials "L.C." beneath it. On the clip side, the initials "R.L."

"The Latin Cobras," Riley informed her.

"Local gang," he told her.

"I've heard of them. Willow told me Nicky de la Natividad might be involved with them."

"Hmm." He looked down at the cross, then over at the

fire captain. "In which case, do I keep it or turn it over to Chief Wiggins?"

Tara smiled faintly. "I thought that, too, about him." The smile faded. "I think we should hold onto it," she told him. "We've already disturbed the crime scene. And if the police get involved . . ."

"More difficult all around," he agreed. "All right." He put it in the kangaroo pouch of his sweatshirt. "Now I'm definitely taking you home."

Disappointed, she looped her hair around her ears and stood. She had sort of been hoping to be included in his snake hunting. "When Willow calls, I'll tell her about this, okay?"

"Oh?" Riley's eyes lit up. "When is she checking in with you?" He had expected to hear from Buffy by now.

"No special t-time," Tara stammered.

Riley had noticed that her speech hesitation had a lot to do with when she was upset or otherwise stressed. He wondered if everything was okay with the two Wiccas in the relationship department. But nice Midwest guys did not meddle in others' personal business.

"Do you have Salma's L.A. number?" he asked.

"Yes." Tara looked bashful. "I didn't want to intrude. Bother them."

"This is worth bothering them about," Riley said. "The Cobras are connected in L.A. Let's give them a call."

She brightened up considerably. Riley was touched by her obvious affection for Willow. He'd been there for the reappearance of Oz, and he would have put money on Oz winning Willow back.

Just goes to show you, life rarely turns out the way you imagine.

Look at me, dating a gal who's not only a demon

hunter, but has prophecy dreams and all kinds of weird connections with dimensions I can't even imagine.

"Giles's house is closer," Tara said. "And he'll want to hear about the fire."

They walked back to Riley's car, climbed in, and watched the fire.

"I think we might be thinking the same thing," Riley said slowly.

Tara eyed the flames. "That Nicky de la Natividad might have died in this fire?" she asked bluntly.

Riley nodded. "If a bunch of Cobras snuck in to start it for some reason."

"A prank?" she said.

"Those lowlifes aren't into pranks," Riley bit off. "They're into intimidation, and bullying, and killing." He frowned at her. "I had a soldier under my command who tangled with them, came back with a knife wound that reached from his left shoulder to his right hip. He almost lost a kidney."

Tara's face was ashen.

She's worried, Riley thought.

So am I.

They drove for a while, and then Tara pointed to a figure stumbling down the side of the road, wearing a familiar black leather jacket. "Hey, that's Spike."

Riley pulled over. Tara opened the door and poked out her head.

"Spike?"

The vampire scowled at her. "What do you want?"

"Where are you going?" she asked him.

"Why is it your business?" he flung at her. "I can't do anything, all right? I haven't hurt anyone. I haven't bitten anyone." He staggered to the right, nearly falling over, and burst into tears.

"Cheryce!" he wailed. He held up a nearly empty bottle of tequila and poured it down his throat.

"Woman trouble. As usual," Riley said to Tara.

She nodded, but only asked the vampire, "Spike, do you want a ride somewhere?"

He fell to the ground on his knees. "People, offering me rides," he moaned. "You should be running in terror from me, not offering to be my sodding taxi service." He wiped his mouth with the sleeve of his jacket.

"She's just like all the rest. Women are just so evil." He looked pitifully at Tara. "Don't you think?"

Before she could answer, he whirled in a half turn and opened his arms. "I'm doin' it," he announced. "I'm standing right here until the sun rises, and I'm going out in flames."

"Spike, get in the car," Tara said patiently.

" 'Spike, get in the car,' " he imitated, sneering at her. "Don't you hate being so good? Doesn't it just wear on you, day after day? Oh, God, I'm so miserable!"

"You know you get like this when you drink," Tara said.

"So bleedin' what." He lobbed the bottle at the street. It didn't break. "Look a' that! Look!" he sobbed. "Nothing's going right.

"Oh, Dru." He wiped his eyes. "Even that bimbo Harmony can bite people. Not me! Not William the Bloody, the scourge of Europe!"

Tara looked at Riley. "What should we do?"

"Hope the sun comes up early," Riley muttered. He leaned across the seat. "We'll take you home, Spike. Otherwise, you're on your own."

Spike's shoulders jerked a few times. "She threw me out. Says I'm only with her because of who she knows, because I want something. Well, pardon me! Of course I want something! Doesn't everyone?"

Finally he nodded.

"Take me home," he said.

Then he passed out cold.

Los Angeles

Buffy stalked the hallways of the de la Natividad house, accompanied by Elfredo.

There had been one more broken window incident in the last few minutes.

But why? she wondered. *The fact that the thing, whatever it is, is breaking windows means it has some kind of solid form. But if it does, why isn't it coming inside? Why just keep breaking windows? What does it have to gain?*

No easy answers occurred to her. The vampire similarity presented itself again, but this clearly wasn't a vampire. Still, was that a common syndrome in the demonic world?

No answers.

Only more questions.

Is it just mischievous? Or is truly dangerous?

The maid who was seemingly attacked—was that only an accident? Did she faint after having been cut by flying glass, or was there something more sinister to that?

Having nothing to fight made her edgy, keyed up.

Elfredo looked like he felt the same way. His brown eyes were narrowed to slits. He moved like a coiled spring, ready to strike at any moment. His handsome face was shadowed with worry.

After a long stretch of no activity, she decided to go outside again.

The thing wasn't coming in. It could smash windows but couldn't pass through them.

So she had to fight it on its own turf if they were ever to leave the house again.

She stopped in mid-pace and turned to Elfredo. "I'm going back out there."

He nodded, understanding. Probably he'd reached the same conclusion. After looking her up and down for a moment, he smiled at her. "You're not just some college chick, are you?"

She smiled. "Not even close."

"What I thought."

"You coming with me or staying in here?"

"I'd just be in the way out there, wouldn't I?" he asked.

"I'm glad you see it my way. I'm going to talk to Willow for a sec, and then I'm going out. If I'm not back in thirty minutes, then you can start to worry."

"If you're not back in thirty minutes," Elfredo echoed, "I figure none of us will last forty-five."

"You could have a point," Buffy said. She left him in the hall and headed for the kitchen.

Sunnydale

Word travels fast in the criminal underground, and the Echo Park Band had ordered the Latin Cobras to escort Nicky to L.A. They wanted to talk to him about how he had survived the fire. A trick like that could prove very useful.

He had gone to Rosalie's to shower while the guys found some clothes for him. With a brown bandana on his head and a long-sleeved shirt and baggy jeans, he looked much more like a Cobra than when he'd gone in to start the fire.

He was one of them now, no doubt about it. He had risked his life for the gang, and nobody would ever dare to question his loyalty again.

Unless, of course, he forgot who his friends were.

None of the Cobras wanted to go home after Nicky, Enrique, and Paco left for L.A. At first, all the talk centered around Nicky, and how the hell he had survived the fire. Rosalie threw back tequila with the *cholos* and fantasized about being Nicky's woman when he came back. She was glad she'd been nice to him. Now that he had done this amazing thing, the other girls would be after him, too.

After a lot of drinking, they straggled down to the beach, in lowrider cars and souped-up trucks. Little King built a bonfire and the gang kicked back, drinking beer and just daring the wimpy Sunnydale cops to tell them they had to disperse. Just as at any other Latin Cobra gathering, food began appearing almost by magic, and more alcohol.

Rosalie started dancing by herself, then was joined by Luisa, who started asking a lot of questions about Nicky.

"Keep away from him," Rosalie snapped.

Luisa laughed. "You ain't got no claim, Rosa," she sneered. "It's not like he married you or anything."

Rosalie ignored her taunts.

It was as she was reaching for another Dos Equis that she remembered the crucifix she had given to Nicky to wear during his mission.

He had been wearing it when he walked, naked, from the flames.

But he had not been wearing it when he climbed back into the SUV.

It must have fallen off in the dirt.

"*Ay, Dios,*" she murmured.

Her throat tight with fear, she surveyed the drunken crowd. What would they do to her if they found out that her necklace had been left at the scene of the crime?

"Hey, Rosa. I saw you with Nicky," Little King slurred, staggering toward her. "He your new guy?" He slugged back some beer and wiped his mouth. He winked at her. "You could do better, honey."

He'd been after her for a while, ever since her old boyfriend, Nando, had been sent to jail for armed robbery. She'd been friendly but distant. Little King frightened her. He was as big as a Samoan, and he had a terrible temper.

He also has a car.

He'd driven it down to the beach.

She took a breath. "Maybe I could do better, maybe not," she retorted. She didn't retreat as he advanced, only raised her face to meet his. His nose had been broken so many times it resembled an accordion. The few teeth he had left were brown. Plus, he liked to chew tobacco, which she found disgusting.

But he likes me, she thought. Her heart was racing. Her hands were shaking.

Enough to help me?

"*Oye, mamacita,*" he said, frowning, "what's wrong with you? Miss your boyfriend already?"

Rosalie felt faint. If Dom found out, or Jose . . . They were the *majordomos* of the gang. They maintained discipline and made sure everybody toed the line.

"What's up, Rosita?" He took her hand and led her to a beach chair someone had just vacated. The smell of roasting hot dogs revolted her. She was afraid she was going to throw up.

"Oh, God," she whispered. She put her head between her knees and took deep breaths.

"Do you need a ride home?" he asked.

Yes! She nodded. "Please. I'm really sick."

"Sure. Don't worry. Hey, Dom," he called. Then he stood and walked over to Dom, who was tall and stocky, carrying a little extra weight around his middle.

Dom talked to him for a few minutes; then Little King

nodded and gave Rosalie a wave. Completely numb, she got up out of the chair and lurched toward Little King, who didn't seem to notice that she was having trouble walking.

He reached down into one of the coolers and promoted a six-pack, smiling at her.

"You'll feel better after another beer," he advised her as they climbed into his ride.

As soon as they got on the road, he turned to her and said, "You gonna have a baby or something?"

She swallowed hard, about to take the biggest chance she'd taken in years, other than driving the getaway car in the heist that had sent Nando to prison. She'd hadn't even been implicated. So maybe she was a lucky kind of person.

"Little King," she said, "you've got to help me." His brows shot up. "I mean, please help me."

He was waiting. Hopefully, she touched his arm.

"I gave Nicky my crucifix to wear when he went to fix DeSola," she began. "And it fell off him or something. I saw it on him when he came back, you know? But not when he got in the SUV with us."

It took him a moment to put together what she'd said. Then he cocked his head at her and said, "Does it have anything on it that can trace it to us?"

She swallowed hard. "My initials," she admitted. "On the back. It was from Nando."

"Your initials are what, R.L.? Rosalie Lopez? Who's gonna figure that out? Don't worry. Nothin's gonna happen." He peered at her. "Is that what this is about, this 'I'm sick' stuff?"

She nodded. "Little King," she continued, her mouth dry, "Nando had a little cobra engraved on the back, too. Like the tatts him and me got over on Western that one night. With the initials 'L.C.' below it." She touched the right side of her pelvis.

Little King blinked. Then he pulled over to the side of the road and killed the engine.

"Idiota!" he shouted. He smacked her across the face.

Rosalie was actually relieved that it was gonna happen now, whatever it was. At least it would be over.

He drove crazy, shouting at her, as they roared back to the oil fields. The fire was still going and there were police cars and fire trucks everywhere. There was no way they would be able to retrieve her cross.

"Are you sure he didn't have it on when he got in the SUV?" he demanded, all traces of the alcohol gone now. The fire reflected in his brown eyes as if it were burning inside of him.

"Yes." Hot tears streamed down her face, mingling with the blood that dripped from the corner of her lips. "He was completely naked, okay? I would have noticed it."

Little King hung a U. Rosalie wiped away the blood and fearfully asked, "Where are we going?"

"Back to the beach," he said. "You're gonna tell 'em."

"No, please." She held out her hands. "You like me, don't you? I—I could be your girlfriend, if you want." She sobbed. "Please, don't take me back. They're all drunk! They'll hurt me bad!"

He shook her off. "You put all of us in danger, and why? Because you wanted Nicky to notice you, treat you special. Well, he's made his mark now and he can have any woman he wants.

"And I promise you, Rosalie, after we're done with you, no one is gonna want you."

"No, *por Dios,* please," she wept.

Stone-faced, Little King kept driving.

Chapter 15

Los Angeles

As SIRENS WAILED AND SMOKE CHOKED THE CELLS, Angel prodded Rojelio Flores to tell his story. Flores kept glancing at the still form of Barlowe, stretched out on his cot. Barlowe's breathing was regular, Angel noted. He was out cold but he'd be okay later, with just a headache and a bruise. Probably safer here inside the cell, unconscious, than he would be out in the population.

"Talk fast," Angel suggested. "Once the police restore order, I'll be kicked out of here."

Flores rubbed his short hair and closed his eyes for a moment, as if gathering his thoughts. "I was taking a walk," he finally began. "I do that about four nights a week, after dinner."

He patted his stomach. "Doctor's orders, right? Sometimes just around the neighborhood, and sometimes I drive over to the ocean, like in Santa Monica or Venice.

Once in a while, Griffith Park, but I like to do that one on a weekend day, instead of at night.

"Anyway, on this night I was walking close to home, up to Seventh Avenue and then going to head over to Broadway, down that to Olympic, and then back."

"Long walk," Angel offered.

"Yeah, I like to go fast. Get a lot of thinking done. But this night that we're talking about, I'm on Seventh, and my shoelace feels like it's coming loose.

"So I bend over to tighten it. I stop by this apartment building, and put my foot up on this bus bench to tie my shoe. And from the apartment, I hear something loud, like maybe shots. But I figure, no business of mine. Plus, no-body's screaming or anything like that."

He sighed, as if the telling was wearing him out. Angel's patience was wearing thin, but he kept his mouth shut.

"So I just keep going, thinking that if it was shots, somebody in the building will call the cops, take care of things. It's a security building, I couldn't get in even if I wanted to. Plus I'm not a fighter, and I'm not armed. Look at me." He held out his arms. His physique was paunchy in spite of the walking. "What am I going to do against someone with a gun?"

"And after all, this is L.A.," Angel said dourly.

"This is L.A.," Rojelio agreed. "Then, when I've gone about another block, I'm about to cross the street, and I look back. There's a police car. It's coming from the direction of the apartment, but past it, toward me. At first, I'm thinking it's here to check out the shooting, and it really was a shoot-ing, and that's kind of scary, you know? But then it passes by that building so I think it's just a coincidence."

Angel nodded, trying not to glance over his shoulder. Flores had to snap it up, or Angel might never get to hear the end of this story.

"Only as I'm about to step out onto Olive to cross the street, the car pulls to a stop right in front of me, practically running over my feet, and cops get out with their guns drawn, pointing them and yelling at me." He wiped his face with both his hands.

"Flores, keep going," Angel prompted.

The man nodded silently. He took a breath. "Another police car comes up beside them, and there's two more guns pointing my way. I hit the ground, like they said. They came over and knelt on my back and handcuffed me and put me in one of the cars."

Angel considered. "Did they tell you why they were picking you up? Mirandize you?"

"Nothing then." He was sweating now, and he kept craning his head to look at the hallway, as if someone might walk in on them. Angel figured it wouldn't take too long to get paranoid in a place like this.

"While I was locked in the back of the car, they drove back to the alley behind that apartment building. I sat in the car alone for about twenty minutes. Everything was quiet, no sirens, no noise. Then they came back out of the building, got back in the car, and drove me here. It was a couple of hours more before I even found out what they were accusing me of."

"Murder in the first," Angel guessed.

"Police say 'homicide,' " Flores said bitterly. "They said I could call a lawyer, but I don't have a lawyer. Lawyers cost money. So the court has to appoint someone, and finally Mr. Preston, he shows up about three minutes before I'm arraigned."

His voice grew shrill, anxious, angry. Angel understood. This man had every right to be outraged, if what he was saying was true.

"No bail, because they're saying I killed this guy,

Nokivov, and then resisted arrest. They said they found the gun on me that killed him. I don't even *own* a gun." His voice broke, and he swallowed a couple of times as emotion threatened to overcome him. Angel felt sorry for the man. Jail was no place for the innocent. "I never heard of Nokivov before, never met him, and sure didn't kill him."

"I believe you," Angel said.

Flores stopped. "You do? Why?"

"Your story rings true," Angel said. "You don't have a record, your wife says you've never owned a gun, you don't do drugs. Why would you kill a Russian drug dealer?"

"Too bad you're not the judge." Flores laughed harshly. "I figured he'd throw my case out in a minute, but he didn't. Ordered me held without bail until my trial. I've met with Preston a few times, but he doesn't seem like any great lawyer to me."

Angel glanced down the corridor. Things seemed to be quieting down, and the smoke was thinning. It looked like the riot was probably being brought under control. Just then, as he stood in the cell's doorway, an inmate carrying a cop's service piece stopped in the hall, saw Barlowe's uniform, and started to come into the cell.

Angel confronted him at the door. "Help you?"

"Out of the way," the inmate said, waving the gun at him.

Angel caught the prisoner's wrist in one strong hand and applied pressure. The guy squealed and dropped the gun. Angel caught it in midair and put it in the pocket of the windbreaker he still wore.

"Don't think so," Angel said. "Go turn yourself in and be glad I didn't break your wrist."

The inmate's face was white. He turned and ran, his footfalls echoing down the corridor until they were lost in the wail of sirens and the din of shouting voices.

Angel went back to Flores. "Not much time left," he said. "So you were framed, you think."

"That's right."

"Have any idea who? Or why?"

"From what I overheard of their conversation," Flores said, lowering his voice, "I think those cops did it themselves. I heard one of them say something about a throwdown, and the others called the dead guy some names, and laughed. Then they lowered their voices again, as if they were worried I would overhear."

Angel nodded. "A throw-down piece."

"A what?" Flores asked.

"An unlicensed, unregistered gun cops sometimes carry illegally, in case they want to do something with a weapon that can't be traced."

Flores nodded. "And they say it's my gun."

"So you think while they had you in the car, they went in to make the crime scene look like you had been there, maybe even planting hairs or threads from your clothing, and trying to eliminate any traces of themselves having been there except to investigate the crime."

"That's what I fear."

"Hard to prove otherwise, if they knew what they were doing," Angel told him grimly.

"So what you're saying is, basically, I'm hosed," Flores said despondently. "They have evidence I was there, they have a gun they say they took from me, there are four of them and only one of me and no other witnesses."

Angel shook his head. "It looks bad on the surface. Maybe I can turn up something, though. Especially now that I know where to start looking. In the meantime, you stay clean and stay out of trouble."

Flores stared through the bars. "I thought that's what I was doing," he murmured.

Angel knew time was ticking by, and he still hadn't broached the subject he'd come here to talk about. "Rojelio, I think you and your son are both powerful telekinetics," he said. "Do you know what that means?"

Flores blinked. "We can move stuff with our brains?"

"That's pretty much right. Did you know that about yourself?"

For a moment, Angel thought the man was going to go through the routine of denying it. But then Flores sagged, as if relieved to have it out in the open, and said, "There have been things happening, lately. I wasn't sure, but I was thinking . . . maybe . . . something like that."

Angel nodded. "Well, I'm pretty sure it is you. You need to work on it. Pick things in your immediate vicinity, and move them around. It's like any other muscle, you need to work it out, to practice using it. That's the only way you'll gain any control over it. I think the stress of being arrested jumpstarted your ability, but without control over it you're making everyone around you anxious."

"I'll try," Flores promised.

The police officer Angel had knocked out uttered a low moan and shifted position on the bed. Angel went to him, helped him to a sitting position.

"Are you . . . ?"

"I'm the guy who hit you," Angel said. "You were about to assault a prisoner for no reason."

"He—he's the one . . ."

Angel read the man's nametag. "Think about this, Barlowe. You really want to deny this man due process, get carried away in the middle of a jail riot and kill someone? If you have a case you can prove, then prove it. You kill an innocent, unarmed man in here, you'll fry just like any murderer."

Barlowe rubbed his jaw, wincing when he touched it.

"Guess you're right," he said. "I was just so sure." He looked at Rojelio Flores, blinking as if gazing into a bright light. He regarded Flores as if something had changed about the man, but Angel thought it was something in Barlowe that had changed. He was seeing Flores anew. "Sorry, Flores," he said. "Guess I got caught up in the moment."

"No problem," Flores replied sincerely.

"Why don't you go get a compress on that jaw?" Angel said. "Flores isn't going anywhere."

Barlowe looked at Angel. "Who are you?"

"Riot squad," Angel said. "I'm almost done here."

Barlowe unsteadily gained his feet. "I don't like it," he said. "But a situation like this, all the rules are changed. You get out of here in the next ten minutes or I will arrest you, though."

"Deal," Angel agreed. Barlowe left the cell, walking uncertainly.

"Quick," Angel insisted. "What are the names of your arresting officers?"

Flores answered without hesitation. "Doug Manley, Bo Peterson, Luis Castaneda, and Richard Fischer."

"Okay," Angel said. "I think you're safe in here for now. Just practice, like I said, and try to bring your powers under control so there aren't any more incidents. Carlos is doing the same thing at home."

"I miss him," Flores said. His eyes were moist. "And Isabel."

"I know. They miss you, too, believe me. Keep your nose clean and maybe you'll be home with them soon."

Sunnydale

Riley and Tara barged in to find Giles sitting in front of his police band radio, intent on the crackles and sputters that issued from it. He was obviously disturbed by something, but so was Riley. It had taken forty minutes to get Spike back to his crypt, out of the car, and situated inside. Forty minutes that Riley didn't think they could spare. He'd been all for just booting the vampire out by the side of the road, but Tara had argued that Buffy wanted Spike treated with decency. Riley didn't get it—it seemed like she had some kind of save-Spike's-soul campaign going, even though it was way too late for that.

Then he'd wanted to finally get Tara home, but she had argued again. With this new information, she said, there might be more work that needed to be done at Giles's house. She would rather stay there with the others, in case there was something she could help with. *For someone so timid,* Riley thought, heading the car in Giles's direction, *she sure can be persuasive.*

On the way, they had tried to call Buffy and Willow, but there had been no answer at the de la Natividad household. Which could have meant they had all gone to bed, Riley knew. But it bothered him nonetheless.

He told Giles about the fire, mentioned dropping Spike off, and showed him the cross they had found. Giles examined it with the magnifying glass he kept in a drawer in his desk.

"There are two sets of initials on the back of this pendant," he announced. "And a rather poor rendition of a snake."

"We know," Riley told him. "We figure the 'L.C.' is for the Latin Cobras. It's the other one I don't have a clue about."

"R.L. . . . Oh dear . . . There's, umm, there's been a homicide at Sunnydale Cove," Giles stammered, indicating his radio. "Quite recent, by the look of the body. According to the police. The victim's name was Rosalie Lopez, and she was a member of the Latin Cobras."

Stone-faced, Riley said, "Tara, stay here with Giles. I'm going to check this out."

"I can help you," she said. "What if a shadow—"

Riley was out the door.

About an hour later, he returned. Giles and Tara, who had been waiting anxiously, answered the door together.

Xander and Anya were also there, sitting on the couch.

There were bruises on Riley's cheeks and his right eye was swollen shut. When Tara's eyes widened, he grinned halfheartedly and said, "You should have seen the other guy."

"Why?" Anya asked. "It's revolting enough seeing you."

Xander hung his head in defeat.

"Riley, what happened?" Tara asked.

"I'll get some antiseptic," Giles announced.

"I got some answers," Riley said, slowly seating himself in Giles's chair, perpendicular to the couch. Grimacing, he said to Tara, "It's like we figured. Nicky set that fire."

"Oh, my God." Tara covered her mouth.

"And he walked away from it unscathed," Riley added. "The leaders of the Cobras—well, not the Cobras, exactly, but the gang they're associated with, the Echo Park Band—wanted to find out how he pulled it off, so they summoned him to Los Angeles."

"Unscathed?" Giles asked from the bathroom, where he was rummaging in the medicine cabinet.

"He should have died. My informant said no one could figure out how he did it." Riley looked at Tara. "You have any guesses?"

She said slowly, "He's the shadow monster?"

"So what now?" Xander asked. "Do we neutralize him with really big fluorescent lights?"

Everybody looked at Riley.

"What happens is, I try to find him in Los Angeles. And the rest of you stay here and patrol, and make sure the shadow monster is really gone."

"Well, that sounds like bloody good fun," said a voice from the kitchen.

The microwave dinged. Through the arch that separated the living room from the kitchen, Spike's head rose slowly into view. He frowned at Riley. "What the bleedin' hell are you staring at?"

"I thought we tucked you in."

Tara said, "Xander and Anya found him wandering around again."

Grunting, Spike went to the microwave and opened it, pulling out a coffee mug. He began to sip.

"I think he was lonely," Anya reported. "He has few friends, as he isn't accepted by other demons, and his social skills with humans are marginal at best."

Spike made a face at her. "Hey. I thought we were mates, you and me. Neutered Demons United and all that."

Anya blinked. "I am not a neutered demon. I am a perfectly functional human woman. For now. If I get my powers back, that will be a different story."

"Neutered," Spike insisted. "Just like me."

Anya squirmed uncomfortably. Xander put his arm around her and said, "It's okay, Ann. I like you just the way you are."

She preened victoriously at Spike.

"You two shut up," Spike said to Tara and Riley.

"So, Los Angeles," Giles said, returning with a bottle of Betadyne and some gauze pads.

Riley nodded. "The rest of you will stay here and patrol," he said again.

"Oh, yay," Xander drawled.

Tara blinked. "I should go with you."

Riley shook his head. "If we're wrong, and Nicky isn't the shadow monster, you're going to be needed around here."

"That's very true," Giles said. "All hands on deck, and so on."

"Hey, maybe we should hit the lifeboats," Xander said brightly.

"No. Let's take it on. I can hit monsters! I'm ready!" Spike said, showing the first enthusiasm any of them had seen from him tonight.

"I like knowing that we may prove to be indispensable," Anya said, considering. "It makes me feel less . . . incapacitated."

Riley looked at Tara. "Try Buffy and Willow again. Tell them I'm on my way. They should try to get some more leads to the gang up there."

Tara nodded. "Okay."

"Take care of yourself, Riley," Anya said. "It would be distressful if you were torn into bits by this creature."

"I'll miss you, too," Riley said dryly.

"Yeah. Safe journeys. Oh, and be sure to say hi to Angel for me," Spike said pointedly. "I'm sure you'll run into him when you catch up with the Slayer."

Riley simply glared at him and walked out. As he left, he heard Xander say, "Spike, you really have no class, do you?"

"None at all," the white-haired vampire replied with satisfaction.

Chapter 16

Los Angeles

CORDELIA HAD A CLOTH BAG FULL OF WOODEN STAKES
strapped onto her back and one stake in each fist. Hanging against her chest was a wide, metal cross on a leather
thong. As accessories went, these were far from anything
she'd seen in *Vogue,* but she hoped they'd come in handy
in case of vampiric emergency.

Wesley was, if anything, even more decked out. He
held a crossbow in his right hand, nocked with a wooden
bolt. More bolts were affixed to a bandolier that encircled
his torso. Around his neck, a vial of holy water dangled
from a velvet cord.

They waited in the tunnels underneath the library, en-
veloped in darkness. Each had selected a doorway on opposite sides of the main hallway that ran through the
unused lower section of the library complex, and they sat,
more or less silent and alert, in the shadows. Cordelia

could barely make out Wesley across the hall. The girls didn't know they were there—at least, she hoped they didn't.

But that was by no means a sure thing.

They were here because Kayley had called, her voice charged with fear.

"It's tonight," she had said as soon as Cordelia picked up the phone.

"What is?" she had asked, before the meaning of Kayley's words really sunk in. "Oh, okay. Tonight? Are you sure?"

Kayley couldn't speak for a moment, just sniffled softly into the phone. "Okay, Kayley," Cordelia said. "We'll be there. Don't worry."

When Cordelia hung up, Wesley was looking at her, his face ashen.

"We don't have any idea where Angel is," the former Watcher pointed out. "I've just tried his phone again, a few minutes ago. What shall we do?"

"Worry," Cordelia answered.

"No," he said, suddenly forceful and commanding. "We'll gird our loins and step into the breach."

Cordelia hesitated. "I don't think I like you in that way, Wesley," she said. "I mean, you're fine to do research and stuff with, and I actually do like shopping with you. But I think we should leave it at that, you know?"

He blinked a couple of times as he took in what she was saying. "No, Cordelia. What I mean is that we shall arm ourselves and defeat Kostov, without waiting for Angel."

"Ohh," Cordelia breathed with relief. "Why didn't you say so?"

They had busied themselves with preparations for battle, raiding the trunk of weapons that Angel and Wesley had put together after Angel's supply had been destroyed in the explosion that took out his office and apartment. Locked and loaded, they headed for downtown and the library building, letting themselves in through the abandoned storefront Cordelia had been shown before. This time, they were able to gain access and they found their way through the warren of tunnels underneath the library.

Cordelia knew it had taken Kayley Moser a lot of courage to make that phone call. Her friends—or, at any rate, the girls she had fallen in with in the streets of L.A., and had been living with for who knew how long—were anxiously awaiting Kostov's arrival. The vampire had promised to turn them all into his kind. As far as Cordelia was concerned, the girls had no idea what they were getting into. They had flirted with some romantic notion of what vampires are like, without ever knowing the reality behind the romance. Cordelia had a better sense of what they were letting themselves in for, but she was an outsider and she knew they'd never accept her version of things.

So the backup plan was to dust Kostov when he arrived.

Wesley had been able, finally, to find a little information on Kostov in some of his literature, although it had taken some digging. The vampire had been sired just over eighty years ago, in the thick ancient forests of Hungary. Europe was then embroiled in a terrible war, the "war to end all wars," it was called, somewhat optimistically.

Kostov was a soldier then, walking a patrol in the predawn hours, tromping over frozen ground. A clearing edged with bare trees, their limbs frosted in snow, marked the boundary of his patrol.

Kostov walked the perimeter of the clearing, according to the stories that had been told, his rifle in his icy hands, and had, coming across a wide, flat stump where some woodcutter had felled an ancient, massive tree in days gone by, seen sitting on the frost-rimed stump a lovely young lady wearing little more than a gossamer veil and a smile.

He had, at first, assumed that he was hallucinating. The cold had finally caught up to him, or mustard gas inhaled in some battle had affected his brain. He walked closer, expecting her to vanish with every step.

But she didn't. In fact, she crooked her finger at him, motioning him on. As he grew nearer, she stood atop the old stump, passing her hands down her own body as if to entice him further. When he came closer still, he could smell her, sweet and flowery. No hallucination. He reached for her.

She slipped into his arms. Put her head against his shoulder, nuzzling her face against his neck.

Sank her teeth into his throat.

Kostov had returned to camp two nights later. There had been an uproar over his disappearance—no enemy troops had been sighted; the guard had simply vanished in the forest. But when he crept into the circle of snoring men and crackling fires, Kostov did not come back as a hero of battle. He came back as a vampire.

He drank deep of soldiers who had once been his friends, comrades-at-arms, and a select few he turned. By morning, the snow around the camp was spattered with scarlet. More than half of the soldiers in the camp, battle-hardened professionals one and all, were dead.

Another fifteen men followed Kostov into the night and, together with the woman who they came to know as Inge, she of the scanty veils, they had formed their own small troop. The soldiers who remained, abandoned that camp as soon as the sun came up and they found the lifeless, drained husks of their fellows, and from that point on the forest belonged to Kostov and Inge.

Now he had come to California, and had befriended a

teenage runaway named Pat. And Pat had invited him to meet her friends.

So Cordelia and Wesley waited. *Party Poopers "R" Us,* Cordelia thought.

Angel stood in a shadowed doorway, waiting.

He had located the police officers named Bo Peterson and Luis Castaneda. Peterson was a tall, beefy blond guy, young-looking, with a weightlifter's build. His head was so big his hat looked like it barely fit over his crewcut hair. Castaneda was skinny, wiry, with dark olive skin and longish black hair. They were both in uniform. During the confusion at Headquarters, Angel had, wearing his borrowed LAPD windbreaker, accessed a dispatch computer and learned where to find them.

Since he had picked them up an hour ago, Angel had stayed with the officers, watching everything they did, which wasn't much. Outside the station, it was a quiet night.

They cruised the streets of their turf in their squad car. Looking for trouble, Angel assumed, but not really going out of their way to find it. Finally, they had stopped on a dark street corner. Angel pulled his Plymouth Belvedere over and stayed in it until they got out of their car.

Then he saw why they had stopped. A tall, lanky young man had been standing nonchalantly near the corner, hands deep in the pockets of his baggy pants. He didn't look frightened when the cops approached, just greeted them with a kind of wry smile. The cops took him by the arms and escorted him into the alley. As soon as they were out of sight, Angel jumped out of his car and took refuge in the doorway nearest the alley.

Listening.

". . . been a slow night," the man was saying. "That's all I made all night."

"Ain't it a shame," one of the cops replied.

"Breaks my heart," the other one added.

"You can't—" the young man said.

"Watch us."

"Man, you got no right to—"

"You're selling dope on street corners and telling us what our rights are?" The cops laughed. "Let's have it."

Angel risked a glance into the alley. The young man was digging into his pockets, and handing a wad of cash over to Peterson and Castaneda.

So they *were* dirty.

That made sense, as far as Flores's story was concerned. So did the part about them shaking down dealers.

Probably the Russian dealer had refused to be shaken down, or tried to fight back. So they'd made an example of him, or killed him in a fight.

And then, needing a fall guy, had settled on the innocent man who'd been taking a walk nearby.

There was an additional benefit to picking on Rojelio Flores—since he had been close enough to hear the shots, they had no way of knowing what else he might have heard or seen. By making him the suspect, they guaranteed that anything he did report would be disbelieved.

Angel went back to his car.

He wanted to talk to the cops individually, not together. So he trailed along behind them until they went back to the station at the end of their shift, and then he followed Peterson back out of the station.

Peterson drove a new Chevy truck to a quiet, lower-middle-class neighborhood in the Valley. When he stopped, he parked the truck in the driveway of a small dark house. He crossed the street and went into a corner store, bought some junk food and a couple of frozen dinners. Then he crossed the street again and let himself into the small house. One light came on, then another, as he walked from room to room.

No other car in the driveway, no other lights on. Peterson was alone in there.

Only problem now was that Peterson was inside his house. Angel would have to get the cop to invite him across the threshold to get inside. That could be tricky.

Or maybe not.

He decided a guy like Peterson, a big, powerful man who was probably used to frightening others, might be susceptible to fear himself. He vamped out, picked up a flagstone from Peterson's front walkway and pitched it through the windshield of the truck. The windshield exploded with a loud crash.

A moment later, Peterson came outside with his service weapon in his meaty fist.

Angel had stepped to the side of the door. When Peterson barreled through it, Angel kicked out with one foot, catching Peterson at the knee.

The cop folded with a sharp grunt.

Angel followed up with a second kick into the downed officer's solar plexus.

Peterson doubled over in pain.

Angel put his vampirish face in front of Peterson's and waited for the cop to open his eyes. When he did, Angel could see the terror there. He didn't mind. He had no respect for Peterson anymore, knowing what he did about the man. He didn't care if Peterson knew he was a vampire. No one would listen to anything he had to say once his crimes were exposed. Angel didn't like to show this side of himself to humans, but when it was the most efficient way to do things, as it had been with Preston, he didn't hesitate.

"We need to talk," Angel said. "Out here or inside, your choice."

"Oh, God," Peterson wheezed.

"Outside or inside," Angel said again.

"What are you?"

Angel bared his fangs. "Outside or—"

"In," Peterson grunted.

They went in.

"Rojelio Flores," Angel said, standing in Peterson's messy living room. "Tell me about him."

"Killed a drug dealer." Peterson crouched on a low, brown sofa. A few minutes had passed while he caught his breath, and he was almost able to sit upright now.

He was shaking as hard as a junkie in withdrawal. He looked as if he was about to scream. But he didn't ask Angel about his face again.

"The truth," Angel said. "Unless you want to play punching bag again."

Peterson looked at him with a plaintive expression. "What do you want?" he asked. "You want me to confess to something? Go to jail? You're holding all the cards, man. I'll tell you whatever you want to hear. But it's coercion. It'll never hold up."

"I just want you to tell me the truth," Angel repeated. "There's no judge and jury in this room, just you and me."

"Okay, truth. He killed a drug dealer. We arrested him."

Angel left his seat facing the couch, headed for Peterson, balling his hands into fists as he went.

He did the vamp thing again.

Peterson burst into tears. "What! What are you? Oh, God!"

"Won't save you, pal," Angel said. "I bite you, you're dead."

"Don't. Don't, okay?" The man was sobbing. Angel felt no pity for him. None whatsover.

"Your choice."

He lowered his fangs toward Peterson's neck. He could smell the blood, feel the heartbeat. He couldn't deny his intoxication.

Cowering, Peterson held up his hands to ward Angel off. Angel pressed his advantage, giving him no space.

"Okay, okay!" Peterson shouted. "Manley popped this guy, Nokivov. Okay? He was a scumbag, you know, Russian *Mafiya,* dealing. A stone killer. Manley did the world a favor by taking him out."

He looked at Angel with tears streaming down his face. "Okay? Only, don't kill me, man! Don't freakin' kill me!"

He flared into hysterics. Angel sat down and waited for a while; when it didn't look as though Peterson was going to calm down for a while, he rummaged around until he found a half-empty bottle of Ronrico. He unscrewed the cap and handed it to the cop.

Peterson took a huge swig and wiped the back of his hand across his mouth. He took another swig and cradled the bottle against his chest.

"My A.A. sponsor's not going to be happy about this," he said sarcastically.

"Doug Manley," Angel prompted.

"Yeah, that's right." False bravado seized Peterson. Angel figured it was the booze. "Manley and this guy, Nokivov, they got into it. Manley had caught him dealing, and wanted some of the guy's action. Happens all the time."

"Easier than actually arresting him?"

"Hey, don't judge unless you're out there on the streets every day," Peterson flung at him.

"I'm out there," Angel replied quietly. "Go on."

"But the guy argued. Pulled a piece. Manley popped him."

"And didn't just call it a justifiable shoot?" Angel asked.

"Couple of problems with that," Peterson explained. He took another drink. "What was he doing inside the guy's place with no warrant, and no probable cause? And he shot him with a throw-down. I.A.D. did a ballistics check, they'd know it wasn't Manley's service piece fired the bullet. So how is Manley going to explain having a throw-down?"

"Could have said it was Nokivov's."

"Could have. But we were nervous, a little panicked. No one was supposed to get shot. Four of us inside this guy's apartment, not knowing who saw us go in or who would see us coming out, after shots were fired."

His face turned red. "Fischer looks out the window, sees this guy Flores tying his shoe outside the building, and bang! There's our fall guy."

Anger flashed in Angel, so strong and so deep he almost vamped out involuntarily. He thought of Carlos Flores and his mother, terrified for Rojelio. He thought of Rojelio, and the hell he was going through.

"Didn't matter to you that Flores was innocent, has never broken a law more serious than jaywalking."

"Everyone's got something in their past," Peterson argued. "No one's pure. Maybe he never killed anybody, but that doesn't make him Snow White."

"That's wishful," Angel said. "Except cops are supposed to believe in due process, I thought. You're out there to uphold the law, not write your own."

"So what are you going to do?" Peterson asked him. "You can't touch me." He raised his chin. He was pretty drunk by then. "Nothing I just said will stand up in court. We'll all deny it. And if you even try anything, I'll tell them about you. Being a . . . a . . . whatever you are."

"Vampire," Angel said. "And you think they'll believe that?" He regarded the dirty cop with all the contempt and hatred he could muster. "You're going down, Peterson. All four of you."

Chapter 17

Buffy was lost in the impenetrable blackness. Elfredo was somewhere behind her, clutching a gun and a flashlight, both of which she figured were useless. He had changed his mind about coming out, but had agreed to wait at the door, not to venture into the darkness. Her greatest fear was that he would shoot at something in the dark, unable to see where she was, and the bullet would strike her.

But he refused to put it away.

So she struck out on her own, away from the house and the gun.

"Where are you?" she called. "What do you want?"

There was no answer. Even to Buffy, her voice sounded muffled. She had heard once that the roar of a lion, on a clear night, could be heard for up to eight miles. But on foggy nights, sound is dampened to the point that the roar will only carry for a mile or so. Lions know when that happens, and are quieter on those nights because their efforts have so little impact.

Buffy felt as though her voice was carrying only a couple of feet. After calling out a couple of times, she gave up, feeling a little silly for even trying.

Who says all the creepies even speak English?

Only her Slayer senses allowed her to hear it coming before it slammed into her, and even they, muffled like every other sense by the black fog, didn't give her time to dodge.

It hit her like an express train. Buffy staggered back under the impact, but had the presence of mind to grab onto it as she fell. It continued on its path, toward the house, she believed—maybe heading for another window. She hung on.

The force of its momentum snatched her off her feet.

It felt as if she was holding onto a limb of some kind, an arm or a leg. Thickly corded with what seemed to be muscle, the thing tried to shake her off as it sped toward its destination. But she kept her grip, and even though her feet had lost contact with the ground, she climbed the thing, hand over hand, finally reaching something that felt more like a torso.

Buffy could see nothing, just the blackness. And what she felt was totally alien—*skin,* she thought, *not fabric,* but like no skin she had ever touched. It was like leather that had soaked in motor oil overnight—slick and scaly and tough, all at once.

She clawed her way across the thing, finally finding an opening of some kind. Hot breath blasted her hand, so she assumed it was a nose or a mouth. Not knowing if it had teeth or a tongue, she risked it and grabbed for the source of the breath.

Her fingers closed on the side of the opening—like a great maw of some kind. She pulled with everything she could, and heard a sound like flesh tearing. Then the thing made its first noise, a high-pitched keening that sounded like it came from everywhere at once. Buffy held on, kept tearing.

The thing stopped and batted at Buffy with several hard, knotlike objects. They could have been fists, but they might as easily have been balls on the ends of stalks. Since she couldn't see, it didn't really matter. All that mattered was that the pummeling hurt.

Going to have to put this thing down fast, before it kills me, Buffy thought. *Might be easier if I could see it, though.*

Since she couldn't, could only vaguely sense its whereabouts and dimensions, she made sure to keep at least one hand on it at all times. If she let go for a moment, it could be lost in the darkness again. She had hurt the thing, and she wanted to press that advantage. Doing her best to ignore the rain of blows, she clung to one writhing arm or tentacle and worked her way up it again. When she had relocated what passed for the torso she drove her fist into it hard, several times, then followed with four solid kicks.

The thing seemed to feel those. Its attack faltered. Buffy redoubled her own. She jerked forward on the arm she held, tucked it under her own arm against her ribs, and dropped backward, into a roll. She kicked her feet out before her as she went onto her back and felt the thing passing over her. As she came up out of her roll she hurled it, hard, against the ground. It hit with a muffled thump and another wail of pain.

She turned to face it again, still holding the one arm, and she threw herself on top of it. This time, she found something that felt enough like a head and neck to take a chance on. Letting go of the arm, Buffy grabbed the neck and twisted.

The thing went limp in her arms.

Buffy stood, panting, hands on her knees, trying to catch her breath.

And the next one hit her.

Detective Kate Lockley looked up from her desk at the precinct, and he was just standing there casually, as if waiting for a bus.

"Something I can do for you?" she asked, icily.

Angel held his hands up in a placatory fashion. "I need you to listen to me for a minute."

Kate gathered some files, sliding them into her brief-case to take home. Her back was rigid. "Give me one good reason," she said. She scooted her chair back to stand up.

"I've got four," Angel told her. He knew she wouldn't take this well. She hated crooked cops—and just to make it worse, her dad had been one. She had once liked Angel, but not anymore, not since learning that he was a vampire, and that he had been involved, however peripherally, in the events that had led to her father's death. "Their names are Peterson, Manley, Castaneda, and Fischer. They're cops. They're dirty."

She winced as if in pain. "And you can prove it?"

"I will be able to, soon."

"Come back when you can," she instructed him.

"Kate, one of them confessed to me. I'm not making this up. You've got to believe me."

"They out of my division?" Kate asked.

"No, 77th Street Headquarters."

"Not my problem then," Kate said, rising. An iceberg.

Angel blocked her path.

"I don't know anyone over there," Angel said. "And anyway, they're a little busy tonight with problems in the jail, as I'm sure you've heard. But they are LAPD, and they're corrupt. They've framed an innocent man for a murder they committed."

Kate listened. She was no fan of Angel these days, but she hated police corruption even more.

"I don't have any way of knowing how many more dirty cops there are in that division," Angel said. "I don't know who to talk to. So I came to the one police officer I know who is unquestionably honest."

She held the files against her chest, aware that she was using them like a shield. "Most of us are, you know."

"I'm sure of that. But I don't know which ones aren't, and it wouldn't do much good to report a corrupt cop to an equally corrupt one."

Kate sat down again, pulled out a notepad. "I'm not saying I believe you," she said with a deep sigh. "But give me those names again."

"But what if Buffy's right?" Willow was asking.

"She almost certainly is," Doña Pilar replied. She stirred the ingredients in a huge cast-iron pot that sat bubbling on the ancient stove. A wretched smell filled the room. Willow wondered how many air quality laws were being broken in this small kitchen. "But we cannot allow that to make us stop trying."

Buffy had suggested that Willow and Doña Pilar stop using magick, in case Doña Pilar's theory that magick was what had drawn the supernatural attacker to the house in the first place was correct. That made sense to Willow, but Doña Pilar had insisted on going ahead and trying to counter the attack with magic of her own. So they had fashioned a compromise—Buffy would try it her way, but if the cause looked hopeless, Willow and Doña Pilar would join the fight.

For the past twenty minutes she had been adding ingredients to her mystical stew and chanting over it. She told Willow what she was putting in, when she wasn't chanting, but hadn't explained exactly what goal she was working toward or what the chant meant. It didn't sound like Spanish, so Willow thought it might have been the language of the Indians who had been in Doña Pilar's part of Mexico before the Spaniards came.

"The time has come. Buffy needs us. Get ready to cover your eyes, child," Doña Pilar warned.

"Cover my eyes?" Willow echoed. She brought her hands to her face, but couldn't imagine what the old woman was talking about.

"Now," Doña Pilar commanded.

Just as she closed her eyes, Willow saw the inside of the pot begin to glow with an impossibly bright light. It was as if the sun had been captured inside Doña Pilar's cookpot.

Willow shut her eyes tight and held her hands over them. But the backs of her hands, her mouth and chin, and the rest of her that faced the pot felt the warmth of the tiny sun.

It seemed to rise up out of the cookpot and float in the air. Willow could feel the center of its heat move across her as it drifted about the room. It made no sound, but she could hear Doña Pilar pad across the kitchen to the single window. She threw open the window and shouted, "Go!"

When the heat dissipated Willow opened her eyes. A small, homemade sun was whisking out through the window into the pitch black beyond, illuminating the world as it went.

When Angel stepped out of the police station onto the street, they were waiting for him. Two cars, both American, dark and nondescript. Four men in each car. All armed.

Angel heard the engines growl as soon as he reached the sidewalk. By the time he got to the corner, where he had parked his own car, they were roaring down the street toward him. He looked up. Windows slid open and guns bristled from the windows. Angel looked about for cover but there wasn't any—his own car was still twenty feet away, and there were no cars parked immediately in front of the police building.

He hit the ground as the guns spat fire.

A dozen slugs tore into him. Sharp bolts of pain racked his body. He stayed on the ground.

The cars raced away into the night.

A handful of police officers scrambled out of the building, Kate Lockley among them. Some ran to squad cars to give chase. Kate and the others rushed over to Angel.

He stood up, squinting against the pain, dusting off his clothes as he did. Blood flecked his shirt.

"Lousy shots," he said with a wry grin.

"Lucky for you," Kate offered, not looking too worried. Or surprised.

"Really lucky," one of the other cops said. "Didn't hit any lethal zones?"

"Couple of them grazed me," Angel said. "Ruined this shirt. But no direct hits. I'm okay."

"Need an ambulance?" the cop pressed.

"I'll drive him to the hospital," Kate said, waving the officer away. She knew full well that he wouldn't need one, but it worked, and the other cops left them alone. She led Angel toward her car. "Did you see their guns?"

"Didn't really get a good look at them," he answered.

"I did," she continued. "A couple of them were what you'd expect to see. Mac-10s. A Glock 19. But two of them were using Kalashnikovs. Not AK-47s," she said, naming a fairly common assault rifle. "AK-74Ms."

Angel was surprised. "Nobody in L.A. fires 74Ms."

She gave him a look. "Nobody except the Russians."

Buffy fought against the newcomer, but she was still winded from defeating the first one. This thing seemed to be constructed in much the same way, at least as far as she could tell with her Slayer senses. She had no way of knowing what had become of the first one—it was lost somewhere in the dark.

But this seemed to be multilimbed like the other, and its breath, when she got close to it, was just as hot and fetid as the first.

She pounded on it, and took a pounding from it. Every now and then she tore a cry of pain from it, and each one spurred her on again. She kicked it hard, three times, then followed with two shots from her right fist, moving in close for an elbow slam.

The thing screamed, a chilling, mind-bending sound like the combined wail of everyone who had ever died.

Buffy shook her head. The sound was deafening. She had to back away from it, putting her hands over her ears, even if that meant she might lose it.

Anyway, as long as it was screaming, it wasn't fighting.

She watched it scream for a long moment, its wide mouth open in an uneven oval shape, before she realized that she could actually *see* it. Subconsciously she knew she had been able to see it before, that she wouldn't really have let go if there had been a chance that it could slip away from her. But it wasn't until now that she was aware that there was some light penetrating the darkness.

Willow and Doña Pilar, she thought. *Good for you.*

She looked up.

Coming from a window of the house—she could see the house!—was the sun. Or something that looked like the sun does, on those heavily overcast days when the sun resembles a pale white bowling ball in a nickel-gray sky.

But this small white orb glowed with the brightness of the sun on the clearest day, and as it moved steadily into the black it seemed to burn the darkness away. The black world grew steadily more gray. The miniature sun hissed like a ruptured steam pipe as it plowed through the artificial night.

Buffy looked back toward the creature, but it was gone, vanishing before her eyes as if the light made it fade away.

Another moment passed and the little sun was gone. Buffy could see a dark night sky overhead once again, with stars twinkling in their proper spots. A gibbous moon hung in one corner. Familiar shapes had returned.

The night had been restored around the de la Natividad house. With it, the things that had attacked the house were gone.

Buffy went back inside. Elfredo joined her, holstering his gun. He was scraped and bloody, his clothes torn, as if he'd been fighting something on his own.

"You okay?" she asked him, concern in her voice.

"It didn't really get me," he assured her. "I don't think. I was sideswiped by something and slammed into the sidewalk, that's all. When I got up again I couldn't find the house. Until the lights came on."

He shut the door solidly behind them. When she looked back, he had a smile on his face.

"The Russian *Mafiya* is one of the deadliest criminal organizations in the world," Kate explained to Angel. Once the other officers had retreated, they had gone back inside the building, and were seated at her desk. Seeing the attack on Angel seemed to have made her more receptive to his story. He had told her the whole tale of Rojelio Flores, as it had been told to him. The coffee she had poured herself, sitting in a mug at her elbow, had no doubt grown ice cold.

"It's largely composed of people who had been criminals in the old Soviet Union, before the collapse, joined by people who had been KGB agents. Well trained and well armed."

Angel knew a little about the KGB. It had been the Soviet secret police—in U.S. terms, a combination of the FBI, CIA, and Secret Service, all rolled up into one deadly agency. Espionage in other countries and surveillance of their own people within their borders—within their own homes, in some cases—fell under the KGB's scope.

"And after the collapse?" he asked.

She shrugged, as if the answer were obvious. "Suddenly no one was paying them to spy anymore. They decided private enterprise was the way to go, private enterprise meaning crime, corruption, extortion, murder. Anything for a buck. Or should I say, ruble?" She tested her coffee, made a face, and set it down.

"If they're here, then I think 'buck' applies," Angel said.

"Oh, they're here, all right," she said firmly. She opened a drawer in her metal desk and rummaged around for something, locating a tin of Altoids, which she held out to Angel. He took one, and then she popped one herself. "They terrorized Russia, but it didn't take long for them to realize that there was a lot more money to be made in the States than there was over there.

"Not that a lot of them weren't already here. We've had gangs of every possible race and nationality working here forever—Armenians, Russians, Colombians, Irish, Sicilians, and on and on."

"One big melting pot," Angel observed, mildly regretful that he couldn't taste the effervescent flavor of the Altoid. His sense of taste was quite specific—he could distinguish different types of blood with the finesse of a wine taster. Everything else was cardboard to him.

Kate continued. "But, as bad as they were before the Soviet fall, they became that much worse afterward. Before, there was always the threat of deporting them. After, with their ranks swollen by KGB killers, Soviet Army soldiers out of work, and so on, they graduated from being one of the most violent criminal organizations in the country to the most violent, bar none."

"Their revenge for losing the Cold War?"

She thought about that. "I don't think politics has much to do with it. The Russian economy is in a shambles, and part of the reason is that there is so much crime and corruption over there, very little of the budget is actually spent on whatever it's supposed to be spent on.

"The Russian *Mafiya* here—and I'm using that as a general term, there are hundreds of criminal gangs in Russia, and many over here—is out of the politics game." She lifted her coffee cup from her desktop and took a sip. "They're playing the capitalist system for all it's worth, lining their own pockets at the expense of private citizens, government, insurance companies, everyone."

"By dealing drugs?" Angel asked.

Kate stretched, looking a bit overwhelmed by all the bad in the world. "Oh, yes. And they rob banks, they commit various kinds of fraud, they're into gambling. They've already pulled off jobs worth more than a billion dollars. They're not here to raise their families under a peaceful democracy. Most of them don't even have families. They're here to steal."

Angel said, "Flores said the guy he was alleged to have killed, Nokivov, was a drug dealer."

"Flores is right," Kate told him. "I ran Nokivov's name through the system. He's got one conviction and he's on parole. *Was* on parole, I should say. Guess he won't be checking in with his parole officer anytime soon."

They shared a grim smile. Angel was sorry things hadn't worked out between them. Well, not so much worked out, as worked at all. There were a lot of things he liked about her—her drive, her determination, her honesty, her courage. But she pretty much detested the sight of him these days. He avoided looking at the picture of her father on her desk.

"So he was a member of the *Mafiya?*" Angel asked her.

"Of one of the Russian gangs, anyway." She set down the printout and leaned back in her chair.

"I shook down one of the crooked cops who killed him, and less than an hour later, two cars full of people tried to kill me with Russian guns." He gazed at her. "What does that tell you?"

"I wish it was a terrible coincidence." She looked ill. "Obviously, Peterson, at least, is involved with the Russians."

"That's what I'm thinking," Angel said. "He called in a favor after I left him. And someone in this building called to tell him I was here. Didn't take long for them to spread the word."

"Which means there's at least one crooked cop in my division," Kate said, venom dripping in her voice.

"Which also means that maybe they weren't worried about being arrested, like he told me," Angel finished. "Maybe they were worried about their *Mafiya* pals finding out who killed Nokivov, so they set Flores up to take their fall."

"It's a possibility," Kate agreed. "There's been some major turf battles lately over the drug business, between the Russian gangs and some of the Mexican and Colombian ones. Maybe they figured by fingering a Hispanic, a Mexican gang would end up taking the rap."

"L.A. You gotta love it."

Her mind was working, going through all the events and examining them from various angles. "Too bad Peterson's confession to you wouldn't stand in court. I'll make sure we stick to all four of these guys like glue. One bad move and we'll take them down."

"Good."

She took a deep breath. "And we'll find out who in this division is with them. In the meantime, watch your step, Angel. You've got some very bad men mad at you."

"It's happened before," Angel said with a wry smile. "But thanks for the concern."

"What concern?" Kate asked. Her face was expressionless. "I just don't want to have to explain you if you end up dead."

"If I end up dead, I'll vanish in a cloud of dust, Kate," Angel reminded her. "No muss, no fuss."

Kate smiled. "That's right. I feel much better now."

"Thought you would."

"You make sure the Flores family is okay," she suggested, pushing back her chair.

"I tucked them away someplace where anonymity is the main drawing card," Angel said. "No one knows where they are. But we need to get Rojelio out of jail. That's probably the worst place for him to be if organized crime is after him—if they think he's got someone believing his story, he'll be a target twenty-four hours a day."

"I'll try to get his charges dropped as soon as possible, and spring him so he can go home. In the meantime, I'll be trying to tie those four losers to their *Mafiya* friends. The last thing this department needs is another scandal."

She rose.

Meeting adjourned.

Without another word, Angel left her office.

Chapter 18

TWICE DURING THE NIGHT, SOME OF THE GIRLS HAD passed by their hiding places. Cordelia and Wesley had pushed themselves back, deeper into the shadows, and held still until the girls were out of sight again, slipping outside to scrounge food maybe, or just to see the stars, and then coming back in again. They couldn't chance being spotted or the whole plan would be blown. She'd have felt a lot better if Angel weren't cell phone-deficient.

Cordelia's legs were cramping now from staying too still. The corridor was quiet so she allowed herself to step from her hiding place, walked a few paces in one direction and then the other, shook her legs out. She set her stakes on the ground and massaged her thighs and calves with both hands. *Sitting still,* she thought, *takes much more effort than one would think.*

Then there was a sound, from the direction of the empty storefront that served as an entrance to the street. Footsteps, coming down the old wooden stairs inside the old store. Cordelia snatched up her stakes and shot back into the shadows.

"Let me take the first shot with my crossbow," Wesley suggested in a tense whisper. "Perhaps we won't even need to get close to him."

Cordelia nodded, even though she knew he couldn't see her. The footfalls came closer, and she was afraid to speak. The pounding of her own heart sounded deafeningly loud in her ears, and she feared Kostov would hear that, or smell the blood that it pumped through her body.

She tightened her grip on the wooden stakes and made sure the large cross was plainly visible on her chest.

At the end of the hall, the heavy door scraped open.

Cordelia had been in the darkness of the hallway long enough for her eyes to adjust to the faintest illumination inside. She could barely see, filling the doorway, the large form of a man. Or what had once been a man. This had to be Kostov, coming to take what had been offered to him.

But as he came into the hallway, the door stayed open. More came in. Kostov hadn't come alone. There must have been seven or eight of them—in the darkness, Cordelia couldn't distinguish how many, but the footfalls, she realized, were multiple, and the men spoke in soft voices, laughing quietly among themselves.

This, she and Wesley had not counted on.

They had anticipated taking out one vampire, who was expecting only to be welcomed with open arms. Dusting a whole troop of them was something else entirely. Her confidence, which had been mostly foolish bravado in the first place, plunged.

But Wesley was across the hall from her. They couldn't talk about a change in strategy without being heard.

Anyway, it was a little late for that.

The vampires came closer.

Across the hall, Cordelia heard, rather than saw, Wesley take in a sharp breath and then step out from his hiding place. The vampires stopped suddenly, and one started to speak. But Wesley's voice hushed them.

"Kostov," Wesley said bravely. "Stop where you are."

"Somebody kill this fool," a vampire snarled. This was presumably Kostov. Addressing him by name had probably been a good idea on Wesley's part—if these guys had been termite inspectors or something, then driving wooden stakes into their hearts would have been a truly horrible idea.

But the counter suggestion, of killing Wesley, made it more or less clear that whoever these shadowy figures were, they weren't the good guys.

Cordelia heard the *thwip* of Wesley's crossbow and the whistle of its bolt as it darted through the air. A vampire screamed, and even in the near dark Cordelia could see and hear the cloud of exploding dust. Direct hit.

"You go, Wesley," she said.

Then she remembered that they had been unaware of her presence, until then.

Oops.

She came out of hiding, stakes in both fists. Ready to face whatever was ahead of her.

And behind her, a female voice called out.

"What's going on?" someone shouted. "Kostov? Who's that?"

It was Pat, coming up the hallway from the other direction. There were more voices from behind her, the other girls, suddenly all talking and yelling.

Crossfire.

Cordelia and Wesley caught in the middle.

This is so unfair, Cordelia thought, as the vampires moved down the corridor toward them. She glanced back.

The girls were coming, too. A couple carried flashlights or lanterns, and in the flickering light Cordelia could see faces set in angry scowls. She thought of one of those mobs of villagers, from the monster movies, storming the castle with flaming torches.

Except in this case, the mob was on the monster's side.

"We only wanted to help," Cordelia said quickly.

Wesley's head swiveled like a spectator at a tennis match. The vamps, the girls, the vamps.

Both closed in. But the vamps were scarier. In the shifting light from the flashlights, Cordelia could see their demonic aspects, long fangs and furled brows and eyes that glinted with malice. No matter how long she knew Angel, she was convinced that she would never get over her innate horror of vampires.

And in front of the pack, one who could only be Kostov. He was taller than the rest, with broad shoulders and a rich mane of silver hair. He seemed nearly to fill the wide hallway with his presence. His jaw was set, mouth a thin line in a handsome face.

Cordelia could see how Pat might have been taken in by him—he looked like the kind of man who, if he smiled, might be taken for a worldly professor, maybe. The type undergraduate coeds get crushes on.

But now, he was all malevolent evil and spookiness, and he strode toward Cordelia, his dark clothes rustling in the shadow. She raised a stake before her in one trembling hand.

He smiled, but there was nothing friendly in that smile. It was all long teeth and hunger.

He stopped, inches from the stake's point.

"Take your shot," he said. His voice still carried the accent of the Eastern European forests of his birth.

Cordelia drove the stake forward with all her might.

But Kostov turned at the last moment. Instead of penetrating his heart, the stake rammed into his arm. He grunted with pain, then drew his arm back, raising it high and yanking the stake out with his other hand. He hurled it down the hallway.

"Not good enough," he said. "I take it you're an amateur at this business."

"I'm not a Slayer, if that's what you mean," Cordelia said.

"But I am a Watcher," Wesley added. He fired another bolt from his crossbow. The wooden shaft thudded into Kostov's chest, but too high to penetrate his heart. Again, he tugged it from his flesh and tossed it aside.

One of Kostov's comrades caught Wesley by the throat and slammed him into the far wall. Wesley's feet dangled off the floor. The vampire holding him opened his mouth, baring fangs, and leaned in toward Wesley's exposed throat.

"Never had me a Watcher," the vampire snarled. "Always wondered if they tasted any different than regular folks."

This one's accent sounds Southern, Cordelia thought. So these weren't Kostov's old soldiers, but another assortment he'd put together here in the States. She found it interesting in a kind of abstract sense, but there was nothing there that would help defuse the immediate situation—which was, she realized, pretty much all bad.

Kostov turned back toward her, the distraction of Wesley seemingly forgotten already. "As I said, amateurs," Kostov hissed. "Still, you'll do for a quick snack."

Cordelia waved her second stake. With her other hand, she held up the cross that hung around her neck. "Hey, I'm nobody's Happy Meal," she warned.

Kostov raised a silvery eyebrow at the stake. "But you come with a toy," he replied. "Which you've already shown an inability to use."

"Just give me one more chance," Cordelia said defiantly, "and I'll show you what I can do with it."

Kostov shook his leonine head. "You've had as many chances as you're going to get, young lady."

He lunged at her. She thrust out the stake but he swatted it away like it was nothing, and one of his hands clamped down on her forearm. His grip was steel. He pulled her toward him, his mouth opening, fangs glistening in the faint illumination, breath hot and rancid. She struggled against him, fear silencing her voice. She could see Wesley, over Kostov's shoulder, trying to fight the one who had him pinned against a wall.

"Take her!" someone called from behind Cordelia. She thought it sounded like Jean, or maybe Holly. One of the girls she had come here to help, at any rate.

So much for the Good Samaritan bit. A different Bible story came to mind, involving Judas.

And then, from the far end of the corridor—the direction from which Kostov and company had arrived—there came the clatter of many feet on the steps. The door flew open and voices sounded. Cordelia tried to see past Kostov, to make out who was coming in now, but the vampire was too wide.

She couldn't see, but she heard the thunder of weapons. Behind Kostov, two vamps burst into clouds of dust.

"Who . . . ?" Kostov demanded. He whirled, releasing Cordelia. She looked over his shoulder. Coming toward them, bearing a gun that fired wooden stakes fed into it on a jerry-rigged ammo belt, was a young black man who wore a dark rag on his head, a plaid shirt, and jeans. He walked with a swagger, and a smile split his handsome face.

"'Sup, vamp?" he asked casually.

Behind him there were several others. They looked like

street people, runaways, gangsters. One carried a cross-bow, one a long pike, another a length of chain with a spiked ball dangling menacingly from one end.

Wesley shook his head, blinked his eyes. One of the vampires who had been dusted was the one who had been holding Wesley up and preparing to chomp on his skinny Watcher's neck, Cordelia realized.

A low growl built in Kostov's throat. He advanced on the young crew. But the teens stood their ground, even when Kostov's comrades turned on them as well.

"Kostov!" Pat called. "We invited you here. These other people are all intruders. Don't forget, we asked you to come here. The rest of you, just get gone!"

Fury rising in her, Cordelia turned to Pat, whisking another stake from her bag. "Listen, girlie," she said, holding the stake at Pat's throat. A drop of blood appeared where the sharpened point dug into Pat's skin. "You're not a vampire but that doesn't mean this won't hurt! You and your pals stay back and let the *professionals* handle this."

Pat's eyes began to glitter with tears. "But we wanted him to come here. We *invited* him."

"You keep saying that like it means something to anyone but you," Cordelia responded. Behind Pat, the other girls stood watching the scene, fear etched on their young faces. Amanda, Jean, Holly, Nicole, and Kayley were breathing fast, openmouthed, eyes wide.

Only Keri and Erin watched calmly, as if this was just one more event in their lives, no more noteworthy than anything else they'd ever seen.

"News flash," Cordelia continued. "It doesn't mean anything. I'm pretty sure I know who those people are down there, and your vampire friends don't stand a chance against them. Now I want you to make sure that your wannabes keep out of the way."

"I don't care what you say," Pat said. "Kostov can take them."

"Kostov doesn't have a prayer," Cordelia countered.

"Got that right," the black man said. "Be vamp dust every which way in a minute." Cordelia glanced his way. He was raising his stake gun again. Arrayed around him, his crew was braced for assault.

Kostov's guttural growl transformed into words, spoken from a throat that barely seemed human. "Tonight we feast, brothers," he announced. He threw himself toward the youths. His fellows came right behind. Stakes and crossbow bolts flew. Two more vampires went up in clouds.

One of the vampires caught a pike that was thrust toward him and yanked its wielder off his feet. The vamp grabbed the kid's head between his hands and began to twist, as if unscrewing the lid from a jar.

The one with the chain swung it, its spiked ball slamming into the head of the vamp. The head disintegrated in a spray of blood and brain and the vamp followed suit, decapitation dusting a vampire as efficiently as staking.

"Yo, thanks," the pike wielder tossed off.

"No prob, dog," chain guy replied.

After another moment, only Kostov remained. He faced the armed youths, defiant to the end. "Out of my way, striplings," he demanded.

"This where I tell you to make me?" the one who was obviously their leader said. "Sounds a little third grade, but hey, I ain't proud."

"Say whatever you like," Kostov replied. "But stand aside or prepare to die."

"Been preparin' for that my whole life. Ain't happened yet. Don't seem likely to happen this time either. Or ain't you noticed you got enough wood aimed at your heart to reforest Africa?"

"If I go," Kostov threatened, "you go with me."

"Uh-uh," the black man said. "You go alone. I got work to do here." He nodded his head toward Kostov. "Dust him."

They all fired at once. Crossbows, the stake gun, single stakes hurled like throwing knives. Cordelia heard the *thunk! thunk!* as the stakes impaled Kostov, but then the sounds were obscured by his wail of pain. A moment later, he was gone.

Pat was sobbing. Cordelia released her. "I know you don't think I'm right," she said gently. "But someday, you'll be glad."

Pat glared at her through tears and didn't reply. Cordelia turned away from her toward the newcomers who had saved them.

"How did you—?" she began.

"Chain there been noticing some suspicious late-night comings and goings around here," the group's obvious leader replied. He pointed toward the man who carried the heavy chain. "Figured maybe it was a nest, so we been keeping an eye on it. Lo and behold, you dogs show up with stakes and weapons, we figure something's about to go down."

"Very perceptive," Wesley said. "Of course, you might have joined us then, and saved us some worry."

"Didn't want to blow our cover," the man said. "Or the vamps might not have shown up at all."

"So, keeping us safe wasn't your main priority?" Cordelia asked.

"Killin' bloodsuckers is our only priority. Keepin' you safe just a fringe benefit."

"And one that we can certainly agree is worthwhile," Wesley said. He was about to say more when he was interrupted by a piercing scream from the girls, still behind them in the corridor.

"Did we miss one?" Cordelia asked. She spun around.

Amanda was crying and sweeping her flashlight about the hallway. "Kayley," she said between sobs. "She was . . . right here, right in front of me. I had my hand on her shoulder. And then she was . . . gone!"

"What do you mean, gone?" Wesley asked. "She ran away?"

"No, she didn't *go* anywhere." Amanda sniffled. "She was there, and then . . . and then she wasn't. My hand just fell. Like she had never been there."

The other girls began to search the hallway with their own lights, calling Kayley's name. But after a few minutes, it became obvious that the search was pointless.

Kayley Moser had vanished.

Chapter 19

ON THE WAY BACK INTO THE LIVING ROOM, ELFREDO clapped her on the back and gave her a high five. He was still grinning broadly.

"You kicked its butt!" he chortled. *"Oye, mama, eres fuerte!"*

Buffy laughed, flushed with victory. "I'm not sure it was its butt I kicked, and there was more than one, but the good news is that we can kick them. They are kickworthy."

"Yes." Elfredo was obviously very pleased.

With the cessation of hostilities, the rest of the household began assembling. Salma's parents appeared, along with some servants. After a time, Doña Pilar and Willow emerged from the kitchen, beaming smiles.

"Will!" Buffy said, hugging her best friend. "Did you two create that fireball thingie?"

"Yup." Willow raised her chin proudly. "I am pleased to announce that the experiment was a success."

"Now, *mi'jo*," Salma's grandmother said to Salma's father, "I know you don't approve, but—"

The silver-haired man embraced his mother. "In this case, Mama, of course I approve. It's just that in the case of Nicolas and Salma, I—"

"Where is Salma?" Salma's mother said. *"Dios mio,* they took Salma!"

"Calma, calma," her father urged.

He spoke in rapid Spanish to Elfredo, who answered likewise and took off.

"They're searching the house," Doña Pilar explained to the *gringas*. Her eyes were shiny with tears. She grasped the crucifix around her neck and murmured a prayer, then crossed herself fervently.

On an ornately carved wooden coffee table, a portable phone rang in its base. Everyone stared at it for a beat. Then Señora de la Natividad picked it up and said in English, "Hello?"

She listened for a moment, her face a dawning mixture of relief and disappointment. "Buffy, for you," she said, holding it out. She began to cry. Doña Pilar and Señor de la Natividad went to her and put their arms around her.

"It's me. Tara," Tara said. "Um, is Willow there?"

Buffy was amused. Was Tara actually too shy to call her own sweetie? "Yes. Hold on."

"Wait! Wait!" Tara blurted. "I have some things to tell you. First of all, Nicky de la Natividad is definitely mixed up with the local gang here. The Latin Cobras."

"Oh." Buffy was sorry to hear that, although at this point it didn't come as a surprise. She was glad to have confirmation because it would give her a direction to go in. But for the family's sake, she was saddened.

"Also? He set the DeSola oil field on fire. For his initiation into the gang. It's all burned up."

"That's some prank. Makes UC Sunnydale fraternity hazing look like kid stuff."

Buffy was aware that the room had gone silent. Everyone was watching her, listening to her, straining for some message about Salma. She shook her head to keep them from anticipating good news.

"It should have been a suicide mission," Tara continued, "but he survived. There wasn't a scratch or a burn on him. The Cobras are taking him to Los Angeles to meet up with the gang they're connected to, to explain how to do it. We think there's some big gang war brewing, Buffy."

"Okay."

"Riley's heading your way to see what he can do about Nicky, since you guys are busy with Salma."

Maybe, Buffy thought. She could hear the bodyguards searching the house. Occasionally they called to one another in Spanish. Buffy didn't speak much Spanish, but it sounded pretty much like, "We are in big trouble."

"When did he leave?"

"Just a few minutes ago. He asked me to call you right away. He didn't want to lose a second."

"Of course," Buffy said, touched that Tara felt the need to explain why Riley hadn't called himself. "Would you like to speak to Willow?"

"Oh, um, y-yes," Tara said.

Willow smiled, realizing at once who it was. She took the phone and said softly, "Hi."

Buffy turned to Salma's parents. But they'd both dismissed the phone call as unimportant, clearly concentrating their attention on the disappearance of their daughter.

Maybe I won't have kids after all, Buffy thought. She had a quick mental image of some little girl begging to spend the night at Aunt Willow and Aunt Tara's, to play with Miss Kitty Fantastico and do witchy stuff.

Elfredo returned to the room and spoke quietly to Salma's parents. Salma's mother broke down weeping, and her husband escorted her from the room.

Willow had hung up the phone. She took Buffy by the arm and led her over to Doña Pilar. In a low voice, she said, "We need to talk. In the kitchen."

"Bien," said the elderly lady.

As unobtrusively as possible, Doña Pilar led the way. Their bubbling pots of toil-and-trouble were scattered everywhere, and a thick spicy odor pervaded the room. Buffy sneezed.

"See?" Willow said. "I *told* you you were allergic to mugwort."

"What do you have to tell me?" Doña Pilar asked Willow. "Please, tell me quickly. Then let's set to work on a finder's spell for Salma."

Willow glanced at Buffy almost guiltily. Buffy totally understood; it wasn't fun to lay more problems on the shoulders of any of the de la Natividads. But while it might make sense to keep Salma's parents in the dark—so to speak—her *bruja* grandma needed to know what was going on.

"Your grandson is involved in a gang," Willow said, not pulling any punches. "A bad one. And he set an oil field on fire tonight. No one expected him to live through the explosion, but he survived without a scratch."

The woman stared straight at Willow for perhaps a full minute. Then Buffy realized she was swaying. She grabbed a wooden kitchen chair and set it behind Doña Pilar, who sank into it gratefully.

"Ay, Nicolas," she keened. The tears came hard. As she sat and cried, she looked somehow younger, like a little girl instead of the ancient woman she was. Her grief washed away the years.

Buffy traded glances with Willow and they waited respectfully. But Buffy's blood was pumping; she hadn't really come down from the battle yet. She was thinking, *C'mon, let's go!* But she wasn't sure where.

"The things that are missing," Doña Pilar said slowly. She sighed heavily, pulling herself together. As her cheeks dried, the age came back to them, the lines seemed to multiply, and deepen. "My grandson has performed a ritual of some sort. From what you are telling me, I believe it to be an ancient Aztec ceremony called the Night of the Long Knives. In it, a warrior invokes the darkest of powers and is bound to serve them."

Buffy groaned. "And now they're loose in Sunnydale," she said, jumping ahead.

The *bruja* shook her head. "If that is where he performed the ritual . . ."

"It is," Buffy assured her.

"Then perhaps that is why they have come there . . . I have never performed such a ceremony, and I'm not precisely clear on all its facets. But the evil inside one is thrown off, and the dark magick one uses in conjuring increases its powers many, many times over."

"And it breaks the windows of your parents' house and kidnaps your sister," Buffy said.

Doña Pilar covered her face. "I don't know. I don't think so, but it might. Or this might be something different. There is much loose in the world tonight, I fear. Not all of it can be laid at the feet of my grandson. Ay, Nicky. *Mi amorcito. Y Salma, mi angelita.*"

Willow put her hands on the woman's shoulders. "We'll get right to work," she said, wearing her resolve face. "This very minute."

"*Sí, sí,*" said Doña Pilar. "Not a moment to lose."

She rose. "Willow, we'll need those herbs in the green jar, eh?"

"What can I do?" Buffy asked, looking around. She picked up a pot crusty with something brown. "I'll just wash these dishes."

"No!" Willow and Doña Pilar both shouted at the same time.

"Buffy." Willow came over to her and gently took the pot away from her. "Maybe it would be better if you found something else to do."

"Okay." She frowned. "Like what?"

"Um . . ." Willow thought for a moment. "Footprints. Outside," she suggested. "A ransom note. You know, stuff like that."

Buffy shrugged. She had an idea of her own. "All right."

Both witches smiled briefly at her as she left the kitchen. She hurried upstairs to her room, snatched the phone off the nightstand. *Please,* she thought, *please have your phone on.* She dialed the number. It rang. After a moment, he answered.

"Yeah."

"Is that how you always answer your phone, Angel?" she asked. "Not very professional."

"Buffy?" She could hear the surprise in his voice. It had been a while since they'd talked. "What . . . where are you?"

"I'm here," she said. "L.A. Up in Laurel Canyon."

He seemed to hesitate. "Work or play?" he asked.

"Most definitely work," she said quickly. "You know me. All work and no play makes Buff a dull girl."

"Right." Noncommittal.

"You sound like you're driving," she said with forced cheerfulness. "Are you driving?"

"I'm driving. Heading over to Cordelia's."

"Oh?" she asked, immediately aiming a mental kick at herself for the way it sounded.

"My place sort of . . . blew up," he said. "I'll tell you all about it later."

"Okay. So anyway," she went on, "there's this situation I thought you should know about."

"What kind of situation?" he asked, with evident interest.

"A couple of them, actually. I came here to bodyguard a girl, a friend of Willow's who seemed to be in danger from some kind of shadow monster. I think that's still in Sunnydale, although a different type of creature attacked the house here, and it also seemed to have something to do with shadows, or darkness, or invisibility."

"But you beat it." He didn't sound surprised. The fact that he understood how strong she really was had always pleased Buffy.

"I beat it. Only then, the girl disappeared. Her brother has already disappeared, so maybe it runs in the family."

"Disappeared like, ran away?"

"I don't know exactly," she replied. "Just gone. I have a lead on the brother—he's mixed up with a Sunnydale gang called the Latin Cobras. And they're all buds with a local gang called the Echo Park Band. So I figure I'll find me some Echo Park boys and turn them upside down, see if Nicky's name falls out. Sounds like what you'd do, right?"

"Sounds just like what I'd do," Angel said. "You're not doing this alone, are you?"

"The family I'm staying with has assigned me a bodyguard," she assured him. "Bodyguard for the bodyguard. He's very good at what he does. I'm sure we'll be fine."

"That's good," Angel said.

"You, uh, want to play? Thought it might be your idea of a good time."

"Ordinarily I would," Angel said. "But I'm just running to Cordelia's to get a change of clothes. These smell like smoke—another long story—and I have to meet an informant in a little while. Unless you need—"

"No, I'll be okay. Just thought I'd ask."

"I hope I'll get to see you. While you're in town, I mean."

She smiled. That was better than escorting her to the county line. "I'll make a point of it," she said. "Or, we will. Me and, you know, Riley. He's on his way over from Sunnydale."

"Oh," Angel said flatly.

"Well, I guess I should go," Buffy said after a moment. "People to see, you know."

"Me too," Angel agreed. "I'm there anyway."

"I'll be in touch," she promised.

"Good," Angel replied. "You be careful, Buffy."

"I always am," she said. They both knew that was a lie. But it was one that she thought made him feel better, so she told it from time to time. She said good-bye to Angel and hung up. She was glad she had called—thinking about calling was always harder than making the actual call. And he hadn't sounded not-happy to hear from her. But he wouldn't be joining her on her excursion, so she needed to make other plans. Which meant that she'd still have to see him, which she expected to be even harder than just calling him.

Although, not seeing him might be even worse.

And she was kind of hoping he'd have volunteered to drop everything just to give her a hand. She knew that wasn't fair—he was probably working on his own cases, and, knowing him, they'd be a lot more important than just two missing kids. Nonetheless, she couldn't help feeling a little resentment that he hadn't rushed right over to see her. Together they had saved the world more times than she could count. Why couldn't he spare a few hours to help her save a friend?

It was all just so complicated.

She returned to the living room, to find Elfredo on the phone. She waited until he was finished and said, "Did you find any footprints?"

He shook his head.

"A ransom note?"

Shook it once more.

"Have you ever heard of a gang called the Latin Cobras?"

Again with the head shaking.

"They're a gang," Buffy told him, "in Sunnydale. And Nicky is . . . involved with them."

He didn't look shocked. Sad, yes. And maybe a little defeated.

"As I told you, it sometimes happens with these rich Mexican boys," he said. "I've been telling his father for years to be careful. But everyone focused on Salma and left Nicky alone. Our culture gives men so much freedom. Females, still very little. We think it's for their own protection."

"In Salma's case, not such a great theory," Buffy pointed out. "The gang that Nicky's involved with has ties to the Echo Park Band. You ever hear of them?"

That set him back. He was most definitely wigged.

"Do we want to call the police?" Buffy asked, mostly to see which way the wind was blowing.

"Not yet." Elfredo held out his hands. "These people, the de la Natividads, are very wealthy, very private. They are living in a foreign country in a city where, if you might excuse me, the police are known to be corrupt."

"Ouch," Buffy said firmly. "Not all of them. And if you want to talk corrupt cops, I'm thinking Mexico would be a better place—"

"All I'm trying to do is explain to you why we're not

calling the police yet. When we have something more concrete to share with them, then, perhaps."

Buffy was dubious. *If it has to be more concrete than a blazing oil fire and eyewitnesses, I don't think it exists on the planet Earth.*

Of course, there is the problem of the shadow monsters.

"So, meanwhile, someone has to go check on the Echo Park guys," she suggested. "Who, I'm assuming, must hang in Echo Park." A fairly rough section of Los Angeles; in her preSlayer, cheerleading days, she wouldn't have been caught dead anywhere near Echo Park.

"I have to stay here with the family," Elfredo said. "Don Armando specifically told me to do so. He's worried that someone will try to kidnap his mother or his wife."

She was perplexed. "But what about Salma?"

He checked his watch. "As we speak, three carloads of my men have been searching for her for fifteen minutes. The moment no one could find her, I dispatched them. And by the way, they can get in touch with the police if need be."

"Oh. Okay." Buffy shrugged. "Then I'll go find the Echo Park gangbangers on my own."

His expression spoke volumes. "Pretty bad guys, huh?" she asked.

"You know of the Hell's Angels?" he asked her.

She snickered. "Of course."

"They won't have anything to do with the Echo Park Band. Too scary."

"Then it's a good thing I'm around."

Elfredo regarded her. "That's true," he said simply. "But this time, Buffy, don't go outside."

"Sorry." And she was. It would be nice to have a nice, quiet evening in this big house, maybe watch something on DVD with a mug of Mexican hot chocolate and some homemade *churros*.

It would also be nice to take a hot bath and spend time with Riley.

But nothing like that was going to happen tonight.

"I gotta," she added.

Elfredo nodded. "I can't come with you," he repeated, starting to dial his phone again. "But I'll send some of my men. Some of my best. Well armed."

"From what we know about what Nicky's mixed up with, those kinds of weapons might not be helpful," Buffy said evenly. "But that's the part I'm good at. If we run into humans, your guys can do the dirty work. If we run into—well, other stuff—I'll take over."

She left Elfredo behind to make arrangements, and walked into the kitchen. Willow was grinding some noxious herbs in a mortar with a pestle while Doña Pilar stood beside her with an enormous book bound in black leather with red lettering.

"Hey." Buffy looked at Willow. "I'm going to drop in on the Echo Park gang. If Riley shows . . ." She hesitated. "Tell him I'll be back later. And hi. Tell him hi."

"Got it," Willow said seriously. "Hi."

Doña Pilar set down the book and walked to Buffy. She made the sign of the cross over her head and murmured a prayer. Then she kissed Buffy on the cheek.

"Go with God, little one," she said.

The banter in the SUV died down as Enrique reached the environs of East Los Angeles, which was not near Echo Park. The meeting was being held in the *barrio,* for reasons that had not been shared with the emissaries from the Latin Cobras.

Enrique and Paco were very nervous. Not so Nicky.

Nobody in the world could hurt him, not even the most notorious gangbanger on earth. He was invincible.

These guys have no idea who they're dealing with, he thought smugly.

During the drive up, he had gradually realized that Enrique and Paco were afraid of him. Nobody had expected him to live through the oil fire. He, Nicky, had become the most important member of the Latin Cobras. He was their ticket to an even stronger alliance with Echo Park.

Nicky was trying to decide what to tell the leader of E.P., whose name was Che. Divulge the secret ritual but hold back on how to obtain the ingredients? Tell them that because he was the grandson of a *bruja,* that only he could do it? To be honest, he didn't even really know which was the truth. He knew it had worked on himself, but not if it could be repeated. But Che was a very powerful man, one of the most influential in Los Angeles. He wanted to be on the guy's good side.

Then Enrique muttered, "Look. There."

The neighborhood was dark. The streetlamps had been shot out, Paco had explained earlier. Beneath a half-crescent moon, buildings lined with hedges and dotted with palm trees stood in relief against the flat black landscape. Radio Latina blared *banda* music from someone's front steps.

"It's the next right," Paco told Enrique. The SUV rounded the corner.

Lights shone from a single-story stucco house. The front window was aglow, the curtains pulled back, and strings of little lights resembling chili peppers were looped along the eaves.

As Enrique pulled up slowly, he flashed the SUV's lights twice. The answer was three guys carrying rifles, who moved from the porch of the house and lazily came down the cement steps in front of it. A big black dog jumped around their legs, excited, and barked at Enrique's car as he pulled to the curb.

"*Hola, mano,*" he said to the guy who walked up to the window. They went through an elaborate handshake. Then everybody relaxed.

"Nicky, these are our brothers, eh? Our *hermanos,*" Enrique said. "Treat them with respect."

"*Claro,*" Nicky said absently. He was already studying the house, wondering if he could try to trade the secret to Che for a high-ranking position in the gang. This was not Che's house, he knew—before he left L.A. to live in Sunnydale, he had been to Che's for summer barbecues a couple of times. Gangbangers grilling burgers, swilling beer, trying to act like suburban Anglos. It was kind of funny, but Nicky had always felt comfortable there, nonetheless.

The door opened, and a guy wearing an eyepatch and holding a rifle, bobbed his head at Nicky.

"It's a party, eh?" Nicky asked, pointing to the house. He was impressed that they didn't hide themselves away from the cops. L.A. cops were a lot rougher on gangbangers than Sunnydale *policia,* he had heard. Maybe not in this neighborhood, though.

Eyepatch shrugged. Without a word, he escorted Nicky up the stairs.

On cue, the door opened.

Nicky went in.

The other two climbed back into the SUV, and it pulled away.

Buffy could not turn down a free ride—not in the endless sprawl that was L.A.—so Elfredo sent two armed guys along with her in his own vehicle. She was a bit disappointed to discover that it was a mundane blue Toyota

Corolla. But that made sense; it was less likely to be noticed.

Wrong. The area they traveled to was the land of rust buckets and flashy lowriders, complete with neon undercarriages. The Corolla was a symbol of the middle class—not a lot of that in a depressed area like this one.

"Where to now?" one of the big muscle guys asked Buffy.

From the backseat, she leaned forward and peered through the windshield, scrutinizing the area. Back in the 7–11 off the 101, she had discovered the Echo Park gang was led by a guy named Che. The guy in the 7–11 had also confirmed their ties to the Latin Cobras. The gang really did hang out in Echo Park, and most of them lived near Glendale Boulevard, just a couple of blocks away.

Also, that there were rumors of something to go down soon, something huge and bad, which had to do with Russians.

All that and three Icees for fifty bucks.

"Glendale Boulevard," she said, pointing to a street sign. "Left here."

The driver—his name was Sandor—complied, and there they were, firmly in gang territory. In fact, as they rolled to a stop at the first intersection, a guy wearing a hair net strode over to the driver's side and rapped on the window.

Sandor pulled a gun before he unrolled the window and stuck it in the intruder's face.

"Sí?" he demanded.

"Hey, I got three guys across the street, pointing straps straight at this car," the other guy sneered.

Shrugging, Sandor cocked his weapon. "I'm not pointing my gun at them. I'm pointing it at you."

Buffy said from the back seat. "Where's Che?"

Hairnet frowned. He said nothing.

"We're supposed to go to the meeting. We're L.C.," Sandor said.

"You? With that accent?" Hairnet scoffed. "Hey, man, Che's not here, okay? They went somewheres else to have the meeting. It's too hot around here, you know?"

Too many cops, Buffy mentally translated.

Then another guy walked up. He had on a thick woolen cap and a plaid shirt with only the top button buttoned. He looked at Hairnet, then down at Sandor.

He spoke to him in Spanish, and Sandor replied in Spanish. Hairnet joined in.

Then the new guy called, "Hey, little girl in the back seat. It's your chance to come have some fun, baby."

Everyone switched to English.

Sandor said, "Watch it, bro. That's my woman."

Oh, please. Buffy mentally rolled her eyes.

Hairnet pulled a gun, and pushed it against Sandor's temple.

"What's going on?" Buffy asked.

"They don't believe we're L.C.," Sandor said calmly. "They've got two hostages from the sit-down with Che. They're gonna bring them out and have them identify us."

"They don't know us," Buffy said in a rush. "Only Nicky."

There was a pause. Second guy said, "Nicky who?"

"Come on. You know. The rich guy," Buffy prompted. "He set the oil derricks on fire tonight. Nicky told us to come up to Che's."

They began discussing in Spanish again. Hairnet said, "Give us your names."

"I'm Anita," Buffy said. "And this is Tomás and Julio."

"Yeah. You're Anita like I'm Albert Gore," Hairnet said. His second-in-command thought that was pretty funny.

The second guy walked off. Hairnet kept his gun right where it was.

"It'll be okay now," Sandor told Buffy. "They're going to call Che to verify."

Uh-oh. Buffy wondered if Nicky really did know an Anita, a Tomás, and a Julio.

She didn't wonder if "It'll be okay now" was Sandor-speak for, "We're screwed."

"Um, excuse me?" she said to Hairnet. "I need to go to the bathroom."

"Too bad," he said. Then he huffed. "Okay. Get out slow. You try anything, I'll shoot your boyfriend."

"My boyfriend?" she said flirtatiously. "Not hardly."

She opened the door. Part of her had been hoping for something like this. Her anger had been simmering ever since Angel had refused to see her, to help her with this. Usually when she felt this way, beating the tar out of some demons helped. But right now, there weren't any demons to be had, only criminals who were most likely in league with demons. *Close enough.*

Hairnet ticked his glance toward her. She held up her hands to show that she was unarmed.

"Okay?" she asked. "Where is it?"

"When Miguel comes back, I'll show you." He smiled slightly, revealing a fine specimen of a gold tooth.

"Oh, okay," she trilled. "In the meantime, I'll show you."

She shot forward with both hands doubled into a single fist and rammed his arm upward like she was serving a volley ball. The gun went off, high and wild.

Hairnet lunged toward Buffy as Sandor threw open his car door, smacking the guy with a solid *whump*.

Shots rang out from across the street. *Must be the second and third guys Hairnet warned us about,* Buffy figured.

She made short work of Hairnet, getting in a strong

roundhouse that sent him to the cracked pavement. As he tried to get up, she sent him back down with a good solid punch to his face. She grabbed the collar of his shirt and twisted, pressing her fist against his throat. She knew that Angel might disapprove of her using Slayer force on a human in "his town." *Tough luck,* she thought. *He's not here. He chose not to be here.* "Now let's talk about Che some more," she hissed. "Where is he?"

"Boyle Heights," Hairnet muttered. "Sleepy Ramos." Before she could follow up, the other two guys dashed across the street, guns blazing. Sandor's fellow body-guard, Emilio, shouted and grabbed his shoulder.

Sandor gunned the engine and tried to run the guys down. One was short, one was tall, and they could both run really, really fast. Another neighborhood, another life, they'd be dreaming of becoming pro baseball players.

As Sandor drove forward, the car clipped the tall one. He went down. The short one aimed at Buffy. She gave up on Hairnet, dodged and leaped back into the back seat. As she slammed the door, Sandor took off.

A firestorm of bullets chased after them; bullets to the left, to the right, above and behind them; it was a complete and total bulleteria. Figures appeared everywhere, like some kind of advanced skill level on a video game, until it would have been funny if it weren't so deadly. The rear window shattered and Buffy let out a shriek, pressing herself flat against the seat.

Oh, yeah. Gang neighborhood.

"You hurt bad?" Sandor asked Emilio.

Emilio rattled off a bunch of Spanish cursewords—Buffy was chagrined to admit how many she recognized—while Sandor picked up the car phone and punched a number.

"*Yeah,*" he said into the phone. "Emilio's gotta go to the hospital. *Sí.*" He continued on in Spanish.

When he hung up, he said to Buffy, "We'll drop Emilio off at the emergency room. Then I'm supposed to take you back to the house."

"But—" Buffy protested. She wanted to get to Boyle Heights.

Sandor looked at her in the rearview mirror. She didn't like the look he gave her, as if he held her responsible for Emilio being wounded.

Which, she supposed, was not all that far off. But Elfredo had told her to do whatever she thought she needed to in order to find Nicky. These guys had signed on for dangerous duty, and they'd known that when they started. Buffy was always saddened when civilians were hurt in the battle against evil, but sometimes it happened. She couldn't let herself think about it too much or it would paralyze her.

"Your boyfriend's there. At the house. Waiting for you."

"Oh." As if that were the final answer.

Which, okay.

She leaned back, then forward again, trying to get a good look at herself in the rearview mirror.

Sandor chuckled. "You look great," he said. "Especially for a chick who just took down a *cholo* from Echo Park."

"Good." Buffy smiled. "Good."

Angel glanced at the sky as he tucked his phone away. Still dark, which was good. Still a couple of hours before sunrise. The night had been long and eventful, and he stank like smoke and sweat and fear, but it wasn't over yet. A long shower would be nice, but he had a feeling that wasn't in the cards.

Buffy's here.

He found himself disturbed by that—disturbed that she had, apparently, been here for a while, without calling him. Disturbed that something had brought her here from Sunnydale, and that something could only be a bad something. She owed it to him to at least call, if not to come and see him, in such a circumstance. Los Angeles was his responsibility, and it was hard enough keeping up on things without people—okay, Buffy—importing them from other towns. It wasn't like the newspapers would report such occurrences, since they either completely ignored the unseen layer of life that they didn't understand or, when pressed, printed only the official "explanations" for events that couldn't escape public notice.

Which left it up to him, his network of contacts, Cordelia's visions, and chance to keep up on the forces that threatened the city and its people.

Buffy could help, but not by coming into town chasing or running from badness and not telling him.

He stepped on the accelerator a little harder, stewing in his anger. *It's a good thing I'm not going to see her,* he thought. *I'd probably say some things I would regret later.*

Riley Finn paced the living room of the de la Natividad house. *Which is,* he thought, *a beautiful house.* But he didn't spend much time looking at it. He was anxious. He paced some more.

Her eyes red and swollen with crying, Mrs. de la Natividad herself had made him a sandwich and poured him a soda, then excused herself. Now he was waiting in a living room that could have easily contained his parents' house back in Iowa.

"Riley," Willow said, "the bodyguard said Buffy wasn't hurt. They're taking someone *else* to the emergency room."

"Yeah," he answered tersely. He didn't care what anyone *said.* He cared how Buffy *was.*

The doorknob turned, and Buffy walked in.

"Riley," she said happily, hurrying to his arms. He held her for a good long time against him, then gave her a long, deep kiss, which she so nicely returned.

"What's been happening?" he asked.

"Not much." She sighed. "I was trying to find Nicky. I did, sort of. He's at a meeting in Boyle Heights."

Riley processed that. "Okay. I've got something, too. Also, not much. But the guy who owns the oil field down in Sunnydale also owns a shipping company. His warehouses are in downtown L.A., and the Echo Park Band was going to hit them tonight. Like the Latin Cobras went after the oil fields."

Perking up, she smiled at him and said, "Let's go. We'll try Boyle Heights first, and if that doesn't pan out we'll hit the warehouses."

His stomach did a little flip. Still, after all this time, with the flips. He loved working with her. Hell, he loved just *being* with her.

They turned on their heels and walked out the front door.

"Bye," Willow said faintly, her hand raised in a gesture of farewell.

Chapter 20

Sunnydale

After Riley left, Giles decided that the Scoobs should go out patrolling. Since he had nothing better to do at the moment, Spike joined them. But it was humiliating, tromping around like a pack of bleedin' Girl Scouts, and he knew he would be making no friends among the demon populace by being seen with humans, so he eventually peeled off.

Dawn was coming. He was grateful for an end to this miserable, sodding night.

Then a strange force drew him to the trailer park . . .

. . . and Cheryce was still lying on the bed, now reading something in French, and she actually frowned when he opened the door and stumbled in.

She smiled expectantly. "You ready to hunt, honey?"

She had told him not to come back until he could sink his fangs into a human.

He said, "Cheryce, pet, do you fancy going to France?"

"What?" She stared at him.

"Some birds, they need a change of pace. I understand that. I hear the catacombs simply reek this time of year— mold from the rains. It'll be fun."

He smiled hopefully.

She did not smile back.

"Come on," he said, *"mon petite crème brûlée."*

Snickering, she closed her book. "Honey, I'm putting you out to pasture, don't you get it?"

"Come outside with me," he said. "Breathe in the stench of the oil fire. And tell me you don't want me."

"I can do that fine right here," she insisted.

He took her hand. "C'mon, my little cowgal." He wrinkled his nose. "The stars are out. The air is filled with pollution. It's London. It's Vegas."

Cheryce shook her head, but she laughed, and Spike figured he was halfway home. When she let him lead her outside, he exulted, but he kept cool. *Just let her introduce me to Woodring,* he thought, *and everything will be fine. But the catch is, she'll never do it if she thinks that's what I want from her. I have to want her for her. And that's not me.*

"You still love me," he insisted.

"I didn't love you in the first place," she shot at him.

But he moved in against her defenses. He kissed her, and she did that thing women do where they stiffen, then melt . . . and then scream . . .

Something yanked her right out of Spike's arms as she screamed, and tossed her back and forth like a rag doll.

"Bloody hell!" Spike shouted.

It was an enormous shadow; as Spike watched, it blotted out the stars and covered the trailer. Nothing but black, empty shadow, nothing that should have form or substance or teeth. But as Cheryce fought against it, blood started gushing down her neck.

Spike leaped forward, grabbed her ankles, and pulled. She screamed in pain, but he kept pulling. Like him, she would heal, but tear her into enough pieces, and one might as well put a stake through her heart.

Finally, he managed to tear her out of the grasp of whatever had her. She tumbled into his arms, a bleeding mess—rather like a pasta dish—and clung to him, sobbing. He unpeeled her and pushed her to the ground, and took the thing on.

Fighting was what Spike had been made for. And this, unlike humans, he could fight. Fully vamped out, he went into action.

His boots had steel toes and he used them to advantage, leaping into the air and ramming both his feet into a neat front kick, then a sidekick, and executing an aerial three-sixty that sent him crashing into it.

The shadow retaliated, slamming him. The vampire flew through the air in a high wide arc, piling into the side of Cheryce's trailer.

As he tried to regain his footing, the thing oozed over Cheryce again, covering her, and she screamed for all she was worth.

People—humans—began pouring from the other trailers. *Trailer trash,* he thought. Mostly white-haired, lined, overweight suntanned meatbags he wouldn't have looked twice at ordinarily. A few pointed at Spike and screamed, but as he shook his head to make the little birdies and stars go away, he didn't much care. Cheryce was in trouble—and if he lost her, he lost any chance to get to Woodring.

He flung himself against the shadow. It was solid. He did it again.

And there was nothing there, except for Cheryce, who had practically been vivisected.

"Oh, my God!" a woman screamed.

Spike made his face go human, and bent over Cheryce. She gestured for him to come closer.

"If I die, you can have my Elvis," she said. Then she went limp.

Spike put his forehead against her chest—well, actually into it, by accident—then threw back his head and hollered, "Nooooooo!"

His cry echoed through the night.

Giles, Anya, Xander, and Tara patrolled the town. Tara walked with Giles, leaving the two lovebirds to bicker and kiss, and she and he discussed various fine points of magick. He thought she was a charming girl, quite shy, but well-versed in things Wiccan, to be sure.

He frowned. "I believe I just saw a very small mucus demon scamper through past the hardware store."

Tara turned to look. Then Anya cried out, "Everybody, run!"

Directly on their heels, three stone demons charged at them, wielding thick stone bats, like animate gargoyle baseball players. The gray humanoid monsters slammed their weapons at the retreating figures, one smacking a fire plug so hard it burst, and water geysered into the air, hitting the power lines overhead.

A sound like thunder boomed, and the entire street plunged into darkness, all the streetlamps flickering and dying at once.

"It's back," Giles said, running around a corner. He paused to catch his breath. The screams of other pedestrians rattled his eardrums. "And it has friends!"

But Tara shook her head. "It's . . . it feels different." She turned around. "Something's different, Mr. Giles. Something is happening."

"Of the bad," Xander added.

"Very bad," Anya agreed.

"We should get back to my apartment," Giles said.

"So we can find out what's going on?" Anya asked.

"So we won't be killed."

"Hey. When I suggested that, no one wanted to play," Xander pointed out.

"That was then. This is now," Tara said.

A man ran by, followed by a strange, lumbering creature covered in white fur. The creature wheeled from chasing the man, and ran straight for the Scoobs.

Point man Xander called out, "Nice kitty, good kitty!" and swatted at the tiger-sized monster.

Its attention diverted, it hunkered down, then sprang into a leap straight at Xander. It connected with his chest, propelling him backward, until he fell onto his back. The back of his head made a hard smack against the sidewalk, and Anya and Tara screamed.

The creature, however, could not stop its forward motion, and its face smashed against the brickwork of the hardware store's exterior. Stunned, it toppled off Xander and lay on its side.

Xander groaned and tried to roll out of the way, but he couldn't manage it. Giles grabbed him and dragged him back into the alley.

Down the street, other monsters and demons capered and cavorted.

All hell was breaking loose.

"Can you walk?" Giles asked, sliding his hands around Xander's upper arms and hoisting him to his feet.

"He's been eating a lot of junk food," Anya supplied helpfully. "He probably weighs more than usual."

"I think I can manage, thank you," Giles gritted. "Xander, please, you must get up. We've got to get out of here."

Xander made some incoherent noises.

"I think he's speaking Fyral," Anya said.

"Actually, he's not." Giles pulled out a stake. "Arm yourselves as best you can. We need to get Xander to safety. And we need to figure out what's happening around here."

"Thinking. Good thinking," Xander muttered.

As the four staggered through a darkened and hysterical Sunnydale, Anya pined for the olden days of mayhem and destruction. Xander was a great boyfriend, but being a vengeance demon had its plus side, too, especially at times like this.

Tara performed a few handy spells to help them get Xander to Giles's house in one piece. They were lurching through the courtyard when the bushes rustled violently. Going to investigate, Anya noted the presence of an old blanket draped across the tops of the branches.

She peered down. Spike was huddled inside, a half-eaten corpse draped across his lap.

"What are you doing?" Anya demanded. "Eating someone's leftovers?"

"This is my bloody girlfriend," he snapped.

"She is," Anya agreed.

"She's been hurt. That thing you've all been ranting about tried to eat her."

"Giles?" Anya called. As Giles approached, she said, "Spike saw the shadow monster."

"You did?" Giles said, interested. He looked at Cheryce, made a face. "Have you turned into a ghoul?"

"That's his girlfriend," Anya said.

"Or a pervert?" Xander offered.

"I couldn't take her into your place," Spike said. "You've never invited her." He frowned up at his fellow Englishman. "She's a vampire, and she needs help. You've got to save her."

"First, tell me about the shadow monster," Giles said, crossing his arms.

"You are such a bad person," Spike retorted. "Always talking about being such a goody-goody, but when the chips are down . . ."

"*Spike.*"

"All right then. We were going for a nice romantic walk, just got out the trailer, and this thing just pounces." He shrugged. "Covered up and gnawed on her. I got a few good punches, some kicks . . . excellent kicks . . . and then the bloody thing just vanished."

Giles frowned at him. Spike snapped his fingers.

Then he looked around. "Interestin' thing is, it seems once it was gone, all these other things started showing up. How do you figure that, Rupert?"

Anya cocked her head, waiting for Giles's answer.

The Brit said slowly, "I'm afraid I have no idea."

"You'd better figure it out soon," Spike told him. "From the looks of things, oil fires and shadow monsters are the least of this town's worries." He grinned. "Neat, huh?"

Giles just sighed.

Los Angeles

"She was just gone," Cordelia insisted. "Poof. Like when you're having a good hair day, and then someone pulls out a camera, and then whammo, your hairdo vanishes right before your eyes. And then, while we're looking for her, those other guys just take off, those vampire-killing street kids. It was like elephants at a Siegfried and Roy show, disappearing all over the place."

"I did notice them walking out," Wesley put in. "So their disappearance isn't exactly a mystery. Still, it would have been nice to have found out who they were."

Angel had an idea of his own about that. From the description Cordelia and Wesley had given him, it sounded like Gunn and his crew. Gunn had seen Wesley and Cord, in the hospital, after Angel's apartment had been blown up, but they'd been unconscious and had never actually met Gunn. And still hadn't, it seemed.

"But this girl was the one who called you and told you Kostov was on his way," Angel suggested. "So maybe she was afraid the other girls would be mad at her, punish her in some way."

"No, she didn't run away, though. She was there one second, and then the next she wasn't. No physical motion involved."

"Cordelia's right," Wesley added. "It was like something out of a magic act. The incredible vanishing teenager."

"So we figured, who do we know who knows about this kind of stuff?"

Wesley glanced at her, a pained expression on his face.

"Besides Wesley," she amended.

Angel rubbed his chin. Buffy had been talking about disappearances, too. Had she specified that they were teenagers? A friend of Willow's, she'd said, so probably. It was almost too big a stretch to think there was a connection between a case that had brought Buffy here from Sunnydale and the events Cordelia and Wesley had lived through while Angel was busy surviving a jail riot.

He really wanted to change out of his tattered and smoky clothes, but Cordelia and Wesley had launched into their story as soon as he'd walked in. He listened, while one part of his mind tried to compartmentalize his priorities. First, Buffy was out there somewhere, and although he knew she was good at taking care of herself, he'd want to check in from time to time. Then there was the fact that Rojelio Flores would be released from prison in the morning, and Angel wanted to try to be at the Flamingo to make sure he got settled in, and that there was no threat from the crooked cops who had framed him for their own murder. And Cordelia thought he needed to look into the disappearance of this runaway girl, Kayley.

And he understood her concern, especially coupled with what Buffy had told him. If girls were disappearing from sight, then something was definitely rotten in Los Angeles.

"And she was really gone, not just invisible?" Angel asked.

"Gone," Cordelia insisted. "Everybody called for her. We looked all over the place. No sign of her." Cordelia paced around her living room, obviously agitated. "Look, I know we deal with a lot of strange things," she continued. "As a kid, growing up in Sunnydale—well, you know, it's on a Hellmouth, so there's all that to deal with. But since I moved here to L.A. and started working with you, I've really been exposed to some major league eepiness."

"Eepiness," Angel echoed.

"That's right. It's like creepiness, but more eerie. But anyway, nothing we've faced is quite as eepy to me as someone disappearing right in front of my, you know, back. What's up with that? Where could she have gone?"

Angel looked at Wesley, who was polishing his glasses on a handkerchief. "You have any ideas, Wesley?"

"Plenty of ideas," Wesley replied. He put his glasses back on. "She walked through a rift in the space-time continuum. Her atoms were dispersed to the four winds. She was teleported to a small village in Siberia. I've no shortage of ideas, it's just that none of them seem to make any sense."

"What about the other girls?" Angel asked. "What are they doing now?"

"I asked," Cordelia said. "But it didn't sound like they

had any definite plans. They said they'd stay there for tonight at least, and think about their next move."

"You think their vampire obsession is cured?"

"Pretty sure, yeah. They're pretty freaked about Kayley, though."

"I'll look into it," Angel said. "Ask around. See if I can find out anything."

Cordelia smiled for the first time since he'd walked into the apartment. She had a great deal of faith in Angel—if he said he'd do something, he took care of it.

"But I also have to make sure Rojelio Flores is safe with his family."

"He's being released today?" Cordelia asked.

"Right."

"But not until after the sun comes up, right?"

"Right," Angel agreed.

Cordelia looked at her wrist, where a watch would be if she wore one. "So you've still got some time to look for Kayley."

Angel nodded, resigned to another busy day. There was also Buffy, and the investigation into the crooked cops, which tied into the whole Flores thing.

Kate had asked him—somewhat reluctantly, he thought—to spend some time digging around into the LAPD, trying to find out who was clean and who was dirty. The investigation she had in mind could only be done by someone on the outside. Angel wasn't beholden to anyone on the force. He didn't have personal relationships with any police officers besides Kate. Cops were the most insular bunch of people he knew, and they would close ranks against anyone they knew was investigating them—especially if it was a fellow officer like Kate.

Angel would report to no one except Kate, and she

would keep what she learned quiet until she knew how deep the corruption went, how high up the ladder of command it climbed. The citizens of Los Angeles were entitled to an honest police force, but for the past few years there had been many strains on the force's credibility. Another scandal now could be ruinous, and Kate wanted to make sure she knew the facts before she brought any charges to light.

He'd managed to locate an informant who claimed to know something about the dirty cops and their ties to criminal gangs, and had set up a meeting with the guy to find out the specifics. He'd done all this through an intermediary, a small-time hood he'd had occasion to run across a few times, and who he'd once saved from a Hrothgar demon with an appetite for bone marrow.

The meeting was in twenty minutes. He had to move.

He said good-bye and left, still stinking.

Boyle Heights, at an hour before sunrise, was not Buffy's idea of a garden spot. Having Riley along helped, but even his sunny presence could only do so much. The area they were in reminded her of a war zone—storefronts were empty, their display windows shattered, their surfaces covered with colorful graffiti the meaning of which she could only guess at. Most of the streetlights were out, or their globes and bulbs shattered. Trash blew along the empty street.

"Nice neighborhood," Riley said sarcastically, echoing her sentiments.

"We're lucky," she said. "Not having to live like this."

"Yeah, I guess the city doesn't make a big deal out of cleaning up the poor neighborhoods, do they? Where Salma's parents live—where Salma's parents could afford to hire someone to do nothing but sweep the streets—the city probably has a truck there to pick up every stray candy wrapper."

"You think the mayor ever sees streets like this?" Buffy asked. "These people might as well be invisible."

Riley craned his head, looking out the window as he drove. "Well, I think Sleepy Ramos is invisible, too."

They had found someone who claimed to know Sleepy Ramos, and who told them what to look for, and where. Sleepy would be standing guard outside the meeting place, they were told—after Riley did some persuading. Only "standing" wasn't exactly the right word. Sleepy would be *sleeping* guard inside an old Plymouth, painted primer gray. He could sleep anywhere—hence the nickname—but he was a light sleeper, so he was given guard duty because the slightest sound or movement would wake him up.

So they cruised the neighborhood looking for the old gray Plymouth. Finally, Buffy spotted it outside a butcher shop, across the street from a run-down Victorian house. "There," she said. "Sleepy."

Riley pulled to a stop behind the car. Buffy watched Sleepy's face in his rearview mirror, and noted that as soon as Riley's car drew into the spot, his eyes opened. So the story was true.

"He's awake," she reported.

"I see."

They got out of their car and walked toward Sleepy, who was already punching a speed-dial button on a cell phone. Buffy dove forward, yanked his door open—it had been locked, so the car sustained some damage there—and snatched the phone from his hand. She heard a small voice from it, saying, "Hello? Yo, hello?"

"Sorry, wrong number," she said, pressing the OFF button and tossing it into the back seat.

Riley had gone to the other side of the car, so Sleepy was boxed in.

"Sleepy Ramos," Buffy said. "We need to talk to you."

Angel drove into a neighborhood he had seldom passed through, called Boyle Heights. It was in East Los Angeles, off Cesar Chavez Avenue. Not too far from his usual haunts or from downtown L.A., but he had a hunch the people who occupied the glittering skyscrapers there had never experienced Boyle Heights after dark.

He turned a corner, a block away from the intersection where his informant was supposed to be waiting. The car was there. But the informant was not alone.

Another car was parked behind it, and two people surrounded it—a tall, solid-looking young man with a military bearing, and a shorter, and quite lovely, blond woman.

Buffy.

Angel parked and got out of his car. "Buffy."

She spun, shock registering on her face. "Angel? What are you doing here?"

"If that's Sleepy Ramos, meeting him," Angel explained. His tone might have been a little cooler than he wanted, but he still felt a little miffed at her. "I might ask you the same question."

"I'm looking for someone," she said. "I think he knows where that someone is."

Sleepy Ramos climbed out of his car as they talked. He had heavy-lidded eyes and thick black hair that looked like he seldom combed it. He looked, Angel thought, like someone who had just woken up. He wore baggy cargo pants and a flannel shirt, untucked, buttoned all the way up. He couldn't have been more than seventeen.

"Yo, man," he said. "You Angel?"

"That's right," Angel said.

"These people harassing me," he complained. "That ain't what we agreed to. You gonna do something about it?"

"He could try," Riley said. Angel glanced at Buffy's boyfriend. His stance was aggressive, his fists balled. He knew Riley didn't like him. He also knew he could take Riley without breaking a sweat.

If the soldier boy doesn't stand down, he thought, *this might be the time I prove it.*

"We're all old friends here, Sleepy," Buffy assured the youth. She turned to Riley. "Aren't we?"

"Works for me," Riley agreed.

"And Angel?" she asked pointedly.

"Fine," Angel snapped.

He turned back to Sleepy Ramos—but Sleepy was apparently no longer interested in talking. He had taken advantage of everyone's attention being off him to work his way around his car, to the end closest to the corner butcher shop. As soon as Angel glanced his way, he began to run.

"Ramos!" Angel shouted.

"Hey!" Buffy called. "We're not done with him!"

Angel shot her a look. "He's mine," Angel said, breaking into a run himself.

Buffy kept pace with him easily. "We can share," she said.

Ahead, Ramos ran into an array of metal garbage cans lined up on the sidewalk. They scattered, and he tipped one of them behind him, across the walkway. The lid hit the cement and bounced, sailing through the window of a laundry. Glass crashed, and an alarm began to blare. The noise was shockingly loud in the quiet premorning air. On the other side of the cans, he ducked into an alley.

"The neighbors are going to love this," Riley panted behind them. Angel poured on the speed, and Buffy followed suit.

As they came into the alley, Sleepy Ramos ran toward

a shimmering golden circle that spanned the width of the alleyway. Angel could barely see the alley on the other side of the circle; it was like looking through some kind of viscous liquid.

"Angel—" Buffy started to say. But before she could continue, Ramos ran headlong into the circle and vanished from sight. Angel braced himself for whatever was coming and dove—

—and Buffy slammed into him, clutching at his legs and knocking him into the brick wall at the side of the alley. They rolled on the ground, scraping their hands and knees and Angel's cheek. By the time they stopped and disentangled, the golden circle had faded into nonexistence.

"You really don't want to do that," Buffy said, wiping dirt off her hands and smoothing back her hair.

"What is it?" he asked.

"I'll tell you later," she said.

Riley caught up to them, glaring at Angel and giving Buffy a hand up. Angel pushed himself to his feet.

"We have some company," Riley said. He cocked a thumb over his shoulder.

A police car blocked the mouth of the alley, its light bar flashing red and painting the alley walls with its firelike glow. Two police officers stood behind the car, guns drawn and pointed their way.

Angel glanced in the other direction, at the far end of the alley. Another police car idled there, two more officers drawing down on them.

"Freeze!" one of the cops shouted.

Angel recognized the voice.

It belonged to Bo Peterson.

To be continued . . .

Nancy Holder is the bestselling author of forty-eight books and many short stories, articles, and essays. Alone and in collaboration with other authors, she has written sixteen *Buffy* and/or *Angel* projects for Pocket Books. Her work has been translated into two dozen languages, and has appeared on the *Los Angeles Times, USA Today, Locus,* and other bestseller lists. She is currently working on the second book of this trilogy with her coauthor, Jeff Mariotte.

She lives in San Diego with her daughter, Belle, their dog, Dot, and two kittens named Sasha and David, and all five consider themselves honorary members of the Hart/Mariotte continuum. In her spare time, Holder belly dances . . . and sleeps.

Jeff Mariotte has written, alone and in collaboration with other various authors, two novels about the superhero team Gen[13], one novel about Xander Harris, two novels about Angel, and the nonfiction *Watcher's Guide, Vol. 2.* He has also written more comic books than he cares to count. He is a co-owner of Mysterious Galaxy, a specialty bookstore in San Diego, and Senior Editor for WildStorm Productions/DC Comics.

He lives in San Diego with a variety of people and animals, and would like to find time to visit the desert.

While helping a friend search for her lost brother, Buffy is drawn into a dangerous web of intrigue. Meanwhile Giles and the rest of the Scoobs are on the trail of a shadow stalker—a trail that leads straight to the city of Angels....

Someone is kidnapping the children of the rich and powerful and sending them off to another plane. With the lives of the kidnapped teens and one dangerously talented young woman at stake, Buffy and Angel venture off into the uncharted dimension to do battle....

UNSEEN

An epic trilogy that crosses the lives of Buffy, Angel, and their respective cohorts as they battle the forces of evil....

#1-The Burning
#2-Door to Alternity
#3-Long Way Home
By Nancy Holder and Jeff Mariotte

Published by Pocket Books

When the spirit of a deceased Slayer visits Buffy
Summers with a warning, Buffy never assumes the
danger might stem from herself. A consultation
with a supernatural being finds Buffy trapped
in the body of her 24-year-old-self, a prisoner in a
terrifying alternate reality where vampires rule
Southern California. In addition to fighting vamps
and navigating her way back to real time, Buffy must
wrestle with the realization that she alone has created
this bleak possible future.

As the Slayerettes back home attempt to guide what
they believe to be her missing spirit back to her body,
Buffy and the alternate fang-fighters plot to launch
a full scale attack on the Vampire King—someone
Buffy knows all too well....

The first-ever Buffy serial novel!
THE LOST SLAYER

Part I: Prophecies—available July 2001

Part II: Dark Times—available August 2001

Part III: King of the Dead—available September 2001

Part IV: Original Sins—available October 2001

by Christopher Golden

Published by Pocket Books

3102

They're real, and they're here...

When Jack Dwyer's best friend Artie is murdered, he is devastated. But his world is turned upside down when Artie emerges from the ghostlands to bring him a warning.

With his dead friend's guidance, Jack learns of the Prowlers. They move from city to city, preying on humans until they are close to being exposed, then they move on.

Jack wants revenge. But even as he hunts the Prowlers, he marks himself—and all of his loved ones—as prey.

Don't miss the exciting new series from

**BESTSELLING AUTHOR
CHRISTOPHER GOLDEN!**

PROWLERS